P9-DCD-257

STORYTELLER

BY

Edward Myers

CLARION BOOKS

NEW YORK

Clarion Books
an imprint of Houghton Mifflin Harcourt Publishing Company
215 Park Avenue South, New York, NY 10003
Copyright © 2008 by Edward Myers

The text was set in 11.5-point Goudy.

All rights reserved.

For information about permission to reproduce selections from this book, write to Permissions, Houghton Mifflin Harcourt Publishing Company, 215 Park Avenue South, New York, NY 10003.

www.clarionbooks.com

Printed in the U.S.A.

Library of Congress Cataloging-in-Publication Data

Myers, Edward, 1950–
Storyteller / by Edward Myers.
p. cm.
Summary: Jack, a seventeen-year-old storyteller, goes to the royal city seeking his fortune and soon attracts the attention of the grief-stricken king, his beautiful eldest daughter, and his cruel young son, and he attempts to help them—and the entire kingdom—through his stories.
ISBN 978-0-618-69541-6
[1. Storytelling—Fiction. 2. Kings, queens, rulers, etc. —Fiction. 3. Fairy tales.] I. Title.
PZ7.M98255Sto 2008
[Fic]—dc22   2007031031

DOC 10 9 8 7 6 5 4
4500271974

And everyone settled down for a great feast. Then musicians played, singers sang ballads and songs, storytellers told stories, and everyone present—even the foxes, geese, dogs, cats, ducks, and rabbits—danced till dawn.

After those festivities, Jack and Stelinda settled into their new life, first living with Jack's family, then in a cottage they built together in a meadow.

Just a cottage?

That's all they needed. It's all they wanted. Well—of course Stelinda brought some of her musical supplies to Yorrow, including several lutes and lots of books and manuscripts. She had some of her other belongings transported from Callitti as well. But she was sick of palace life, so a cottage pleased her very well indeed. A cottage just like the one we're sitting in now. A cottage big enough to live in and raise a family in—and big enough, many years later, to welcome any grandchildren who wanted to visit.

And they lived happily ever after?

Happily? Yes. Ever after? Well, no one quite manages that trick. No matter how deep and broad a couple's happiness, life's river doesn't flow forever, does it? But I'll tell you this: Jack and Stelinda have done very well together. They have never once regretted Stelinda's refusal to be queen. They haven't been happy all the time, of course, but most of the time, which is sufficient. They have flourished in their work—Jack by telling stories, Stelinda by writing poems and songs, both of them by helping each other and many other people practice these arts. And they have thrived and delighted in their life together as a couple, as parents of their now-grown children, and as grandparents of the next generation in their family. Their life has been good.

You're sure of that?

Positive.

How do you know?

Well, I give you my word. That should be good enough, don't you think? If not, you can always ask your Grandma Stelinda.

I trust you, Grandpa Jack. But I'll ask her anyway.

Good. She has her own tale, and she tells it well. And of course she's a far better poet and singer than I am.

Listen. For each of us, life is a story. There are characters, conflicts, plot developments, crises, interludes, twists, and resolutions. Sometimes the story makes sense; sometimes it doesn't. But there's still value in the story itself, even when you can't add up the parts and understand the whole. A good story can lead you toward insight—perhaps wisdom—regardless of whether or not you fully understand it. Maybe that's why storytelling has always been so important to me.

Let me explain something. In some ways, nothing can be more preposterous than telling stories. You think up some odd little ideas. You make some noises with your tongue and mouth. You share your dreams and ideas with other people—your listeners. Everything I've told you about Jack Storyteller is true, yet the truth doesn't make his story any less preposterous. The same for any other story. Yet somehow it works. The dreams spread from your mind to theirs. The sounds you make, the stories you tell, release the dreams into the world.

I told you earlier that Jack once feared he was only the stories he told. He feared that he was nobody outside those tales. But Jack was simultaneously himself and the stories in his head, and this is true for all of us. Our stories are our lives. We are our stories.

I'm an old man now, and tired. I need to rest. I've told a lot of stories in my day . . . maybe more than I should have. I'll happily tell you more about Jack and Stelinda—they've had all sorts of other adventures—but those will be stories for another day, another telling.

For Robin and Cory,
storytellers

A Rainy Day, a Cottage, a Fire on the Hearth . . .

Sitting close together in rough-hewn wooden chairs, an old man and his grandchild watch the embers glow, listen to the rain tap at the windows, and find solace in this warm, dry place and in each other's company.

Breakfast dishes clutter a nearby table. A kettle of cider hangs from a hook over the fire, where it simmers almost inaudibly. A shiny black bird dozes on a perch not far from the fireplace. An old woman, seated at a large loom near the back wall, weaves cloth and sings softly to herself.

"A perfect morning for a story," says the old man. "Don't you agree?"

"That's fine," answers his grandchild.

"Meaning—you'd like to hear one?"

"Yes, that would be fine."

There's a brief, not altogether comfortable, pause, as if they should discuss the matter but neglect to do so. Then the old man begins: "Once upon a time—"

"Please don't start like that," the grandchild interrupts.

"I beg your pardon?" The old man isn't offended so much as puzzled.

"I'm tired of stories starting that way," the child explains. "Can't you start some other way?"

"Yes, of course," says the grandfather. "I know many ways to start a story. How about this: Once, long ago—"

"Good. I like that much better."

"Very well, then." He pauses and starts over. "Once, long ago, a magic frog—"

"No magic frogs," the grandchild says abruptly.

"Pardon me?" asks the old man.

"I'd rather not hear a story about a magic frog."

"No? You've always liked them in the past."

"Today I'd like a different kind of story—one I've never heard before."

"All right," the old man responds. "How about a story in which a witch—"

"I'm tired of witches."

"Hmm . . . Fair enough. So perhaps a story about a dragon—"

"No dragons, either. I'm really sick of dragons."

Now the old man grows perplexed. "No magic frogs, no witches, no dragons. Well, I have to admit that rather complicates my task." He sighs and falls silent for a moment. At last he says, "I'm afraid you've ruled out most of the stories I can tell you."

"Don't you know any others?"

"I know a thousand stories, rnaybe more, but none seems likely to please you. You've stopped me from telling every story I've started. Is it possible that you won't like any of them? Is it even possible that you consider yourself too old for my stories?"

"No, I like your stories," the grandchild states firmly, "but I want one that's—that's new."

"Ah, one that's new. I see. That clarifies the situation. All right, how about this one: a story about a storyteller."

"A storyteller?"

"Indeed."

"Is it new?"

"Well, I've never told it to you—or to anyone else, for that matter—so in that sense it's new. And it's a story that's close to my heart. Closer than you can imagine."

"Tell it, then."

"All right, I'll do just that."

ΟΠΕ

❧ I ❧

Long ago—but not so long as you'd imagine—a storyteller earned his bread by telling stories. He told stories to farmers and villagers; to children and grownups; to beggars, traders, sailors, and warriors; to kings and queens. The storyteller told his stories. The people listened. And for the gift of amusing them, the people paid him—with eggs or apples if they were poor, with a candle or a pair of wool mittens if they were better off, with gold or jewels if they were rich. By this means, the storyteller made his way through life and through the world.

Yet the payments he gained weren't the sole reason for his telling stories. The storyteller did more than just ply his wares—as if words were simply goods to sell! No, he told his stories for the love of storytelling. Just as a weaver delights in the click and clack of the shuttle shooting back and forth across the loom and thrills at the sight of the tapestry growing long and wide before him, so, too, did this storyteller enjoy weaving the tales he told. The storyteller loved telling stories, and the people loved hearing them.

So he told stories about demons, ghosts, and witches. He told stories about an old woman who lived in a cottage shaped like a bird's nest. He told stories about a one-eyed robber and his buried treasure. He told stories about a bird who fell hopelessly in love with a fish. He told stories about a princess who battled an evil king using no weapons other than the songs she sang. He told stories—

But I'm getting ahead of myself. The storyteller did everything I've told you, but not during his early years. Like anyone else, he went through a long apprenticeship before he practiced his trade. He had to learn the stories, how to shape them, how to tell them. He had to learn how to please his listeners—when to amuse them, when to surprise them, when to frighten or perplex them. So, like any other story, the story of this storyteller must begin at the beginning, and that's where I'll start.

His name was Jack. That's an ordinary name, one that fit him well, for Jack was indeed an ordinary boy. He grew up in an ordinary family and lived in an ordinary village, Yorrow by name, in the Realm of Sundar. There Jack did what countless children had done for as long as anyone could remember: he helped his parents run their farm, he played during the brief times when he wasn't working, he collapsed in exhaustion each night, and he awoke the next day ready to start all over again.

In appearance, too, he was ordinary. He stood about the same height as most boys his age. His facial features were pleasant without seeming handsome. A thatch of brown hair roofed his head. His eyes were brown as well. Indeed, Jack looked much like any other country boy in Sundar.

He behaved well and worked hard to help his family. He had to. Life was difficult throughout the Realm, and dangerous. Every family provided for its own needs; failing to do so meant hardship, hunger, even starvation. Not only the adults but all the children, too, labored to plow the soil, plant the crops, herd the goats, feed the hens, gather the eggs, weed the garden, carry the water, mow the hay, harvest the crops, shear the sheep, spin the wool, weave the cloth, sew the clothes, and do whatever else needed to be done. Jack did his part, just like everyone else.

Something about him wasn't ordinary, though: his stories. For even during his earliest years, when Jack had just barely begun to talk, he told stories.

What kind of stories, you ask?

Well, you can't expect much from a child who's barely old enough to say his own name. But I'll tell you this much: Jack's first full spoken phrase was "Once upon a time . . ."

The truth, however, is that even Jack's kind, loving parents had little use for his stories. All that mattered was surviving the latest hardships. A storytelling boy was a luxury that no one viewed with patience, much less delight. Yet as he grew older, Jack couldn't ignore his own stories. They came to him unbidden. They whispered to him in the night. They accumulated in his head. They crowded out his other thoughts. Jack's mind became a hive buzzing with stories.

"Once upon a time," seven-year-old Jack told his sister Gwynne as she lay ill one autumn, "a girl named Gwynne caught a quail in a trap she'd set. But the quail cried out, 'Please! Set me free and I'll protect you for the rest of your days. You'll never be sick, for my magic feathers will heal you.' And the quail plucked a feather from his wing and gave it to Gwynne."

"Once upon a time," eight-year-old Jack told his brother Alfred, when Alfred fell into the well and floated, cold and frightened, far below in the water while Gwynne ran off to get help—"Once upon a time, Alfred fell into a well and waited for someone to come and pull him out. And while he was down there, Alfred heard a voice say, 'You! What are you doing in my well?' Terrified, Alfred stammered, 'W-w-who's there?' 'I am,' said the voice. 'I am Samantha, the water sprite who lives in this well.' 'Are you a *good* sprite?' Alfred asked nervously. 'Or an evil one?' Samantha replied, 'Oh, very good, and I'm here to help you. I'll teach you a song that will keep you warm until your rescuers arrive.'"

"Once upon a time," nine-year-old Jack told Father following Grandmother Hilda's death, "a woman named Hilda got sick, died, and left her son, Edmund, lonely and sad. So after the burial Edmund planted an oak tree over Hilda's grave. And the roots grew downward and hugged Hilda. And the tree pulled Hilda into itself and grew big and strong, so that Hilda was the tree and the tree was Hilda, with great limbs reaching outward toward everyone and everything. And Edmund often climbed the tree and rested among the branches, and in that way he never lacked for an embrace."

"Once upon a time . . ."

Where did these stories come from? Jack didn't know. What did they accomplish? He didn't know that, either. By the time he was ten years old, he had only just begun to explore his storytelling skill; he didn't understand it yet. All he knew was that the stories welled up from somewhere deep within, and they demanded his attention until he released them into the world.

2

Now let's jump ahead a few years to when Jack had reached the age of thirteen. The oldest of six children, he still spent most of his time doing farm work. The intervening years had been a time of scarcity throughout the Realm of Sundar. A long drought had limited what the farmers could produce even for their own needs. There wasn't much food, if any, to sell to other people. To make matters worse, the Realm's king, Alphonse, taxed them harshly. A farmer who harvested ninety bushels of wheat owed thirty to the king. A shepherd whose flock gave birth to thirty sheep owed ten. A potter who made sixty pots owed twenty. King Alphonse claimed fully a third of what anyone produced. Such was life during Jack's boyhood.

These hard times hadn't prevented Jack from telling stories. On the contrary, he often used his storytelling to cheer up his family when nothing else was going well. He told a story about a tree that bore apples all year round. He told a story about a cheese bigger than a barn. He told a story about a magic basket that, despite its small size, contained baked potatoes, a crock of soup, some roasted hens, and even some cakes and cookies—so much food that no matter what you removed, the basket stayed full to the brim. He told a story—

You get the idea. Did these stories fill anyone's stomach? Of course not. But they gave his family hope, and they expressed his love for them.

Then an event took place whose consequences Jack wouldn't fully understand for a long, long time.

For most of his thirteen years, Jack had heard villagers speak of an old woman known simply as the Woman of the Woods who lived in the forest bordering Yorrow. Some people said she was just a crone who disliked human company. A few claimed she was a witch. Many believed that there was no Woman of the Woods at all—she was nothing but a character in an old folk tale. Jack himself tended to agree with this last group. After all, in some accounts the Woman was fat; in others, thin. In some she lived inside a hollow tree; in others, behind a waterfall. In some she ate only sparrows' eggs; in others, the marrow of children's bones. Given all these contradictions, what chance was there, really, that this woman existed?

Still, Jack delighted in these stories for the simple reason that he liked to hear them. He enjoyed their strangeness. He was amused by the web of words that this old woman, whether real or imaginary, inhabited like a rare and remarkable spider. Beyond that, he didn't think much about her.

One afternoon, though, while collecting firewood at the edge of the Twilight Woods, Jack spotted a wild rabbit and started tracking it among the trees. He imagined cornering it, killing it with a stone, and carrying it triumphantly home to his parents, who would then prepare a tasty stew for the whole family. But Jack's efforts quickly came to nothing. The rabbit escaped. At that point, Jack realized that he was lost. His efforts to find a way out only led him deeper into the woods. Worse yet, the afternoon light began to fade, and Jack understood with growing alarm that he'd have no choice but to spend the night alone in the forest.

How did he react to this insight? He panicked. He raced around, tripping on roots and smacking into low-hanging tree branches. Then, since panic hadn't solved his dilemma, he lay down, wept, wailed, and pounded the ground. Finally, wearied by this outburst, he sat up. The forest still surrounded him, now even darker than before. At this point, panic and self-pity gave way to a new feeling: dread.

The forest was known throughout Yorrow as a perilous place infested not only with snakes, wolves, and bears but also with gnomes, goblins, demons, and witches. How could Jack survive a night here?

At about this time, however, something caught Jack's eye: a light. Dim but unmistakable, a yellowish glow seeped through the trees and underbrush and reached the spot where he now stood. This light struck him as one of the most beautiful sights he'd ever seen— as welcome as his mother's voice calling him in from the fields for dinner. Jack rushed toward it, shoving his way past tree branches and jumping over fallen logs.

Then he stopped short.

Right before him in a clearing stood a cottage unlike any he'd ever seen. It wasn't a normal peasant cottage, boxy and thatch-roofed. It was round, built of interwoven branches instead of boards and bricks, and looked like nothing so much as a large upside-down bird's nest. Moss grew in the seams between the branches. Ferns sprouted from the rounded roof. An oval window leaked light into the evening. A doorway sat to the right of the window.

Unsure of what to do, Jack pondered the situation. Should he knock at the door and announce himself? Or should he back off and return to the forest?

For years, he had heard stories about lost children who knocked on cottage doors in dark forests and ended up meeting a witch. The cottage door would swing open, shrieking like a rat caught in a trap. A dried-up old woman would call out, "Come in, my dearies," in a voice as squeaky as the door. And within a short while the children's worst nightmare would come true. Didn't it make sense, then, for Jack to flee? To avoid the shriveled-up crone? To seek instead the safer company of snakes, wolves, and bears?

Without knowing why, Jack knocked firmly, twice, on the door. Nothing happened.

Jack reached over to knock again—just as the door swung open.

An old woman stood gazing back at him. Her body was plump, her face soft with wrinkles, her eyes the palest blue, her hair so long and white that it streamed like a waterfall across her shoulders and down her back and sides. "Yes?" she said in a voice that didn't squeak or screech but only sounded high and breathy.

"Hello," he said. "I'm lost."

The woman shook her head in dismay or sympathy. "Well, that's a pity. Enter my palace and warm yourself—I'll give you something to eat."

Jack hesitated once again. Palace? This woman looked harmless enough, but she was undoubtedly the Woman of the Woods. Visiting her might put his life at risk. Even so, Jack's curiosity got the better of him. His hunger, too: he hadn't eaten anything since midday. So he stepped inside and seated himself at her table.

"Here you are, lad," the Woman said, setting down a bowl of fern-head soup and some rough, nutty bread.

Jack started at once to gobble his portions. Only when his hunger eased a bit did he stop and look around.

The house was less unusual inside than out. Except for the curved, woven-branch walls, it could have passed for any other poor person's cottage in the Realm. A copper kettle, a knife, a wooden spoon, and two earthenware bowls sat on a simple shelf. An ax rested beside the doorway. A storage area near the ceiling held stocks of dried plants and baskets of supplies. An open hatchway in the floor led to what was likely a root cellar. The only source of light was the flickering fire on the hearth.

What made this scene remarkable wasn't the house, however, so much as its inhabitants. For in addition to the Woman, many creatures lived there, creatures of the sort that most people would have worked hard to keep out. Mice scurried up the walls. Weasels slunk about underfoot. A couple of hares loped back and forth across the room. A squirrel peeked out of a ceramic bowl near the hearth. Birds fidgeted in the rafter-like branches overhead. The Woman ignored almost all this activity and paid little attention to the creatures' noise. But as the squeaking, squealing, chirping, and chittering swelled into an intolerable din, the Woman suddenly clapped her hands and announced: "Gentle ones, *enough!*"

The creatures fell silent, stared at her, and then retreated, some seeking refuge in the woven walls.

"These are my subjects," stated the Woman. "Like most subjects, they are unruly and need gentle reminders to behave themselves. But they thrive on kindness and expect nothing less from their queen."

"Queen?" Jack said in bewilderment.

She nodded. "This is my kingdom. I am Queen Celestina."

Jack wasn't sure how to react. Queen Celestina looked anything but regal; in fact, she resembled any other woman of her age and humble circumstances. But her attire—so odd! Her crude clothes, fashioned out of homespun fabric and grassy materials, were tattered and dirty. A necklace of tiny snail shells ringed her neck. A bracelet of braided weeds clung to each wrist. A crown of woven leaves encircled her head. Despite her claims of royalty and the strangeness of her appearance, Jack saw nothing dangerous or hostile in her behavior.

Celestina offered Jack a second helping of food, then a third. She draped a cloak over his shoulders. She heated water and brewed strong tea for him to drink. "I trust you're feeling better now," she said. "But tell me: what, dear boy, has brought you as an emissary to my realm?"

"I'm not an emissary," Jack said. "I just got lost in the woods. I'm a villager. My name is Jack."

"Jack. Jack, indeed. A good name for a villager. And which village do you call your home?"

"Yorrow," Jack said.

"Yorrow," Queen Celestina repeated. "A fine village, Yorrow. I ruled over Yorrow many years ago—indeed, I ruled over the entire Realm of Sundar—but just briefly. Now I rule over mice, rabbits, and weasels." She held out both hands affectionately. "Bless you, my dear subjects," she said. "Bless you all."

Jack didn't know what to think. On the one hand, this old woman seemed gentle, kind, and harmless; on the other hand, she was nutty as an oak tree in October, and her rambling comments made him uncomfortable. To put himself at ease, Jack asked, "So what do you do here, you and your loyal subjects?"

She smiled knowingly. "Oh, we tell stories."

"Stories?"

"All kinds of stories. That's our greatest wealth here, stories."

"I tell stories, too," Jack said on impulse.

"That's a good lad!" Queen Celestina exclaimed. "What could be better than lots of stories?"

This exchange pleased Jack; as odd as he found her, at least they shared this interest. "I like stories more than anything," he told her.

He was unprepared for Celestina's response. His words, like firewood heaped on glowing embers, sparked a flame in her eyes and gave brightness and warmth to her voice. Almost at once Celestina started to tell a story. And though Jack wondered if he'd get burned by the intensity of the Woman's voice, he felt cheered by the light she cast and comforted by the heat this tale brought to the small, dark cottage.

❧ 3 ❧

Once upon a time I was queen of Sundar (she began). Do you doubt my words? Well, then, doubt them. But what I'm telling you is true.

I grew up in a castle whose splendor surpassed all others. Towers rose so high that their pinnacles could snag the clouds. So many rooms filled the castle that no one had ever counted them all. The whole place swarmed with servants: lords- and ladies-in-waiting, cooks, provisioners, tutors, and guards. There were even servant playmates—children assigned to amuse and entertain me—for my parents, King Edgar and Queen Lydia, wanted every possible happiness for their only child.

"Oh, look!" exclaimed my mother at a party honoring my sixth birthday. "Your friends have come to give you gifts!"

Seated at my parents' feet before the royal thrones, I watched as scores of children approached me in the Great Hall. Each child carried a velvet pillow, and each pillow held a birthday present.

Such presents!

Two pure white canaries in a golden cage.

A miniature rocking horse painted with gold and studded with sapphires, emeralds, and rubies.

A little mechanical man who, when cranked up, announced, "I love you, Celestina! I love you, Celestina!"

A kitten with a golden collar.

A music box that played my favorite tune.

Gifts and gifts—gifts that took me all morning to receive.

"What a nice present," I stated, thanking each child in turn. "I'm so happy."

In truth, I couldn't have been more miserable. These *children* weren't giving me gifts; they were only delivering what my parents had arranged to have bestowed upon me. This procession of hired playmates did nothing but rub salt into the wound of my loneliness.

The only gift I wanted was a brother or a sister—I didn't care which. Someone who would sing songs and play games with me for fun, not for hire. Someone I could tell stories to, and who would tell me stories in return.

Imagine my surprise when my wish came true soon after that— and more fully than I'd ever thought possible. My mother gave birth not to just one child but to twins: Mackaroe and Mortimer, as my parents named them.

I was jubilant. I had attained the only riches I'd ever wanted. I reveled in my brothers' presence in my life. I nagged their nurses to let me help feed, bathe, and dress the babies. In some ways I was more the twins' mother than Mother was. I taught them how to walk. I taught them how to speak. I told them the bedtime stories that put them to sleep. I couldn't have been happier with my new companions.

As they entered boyhood, Mackaroe and Mortimer delighted in my attentions and grew fond of me. They saw little of our parents, who spent most of their time governing the Realm. Although the nurses provided most of the twins' care, I was their closest friend.

They turned out to differ greatly from each other. Though twins, they looked, spoke, and acted as if born into two different families. Mackaroe was fair haired, blue eyed, lean, and muscular. Though outwardly quiet, he tended to be intense: impatient, restless, and capable of anger. I never knew what he was thinking. Mortimer, by contrast, was dark in eyes and hair color. His temperament seemed darker, too—not sad so much as brooding. He talked more, and more openly, than his twin. He was emotional, and his moods could be difficult, but with Mortimer I always knew where I stood.

The truth is, I loved them both. We spent all our time together. We played tricks on one another. We got into trouble together with the tutors, the stewards, and the Royal Guard. We made the castle our playground.

And we told stories. Stories about the ghosts we thought haunted the castle. About a witch who lurked unseen in the kitchen. About the huge serpents that prowled the water in the moat. About the magical birds that roosted in the palace gardens.

We told stories about each other as well. About how Mackaroe, who was fascinated with swords, armor, and military prowess, would grow up to be a brave warrior. About how Mortimer, who preferred the arts, would someday become a painter, a sculptor, and a great patron of artists throughout the Realm. About how I, who loved stories, would create an empire of stories, a land in which everyone cherished both the teller and the tale.

What we didn't tell, however, were stories about what might happen to us if our parents died. Some stories are too worrisome even to contemplate. What a shock, then, to find our lives upended in this way just ten years later, when I was twenty and the twins thirteen.

While traveling somewhere in the Realm, Mother and Father both died suddenly. The circumstances were unclear. What I heard at the time was that my father, while walking on a steep, rocky trail, fell and suffered mortal injuries. My mother then hurried to assist Father and fell to her death. This explanation baffled me. My parents were both strong and sure-footed. What else was I to believe, though, when the royal councilors presented me with the appalling news of my parents' deaths?

Well, I did what I was destined to do. Being the oldest heir, I assumed my rightful place as queen. Yet only three days later, I was queen no longer. My understanding of the reason why came too late.

Certain nobles—my allies within the court—informed me that my parents' deaths had been no accident. Mother and Father had suffered their injuries not from falls but from soldiers' weapons. My parents' enemies within the royal army had overthrown the monarchy. Believing that Mother and Father had neglected Sundar's military interests, these traitors had killed them to install a puppet king responsive to their own ambitions.

Who, though, would be that puppet?

Apparently, I qualified—but just briefly. Once I'd learned the truth about my parents' fate, I did everything possible to identify their killers, bring the criminals to justice, and return the Realm to its proper course. My enemies had better spies than I did, however, and they soon detected my moves against them.

Within a day or two, I ended up in prison. I—and my brother Mortimer.

Who, then, would be the Realm's new ruler? Who would cooperate so fully with the military leaders that they would tolerate him?

The answer: our brother Mackaroe. He, in his sympathy for warriors, would be the pawn in their game.

Languishing in the castle's dungeon, I received news that I'd soon die beneath the blade of Moribundo, the royal executioner. Mortimer would die as well. Thus our potential for causing trouble would vanish like flowers snipped from a vine.

So how did I escape this fate?

One night, as I huddled in my cell, I heard footsteps in the corridor and felt the door tremble as someone threw back the bolt. Who could possibly intend to visit me?

It was the man who inspired my deepest dread. Massive, hairless, and heavily scarred: Moribundo. His hands were as large as a bear's paws. His eyes gazed at me through holes in a black leather mask. I tried not to look, so fearsome was this man's appearance. I covered my head and waited for the final blow.

"Up, m'lady," said the executioner. "Up wit' you."

I didn't understand the words.

"If you wish to save yer life, get up *now*." He motioned with his huge hands.

"You're rescuing me?" I asked, incredulous.

"Not if you don't 'elp me do it."

I forced myself to stand.

To my astonishment, Moribundo unlatched the shackles anchoring me to the wall. "I thank you with all my heart," I told him. "But please explain—what accounts for this act of mercy?"

He shook his head. "That's not a question I'm at liberty to answer."

I never learned more about what had prompted Moribundo's actions. What I *can* tell you is that he led me through the dungeon and showed me out through a doorway I'd never known existed. Then he hid me within the foul cargo of a cart loaded with rotten food, and he sent me on my way.

Somehow, I endured the oppressive voyage. At least it had a better destination than the one I'd nearly reached. Dumped with the rubbish in a refuse heap, I played dead for a while, listening to the cart rumble off. Then I pushed my way out from under the stinking scraps, got up, and looked around.

I was at the edge of a forest. A lush, dark forest. A forest that has been my home, my haven, my kingdom ever since.

ᚎ 4 ᚏ

As the Woman of the Woods finished speaking, Jack grew aware of his surroundings once again. The fire hissed on the hearth. A few mice squeaked nearby on the floor. The wind muttered outside the cottage.

Jack had enjoyed the Woman's story from start to finish. At the same time, he decided that *what* she'd told him could never have taken place. The castle of uncountable rooms . . . the servant playmates . . . the gifts that took all morning to receive . . . the twin princes, Mackaroe and Mortimer . . . the king and queen's mysterious deaths . . . the royal executioner, Moribundo. It was more than Jack could even begin to believe. Hearing Queen Celestina's story confirmed everything that he'd suspected about her: the old woman's mind harbored as many mad thoughts as her cottage housed unruly rodents.

"So now I am queen of this forest realm," said Celestina, "and these are my courtiers." She motioned regally with both hands.

The mice, weasels, rabbits, and birds stared back at her.

Jack wasn't sure how to reply. "No doubt they're loyal subjects," he said.

"They are indeed."

"And they love their queen."

"They do—just as I love them."

"They respect you, too."

"Indeed, though I have so little to offer them. Nothing, really, except a few scraps of food."

"And your stories," Jack reminded her.

Celestina nodded gravely. "My stories. True. For what is a king-dom but stories? Stories about the struggles of the past. Stories about the promise of the future. Stories about the love between the rulers and the ruled."

Jack wondered if she'd start in again. What time was it, anyway? Surely close to midnight. But the time really made no difference: he couldn't go anywhere in the dark; he'd have to wait till morning. He settled comfortably in his chair. "Could you tell me another story, then?" he asked.

"Of course," she answered. "I'd like nothing better."

She told him a story about two children, lost in the woods, who were rescued by a snow-white deer that let them cling to his huge antlers for support and ride on his head.

She told him a story about a woman with hair so long that she knotted it into a net, cast it into the sea, and caught fish to eat.

She told him a story about a man who toppled into a magic lake and emerged radiant, his body so intensely aglow that forever after-ward he could sit in the dark and read a book by his own light.

She told him a story about a bird and a fish who fell in love and struggled hard to find a realm in which they could live together.

She told one story after another. Jack listened as if bewitched, losing track of time as the moon rose and the stars wheeled overhead. All that mattered was the stories.

Finished with one, she'd begin another: "Once upon a time . . ."

Jack awoke with a start. He forced his head up and looked around. A crude table. The hearth, its fire now dead. A few pots and plates. In the corner, on a rough bed, the Woman of the Woods—Queen Celestina—fast asleep.

Blades of sunlight slashed through the woven cottage walls.

If he hadn't seen the place before him now, Jack would have thought he'd dreamed it. And the stories: had he dreamed those? Or had Queen Celestina really told them? Stretching, Jack got up, walked to the doorway, pulled open the door, and squinted at the brilliant day. It must have been nearly noon!

"What's the matter?" Celestina called out.

Jack turned to see her getting up, disturbing two weasels, a rabbit, and a scattering of mice that had been nestling against her.

"I have to go," Jack said abruptly.

"Go?" the old woman asked in bafflement. "You just barely arrived."

"I'm sorry, and I thank you, but I can't stay any longer."

Queen Celestina shook her head. "Very well. I'd never keep you here against your will. But what about the stories? I have so many more to tell."

"Some other time!" Jack shouted as he headed off.

☙ 5 ❧

What choice did Jack have? Even if he succeeded in leaving the woods without difficulty, he'd reach home almost a full day late. If he had problems finding his way, he'd be delayed still further. Jack dreaded his parents' response no matter how quickly he returned to Yorrow. Thus he left Celestina's cottage, struggled for a long time to locate the path, walked for hours, emerged from the forest, and finally arrived back at his family's farm.

Of course his parents scolded him—not just because he'd missed a whole day's work, but also because they'd worried so much about his safety.

"How were we to know what had become of you?" Jack's father demanded.

"We thought you'd been devoured by wolves!" his mother lamented.

"I was safe," Jack told them quietly.

"Safe, you say. Safe, in the Twilight Woods?" Father trembled in anger. But then he steadied himself, reached out, said, "Come to me, son," and embraced Jack. Mother came over, too, and hugged him. "We just didn't want to lose you," Father said.

"The woods are so dangerous," Mother added, "and we feared the worst: bears, serpents, demons. . . . You might even have fallen prey to the Woman of the Woods."

"I found her," Jack said.

At once his parents pulled back. "What did you say?" asked Father.

"The Woman—I found her." Jack couldn't help chuckling at the shock on their faces. "I found the Woman of the Woods."

Now everyone in the house assaulted Jack with questions.

"What does she look like?" asked Sally.

"Did you talk to her?" asked Fergus.

"Is it true she's a witch?" asked Eleanor.

"Did she try to eat you?" asked Alfred.

"Please, please!" he told them. "I'll explain, I promise!"

So he did. Jack told the story of how he'd gotten lost, found the Woman, and spent a night in her company. He told the story of what she was like—how her cottage resembled a bird's nest; how it teemed with mice, weasels, birds, and rabbits; and how she held sway over these woodland subjects and called herself Queen Celestina. He told them her own story—how she'd lost her parents, inherited a kingdom, and lost that, too, only to gain another, humbler realm.

Finally finished, Jack gazed at his family.

"Oh, Jack," his mother said, shaking her head. "How I wish I could be angry with you."

"As we surely ought to be," Father added.

"Not just for getting lost," Mother went on, "and for missing a whole day's work—"

"But for telling such outlandish stories!" Father exclaimed.

"I want to be angry," Mother said, "but I'm not. Not when you tell such fine tales."

A moment passed before Jack could grasp what had happened: no one in his family believed him. He felt offended by their disbelief and wanted to set them straight. What he'd told them about the Woman of the Woods was different from her strange, unlikely tales. *This happened!* he'd exclaim. *This really happened.* Instead, he chose to keep quiet. He had somehow escaped punishment and didn't want to push his luck.

He realized something else, too: his family might not have believed him, but they still enjoyed his stories. They listened and let themselves be caught in the net he'd cast.

And that, Jack decided, was what mattered most.

So what did Jack do? I mean about the stories.

Well, he kept telling them. For that's what he loved most.

That's all he did—tell stories?

No, of course not. Remember: Jack was a farm boy, and a farm boy rarely gets a break from his chores.

So when did he tell his stories?

At day's end. There was no entertainment in Yorrow—no concerts to hear, no magicians to watch, no parties to attend. Jack and his family worked from dawn to dusk. But after sunset, they couldn't keep working, could they? They had no light but the hearth fire, for they couldn't afford even a single candle.

So they just went to bed?

Sometimes. The younger children did, certainly—they nestled under their blankets and fell asleep. But the older ones, Jack and Gwynne and Sally, often stayed up awhile with their parents. And guess what they liked to do?

Tell stories!

Right. They sat before the hearth and told stories. And guess who told the most?

Jack!

Right again. His family often stayed up much later than they would have otherwise, listening to Jack.

❧ 6 ❧

In some respects you could say that Jack lived two separate lives. By day he lived in the farm-and-village world, a world in which he worked the fields, herded animals, carried water, chopped firewood, and helped his family. Each night, however, he lived in the story world, a world in which goats could fly, eggs grew on trees, gold coins fell like hail from the sky, dukes traveled the land in disguise, and children flew kites so huge that they were lifted from the earth and carried away through the clouds. Life by day and life by night— the farm-and-village world and the story world—each gave Jack its own real but greatly differing satisfactions.

Three years passed. And as they passed, Jack realized that he was growing more and more comfortable in both worlds, and he was learning more and more about what each world required of him. Then, at age sixteen, Jack reached another insight about storytelling.

I should mention that one of Jack's stories at the time concerned a man named Garth Golden-Eye. As Jack told the tale, Garth was a robber, greatly feared for his evil deeds, who had grown rich off the gold doubloons, ducats, and guilders he'd stolen. Having lost an eye in a fight with an uncooperative victim, Garth had recovered from his wound but ended up with a hideous empty socket. He had inserted a gold ducat into the space where the eye had been, inspiring the nickname that intensified his reputation as a terrifying outlaw.

Now, it's true that such a man had once lived in the area. But no one had seen any sign of him for several years, so it seemed probable that Garth Golden-Eye had died. What, though, had become of the robber's ill-gotten treasure?

The answer to that question was the heart of Jack's story. "There's a hill not far from here," he told some villagers one night, "and on that hill there's a tree. Beneath that tree there's a stone, and beside that stone there's a stump. Forty paces north of the stump there's a mound of moss. Three feet under the mound there's a buried chest, and in—"

Before Jack could finish his sentence, four of his listeners bolted from the room. Jack told the rest of his story; then everyone else left, too, heading out to the fields.

Jack couldn't believe what had happened. He didn't know anything beyond the usual rumors about Garth Golden-Eye. He certainly didn't know where the robber might have hidden the spoils of his crimes. Jack had merely made up a story. He'd even made up the part about how Garth had lost his eye. Yet now dozens of villagers were scouring the countryside! What a strange machine he had wound up and set in motion!

People dug and dug. In fact, they dug up every clump of moss in the area.

Jack grew concerned. What if nothing came of all these efforts?

"I hope you're ready for what happens next," Father told him. "A lot of folks will be angry when they come back empty-handed. Telling a story doesn't make it true."

"But what if it *is* true?" Jack asked hopefully.

"Be careful, Jack," said Father. "If you jump off a cliff convinced you're a bird, flapping your arms won't make you fly."

Jack knew that his father spoke the truth. Yet he kept telling the story about Garth Golden-Eye, and he started to believe it himself. Garth had relieved many people of their belongings. Surely the old robber had stashed his treasure *somewhere*. Why not three feet under a clump of moss forty paces from a stump, beside a stone, beneath a tree?

One day, some villagers came sprinting into Yorrow. "Where's Jack?" they yelled. "Where's Jack the storyteller?"

Jack flinched. His storytelling days were over. These people would now punish him for wasting so much of their time and effort. Yet as they reached his family's cottage and burst in, Jack heard their shouts: "We found Garth's treasure!"

"Found *what?*" Jack asked.

"*This!*" a tall man said, showing off a fistful of coins.

Within minutes the truth emerged. Five men and three women had located a suspiciously shaped clump of moss, dug beneath it, and unearthed a half-rotted wooden chest. Inside were coins, jewels, and gold ingots.

These people were now rich.

Jack felt pleased that his story had somehow pulled several families out of poverty, yet he felt astonished, too, that embroidering the cloth of fact had somehow created a fabric of truth. He couldn't make sense of these events. This much was clear, however: after his fellow villagers dug up the box of Garth Golden-Eye's doubloons, ducats, and guilders, everyone in Yorrow listened with great eagerness to his stories.

As the commotion over Garth Golden-Eye's treasure subsided, Jack reflected on what had taken place. He hadn't made a penny from the recent turn of events. He *had* gained something, though, because of the stories he'd told.

In Sundar's smallest villages, most people generally had only one name. If you spoke of Keith, Gwendolyn, Edwin, Wilfred, Beth, or Trevor, everyone would know whom you meant. There might, of course, be two Beths in town, but you could easily clear up any confusion by referring to "Old Beth" or "Young Beth." In larger villages, however, the situation grew more complex. Three Beths might live in the same neighborhood. The solution: people used their trades as surnames. Beth the weaver was Beth Weaver. Beth the butcher was Beth Butcher. Beth the kettlesmith was Beth Kettlesmith.

Jack, having grown up in such a small village, had never had a surname. Even a common name like Jack had been all he'd ever needed. But now his name grew longer, better, stronger. Best of all, it told the world who he was and who he felt proud to be.

Not just Jack. Jack Storyteller.

⚘ 7 ⚘

So the months came and went, and with them the many tasks that yapped at Jack's heels like a pesky dog. Jack might have become Jack Storyteller, but this new name offered no relief from his day-to-day work. All along, however, something gnawed at him.

He wanted more from life—something deeper and more powerful.

"I've decided to seek my fortune," Jack told his family one morning shortly after celebrating his seventeenth birthday.

His family just stared at him.

"I intend to explore the world," Jack went on hurriedly. "I want to see what it offers me and find out what I can offer in return."

Father asked, "You'll go tell your stories?"

Jack nodded. "Yes, I'll tell my stories."

"To an eager world?"

Jack felt uncertain. Was Father mocking him? "Eager or reluctant," he said, "the world will hear my stories."

"What about us?" Mother asked him. "We need you here."

Jack spoke his mind: "But isn't this what lads do? Go off to seek their fortune?"

Father chuckled quietly. "Well, perhaps they do in stories," he said.

"Perhaps they do when there's no field to plow or goats to herd," Mother added.

Jack felt terrible. "I'm sorry."

"If you're sorry," Father told him, "don't go."

Jack would have given anything to be able to say *Oh, never mind. I'll stay.* He knew that he was letting his family down. He dreaded the consequences for them. Yet somehow he couldn't say *Oh, never mind.* Instead, he said firmly, "I must go and tell my stories."

Silence filled the room like smoke.

"Go, then," Mother told him suddenly.

"Go," said Father. "We won't stop you."

Then his parents left the cottage to resume the work awaiting them in the fields, and his brothers and sisters left, too, to perform their own tasks.

Jack felt bewildered and uncertain. He wanted to call out, to explain why his quest was so urgent, to convince his family that he'd prove himself, that he'd accomplish great deeds and return victorious to Yorrow, that he'd ease the burden on his family despite having chosen a path that seemed like abandonment. But he didn't call out. He didn't explain his quest. Confused and sad, Jack merely watched as they walked away.

❦ 8 ❦

Jack felt deep sorrow over disappointing his family, but he also felt delight and relief that his parents had let him go. He could scarcely restrain his excitement as he imagined the adventures ahead. Even so, he didn't leave. For days he remained in Yorrow, desperate to be off yet helpless to depart. But why? Was he afraid? Was he doubtful of his goal? Was he alarmed about what he might encounter out there in the world? Then, without warning, Jack understood that he still had someone else to bid good-bye.

"I've come to say farewell," he told the Woman of the Woods when he reached her cottage late that morning.

"Farewell?" asked Queen Celestina. "You haven't even said hello."

"I mean I'm leaving," Jack said, flustered.

"Lad, you've just arrived."

"I'm leaving home. Leaving Yorrow. I'm off to seek my fortune."

Celestina set aside the big spoon she'd been using to stir a potful of soup. She motioned for Jack to sit at her table, and she sat down across from him. "You're the right age now," she said. "Sixteen? Seventeen? But how, exactly, will you seek your fortune?"

He shrugged. "By doing the only thing I do well—by telling stories."

"Ah, yes, stories."

Jack warmed to his subject. "I'll tell the stories that come to me."

"You have no choice, really."

"No choice at all—and I must be off."

"You won't even stay long enough to hear one of *my* stories?"

"I'd love to, but I can't. I have so many of my own to tell."

Celestina smiled at him. "You do indeed. Go, then," she said, motioning cordially toward the door. "The telling can't be stopped, and you will surely find your listeners."

"Thank you for your kindness."

"It's nothing. Go in peace."

Jack knelt as if before a queen and arose only when Celestina touched him on the head. Then he left the cottage.

The old woman called after him: "Jack Storyteller!"

He stopped and turned to face her.

"Add some good plot twists," she shouted. "But not too many."

"I shall!"

"Invent characters who tell their own stories."

"I promise!"

"Tell stories that make people laugh or cry—"

"I promise that as well!"

"—or even sneeze."

Jack was puzzled. *"Sneeze?"*

"Be off!" yelled Queen Celestina, shooing him away. "The world awaits you!"

The next morning, Jack said good-bye to his parents, his brothers and sisters, and everyone in Yorrow, and he set off on foot with a leather bag on his back, a few coins in his pocket, and a lot of untold stories inside his head.

†WO

What happened on his journey?

Well, that's not just a single story, but lots of them—stories that Jack himself couldn't have made up.

Because they were so strange and amazing?

On the contrary—because they were often so ordinary. A young person setting out to seek his fortune is, in its own way, one of the oldest stories of all.

So tell me!

Well, there are many stories, not just one. How Jack fell in with traveling companions who claimed to be friends but stole most of his belongings while he slept.

What else?

How Jack, striving to regain his footing on the path of life, reluctantly sought help from an ugly man whose appearance scared the boy but who nonetheless treated him with great kindness and generosity.

Go on.

How Jack, wandering from village to village, found his luck reversed not once or twice but time after time.

So what happened?

I could tell you these stories, but I'll hold off. I can't tell you all the stories. What matters most is simply that Jack kept going, survived many close calls, went on his way, and, with each passing day, practiced his storytelling art with more and more skill.

❦ 9 ❦

For several days Jack had been walking from town to town, earning meals and lodging in exchange for stories. Now, following the directions that people had given him, he veered off the main road and entered the forest of Sycamora. This path was supposed to be the quickest route to Callitti—the Royal City. And so Jack left the sunny road behind and forged a more uncertain route into the thickest, darkest woods he'd ever seen.

This place was so gloomy that Jack sometimes thought dusk had fallen, for the trees overhead formed a canopy as dark and tight as the hoods that prisoners wear while awaiting execution. Then, just as he'd start to panic, he would abruptly enter a small clearing and discover that the sun still shone brightly in the sky above. In one such clearing, Jack sat down, weary yet uneasy, to rest. He had started to doubt the wisdom of entering the forest in the first place. He wondered if he might do well to retrace his steps—if, indeed, he could find his way out of the woods at all.

"Once upon a time!"

Jack looked up in alarm. Who had spoken? He couldn't see anyone nearby. Had he heard his inner voice—his mind telling him a story?

The voice spoke again: "I said, *Once upon a time!*"

At that moment Jack noticed a bird perched on a branch no more than three paces away. Smaller than a crow but just as black, the bird looked as if a piece of the night had sprouted feet, wings, tail, and head. Its beak was a shiny dark blade that jutted from its face. Its eyes glistened like two black beads of rain. It looked alert, curious, and aware of everything.

Jack stared at the bird, then glanced about. Surely this creature couldn't have spoken.

"Let me try again. *Once! Upon! A! Time!*"

Seeing the sharp black beak move at the same instant that he heard the words, Jack realized with astonishment that the bird had indeed spoken. He stood, a shiver snaking up his spine. "You can *talk*."

The bird tilted its head back and forth, staring at Jack first through one eye, then the other. "I certainly can—the same as you," it stated bluntly. "I get a thought and I open my mouth. The rest is talk, talk, talk!"

For a moment Jack felt the urge to flee. This creature was surely a bird-shaped demon. Yet Jack stayed where he was, hostage to his own curiosity. "Who *are* you?" he inquired.

"By name I am Loquasto. By nature—well, *there's* a story."

"I didn't know birds could talk," Jack told him.

"Most don't," replied Loquasto. "There's all that chirping and cheeping, of course. One might call that talk. Parrots and cockatiels have a little more to say. 'Hello! Hello!' 'Who's the best little birdy?' 'Lunchtime, lunchtime!' But it's all so . . . *limited*."

Jack shrugged. "Well, many folks would be amused by a talking crow."

"A crow? A *crow!*" Loquasto protested. "I may be gabby, but I'm no crow. I'm a midnight mynah and proud of every feather."

"I meant no offense," Jack assured him.

"None taken. Just don't call me a crow."

"Agreed," Jack said. He was impressed by this talkative bird. It even occurred to him that if he and Loquasto traveled together, both would gain some conversation. "Well, I'd best be going," he said, "but perhaps you'd care to join me."

"That depends," Loquasto said. "Where are you going?"

"I'm off to seek my fortune in Callitti."

The bird looked aghast. "The Royal City? Then it's ill fortune you seek."

"What's so bad about Callitti?"

"What's so bad? Who's got the time to say it all?"

"I'll have some fine opportunities in Callitti," Jack said. "You see, I'm a storyteller, and in a big city I'll find an audience—"

"Who's the king of Sundar?" the bird asked abruptly.

"Alphonse."

"Who has plunged his people into misery?"

"Alphonse."

"And who lives in Callitti?"

"Alphonse."

Loquasto ruffled his feathers in exasperation. "So why insist on seeking precisely the place that you should most urgently avoid?"

"I don't know," Jack said with a shrug. "But in many stories I've heard, young lads seek their fortune by going to a royal city."

"Well, then, you're even younger than I thought—"

"I'm seventeen."

"—and you have much to learn."

Jack persisted. "So teach me what I need to know! Come and share my journey."

"Thanks, but no thanks."

"We'll talk and talk."

"I'd do so gladly," the bird replied, "if you'd chosen some other destination. But the Royal City? No, thank you—I'll pass."

Jack was disappointed but saw no alternative to leaving. Loquasto's comments worried him; still, he wasn't ready to change his goal just because of a chatty bird's opinions.

And so, after bidding the midnight mynah farewell, Jack headed deeper into the forest.

❧ 10 ❧

Jack continued on his way for much of that afternoon. Although unsure how to reach his destination, he felt his confidence surge again, and he strode forth, unconcerned about the fading of what little light lingered in the forest.

Now, sometimes a young man's head tells him a bright story even while his gut tells him a tale full of shadows. As Jack walked through the forest, his head told him: *The woods are beautiful, the path is straight, and the birds sing sweetly in the trees*, while his gut told him: *Beware!* Jack heard both stories, but he listened to the sunny tale, for he enjoyed it more, and he ignored the other.

Still, he shouldn't have felt surprised when a band of robbers stepped out of the gloom and pointed their crossbows and swords at him. And he shouldn't have been shocked to see that one of the ruffians had only one good eye, while the other eye was nothing but a gold coin shoved into the socket.

"Garth!" exclaimed Jack.

"Good evenin' to ye, laddie," Garth replied, stepping closer, his sword drawn. "An' who might ye be, addressin' yer elders in so presumptuous a fashion?"

"My name's . . . Jack."

Garth looked him over, prodding at Jack's tunic, cloak, and leather pack with his sword blade, no doubt trying to decide whether a humble farm boy would possess anything worth his efforts to acquire. The robber was older than Jack had imagined, with stringy gray hair on his head and silvery whiskers that sparkled on his jaw like frost on an October pumpkin. But Garth's age did nothing to ease Jack's worries. If he was lucky, Jack told himself, Garth Golden-Eye would realize that he lacked anything of value and would let him go. On the other hand, Garth might feel outraged by the inconvenience of stopping a wayfarer so unworthy of his trouble. Worse yet, he might grasp the connection between Jack and the boy who had revealed the whereabouts of his buried treasure.

"Jack," said Garth brusquely. "Jack *who?*"

Jack shrugged. "Just Jack."

Garth nodded, circling his prey. "Just Jack," he repeated, mimicking the young man's accent. "A simple village lad, are ye?"

"I don't believe 'im," said one of the other robbers, a huge man with wild hair and a tangled beard.

Garth nodded again, now gravely. "'ardly worth me bloomin' trooble—that's what ye're wantin' me to think, ain't it so?"

Jack was too terrified to answer.

Another ruffian—a toothless young man—reached out with his dagger. "Just slit 'is bloomin' froat and be done wit' 'im!"

Garth ignored his minions. "Well, then, Just Jack, tell me what village ye're coomin' from."

With Garth's sword point at his neck, Jack blurted, "Yorrow!"

"Yorrow indeed," Garth noted with a smile. "Joost as I thought. It's 'ow ye say yer *R*s—loud an' long as a r-r-r-roll o' thoonder." He paused as if rummaging through the musty old trunk of his mind to locate a memory he'd stowed there for safekeeping.

Now some of the other robbers grabbed Jack and held him. What troubled Jack even more than his captivity, however, was how closely they stared at him.

Suddenly, the bearded man spoke the words that Jack had dreaded most: "It's 'im! Jack Storyteller! The bloke who told the tale. The tale what led to—"

"Me losin' all me loot," Garth stated flatly. He shoved his one-eyed face close to Jack's. "Listen, lad, an' listen good. Ye're the bane of me 'ole life. Ye're the fly what's swimmin' in me beer. Ye're the worm what's crawlin' in me apple. I worked many a year to amass me fortune, and ye're the one who gave it all away."

"But I didn't mean to," Jack protested.

"Didna mean to? Didna *mean* to!" Garth said with a laugh.

"I just made up a story. I didn't know you'd really buried your loot."

"So much the worse fer ye, lad, sooferin' a dismal fate fer soomthin' ye didna *mean* ta do—"

"Garth Golden-Eye!"

None of the men present had spoken. Yet Garth's name wafted through the forest, loud and clear.

"Garth Golden-Eye!"

The robbers glanced about.

"Stop yer tricks," Garth ordered, sounding peeved.

"Garth Golden-Eye!" The voice spoke again, its source unclear but its words altogether plain: *"Begone, Garth! Flee, all you walking rubbish heaps!"*

"What's that?" asked the bearded robber, sounding alarmed.

The toothless youth tightened his grip on Jack. "'Tis nothin'— just a trick. 'e's frowin' 'is voice."

At that moment, Jack realized that the words had emanated from a nearby tree. Gnarled and scarred, this great oak had limbs that stretched out like huge menacing arms. A large hole and two smaller ones in the trunk resembled a vast mouth and two hideous eyes.

"Flee, evil ones," shrieked the tree, *"or this forest will become the teeth that bite you—"*

"There i' 'tis again!" shouted the bearded robber.

"And the throat that swallows you—"

"Pay no attention!" Garth cried.

"And the gut that devours you!"

"Where's it coming from?" asked the youth.

"It's that *tree!*" one of the others shouted. "That one—there!"

Jack felt as terrified as his captors looked. Some stared at the tree; some drew their swords; some simply cowered. Only Garth kept his attention on Jack. "If this is yer doin'," he warned, "ye'll die even sooner than ye thought."

But at once the voice came again: "*Speak not of any death but your own, Garth Golden-Eye! For you, too, will perish—but first I'll leave your good eye in the same sorry state as the bad one.*"

This threat seemed to alarm the robber. "Me eye?" he asked, suddenly close to panic.

"*Indeed—your remaining eye.*"

Garth abruptly staggered back, faltered a moment, then sprinted away. His henchmen, terrified to see their leader flee, turned and followed.

Jack was stunned by this turn of events. One moment he had stood at the brink of doom; the next, he was safe.

Or was he?

"*You, Wayfarer!*" said the great oak, its voice booming out of the hideous mouth hole.

Jack trembled, too terrified to run. "What do you want?" he asked fearfully.

"*Simply this: Tell me why you have ventured so foolishly into my domain.*"

"My name is Jack Storyteller," Jack said, his voice wavering. "I mean no harm."

The tree gave an echoey laugh. "You *mean no harm. But what of the harm that others would so eagerly do to* you?"

"Well—"

"*Answer me!*"

Shaking hard, Jack said, "I have to take some risks. I have to accomplish what I've set out to do."

40

"*Indeed!*"

"And so I'm on my way—"

"To Callitti," said a familiar voice as a midnight-hued little bird emerged from the tree's gaping mouth hole.

Jack stared. "Loquasto?" he managed to say.

"At your service."

"I should throttle you!"

"Don't be ungrateful."

"You scared me half to death!"

Loquasto flared his wings, glided over, and alighted on Jack's wrist. "Isn't it better that I scared you *half* to death," he asked, "rather than allow the robbers to do the job completely?"

"Of course."

"Is it possible, too, that thanks might be in order?"

"Indeed," Jack said. "I thank you with all my heart."

"That's better," replied Loquasto.

Jack was uncertain what to say next. "I appreciate what you've done on my behalf," he told the bird at last. "It's late, though, and I'd best be on my way."

Loquasto pecked Jack's hand—only once, but hard.

Jack pulled back in pain. "What was *that* for?"

"For being such a fool," the bird stated. "Best be on your way indeed! Go, then. But don't imagine for a moment that you'll go alone."

"You're coming, too?"

Loquasto pecked him again.

"Stop it!" Jack exclaimed.

"I'll peck you from dawn to dusk," said Loquasto, "if that's what's necessary to knock some sense into you. Of *course* I'm coming."

So they set off again. Sometimes, Jack decided, you need a talking bird to set things right.

So they traveled together?

Loquasto wouldn't have it any other way.

Did Jack understand how much the bird had helped him?

Oh, yes. He knew that Loquasto was a remarkable creature, and Loquasto had certainly proved himself a valuable companion.

How long did they travel together?

Many days, but that's another story.

Please tell it.

Well—

Tell me the story.

All right, then. But first you have to hear what the bird told Jack. For as they headed through the forest, Loquasto told Jack the story of his life.

❧ II ❧

I was born two years ago (Loquasto began), one of six birds in my mother's brood that spring. You want to know what a hatchling's life is like? Well, here's the truth. Within a few months I had learned to fly, and then I joined my parents and my brothers and sisters in the endless tasks of gathering food and defending our territory. That's a bird's lot in life. Do I sound displeased? All right, I'm displeased. From my earliest days I've been restless.

"Is this . . . *it?*" I asked my mother one day. "Picking fruits and berries? Chasing off other birds? Calling out the same thing, over and over?"

"This is what we do."

"But is it *all* we do?"

"Of course—what else is there?"

I didn't know. To be honest, it didn't seem like enough. Wasn't there more to life than this endless routine? "I want more," I told her. "I want to see the world. I want to meet different kinds of animals and talk with them. I want—"

"You want too much," Mother told me.

"But I think—"

"You think too much."

"Mother—"

"You talk too much."

Well, that was true enough, but my longings were part of me—as much a part as my wings, beak, and beady eyes. And one longing, especially, I felt compelled to fulfill.

Look at me. I'm a bird, right? Like any other bird, I didn't want to spend my life alone. I wanted a mate. There were plenty of birds around—many of my own kind. I spent time chatting with them, but does chatter make a good life? Sorry; it's not enough.

Then something happened that changed my life forever.

Picking berries down by the lake one afternoon, I spotted the loveliest creature I'd ever seen. Her feathers glistened orange-yellow in the sunlight. Her wings, though exceptionally small, moved with grace. Her tail was lush, fuller than any I'd ever seen before. And her eyes—the largest, saddest eyes in the world. The sight of her filled me with longing. I knew at once that I'd found my soul mate. I wanted nothing more—and nothing less—than to spend my life with her.

There was only one problem: she was a fish.

Being young and new to the world, I had misunderstood what I'd seen. What I'd thought were feathers turned out to be scales. What had looked like wings were actually fins. What I'd believed to be her tail was indeed a tail, but a tail far different from a bird's. And her slow, stately motions? She wasn't flying, she was swimming.

"Why do you stare at me so?" she inquired as I gazed at her from near the water's edge.

"Because it's you I see—the one I love."

She stared back at me. "And I, too, now gaze at what my heart desires."

Her name was Artemisia, and she was the daughter of the fish king and queen. Their domain encompassed the whole lake, which they shared in harmony with the fish and other creatures there. Artemisia led a peaceful life—peaceful to the point of boredom. In truth, she felt restless and unhappy, just as I did. She felt a growing desire for something more.

Now we had found it, each in the other.

But what to do? If a bird and a fish fall in love, where will they live?

You might say, "Surely there's a way. Try hard and you'll find it."

Well, we tried. We tried and tried. I hopped into the lake and, forcing myself under the surface, made every attempt to enter my beloved's realm. But two awful truths struck me at once. First: birds float. I'd claw my way down a short distance, then bob right back to the surface. Second: birds need air. One beakful of water and I came up sputtering. After just a few minutes in the lake, I flopped about, skittered back to land, and lay panting on the shore.

Artemisia tried, too. Flipping out of the water, she landed in the dirt with an impressive *slap*. Now we were together. But within moments she began to gasp. Her body trembled. Her eyes dimmed. Only with the greatest effort did I roll her back into the lake. Several long moments passed before she roused, started to breathe again, and resumed swimming.

"What are we to do?" I asked.

"We must see each other as we are," she replied, "not as we wish to be. Although we share one spirit, we come from two different worlds and must remain apart."

"But somehow—"

"Let us love each other but accept that we shall never live together."

I couldn't bear these words. "Artemisia—"

"I will always love you." At once she swam away.

I never saw her again.

ᔧ12ᔧ

After Loquasto finished his tale, Jack didn't know what to say. What could he say to console Loquasto for the loss of his beloved?

Jack strode through the forest for a while with Loquasto on his right shoulder. Finally, he blurted his thoughts: "Perhaps someone in Callitti can help you."

"*Help* me?" huffed the bird. "Since when do people in Callitti help anyone? Since when do they cause anything but pain and grief?"

"They can't *all* be so terrible," Jack said. "There must be *some* goodhearted souls there."

Loquasto cawed in amusement. "You're such a trusting lad."

"I'll do anything I can to help bring you and Artemisia together."

"That's thoughtful of you," Loquasto admitted "Though from what I've seen so far, I'd say that *you* need far more help than I do."

Jack shrugged. "Let's help each other, then."

"Fair enough."

So Jack and Loquasto hastened together toward Callitti.

I'm pleased to tell you that during the rest of their journey, the two travelers encountered no threats as dire as Garth Golden-Eye. I must add, however, that their voyage didn't lack for mishaps and adventures. I could tell you many stories. Someday I'll do just that. For now, though, I'll say simply that they continued their journey, they suffered many discomforts, they avoided the worst kinds of trouble, and they soon approached Callitti.

The Royal City! For as long as he could remember, Jack had heard stories about this place—about its size, its beauty, its wealth—but he had never imagined he would see it himself. Now he shook with excitement as he and Loquasto emerged from the forest and gazed at it across the farmland. Massive stone walls—gray-brown in hue and as rough as a beast's fur—surrounded Callitti. Lesser dwellings—the houses, shops, storehouses, stables, bakeries—huddled against these walls like bear cubs seeking the protection of their mother. Inside them was the city itself: the vast keep, the armories, the soldiers' quarters, the yards, and many buildings and towers. Over all these rose the palace, rearing up from the city's heights. The sight of this great city inspired Jack to feel both excitement and dread.

He and Loquasto now headed for the city gates. They weren't alone in doing so; the road was full of people even at the late hour of their arrival. Some carried baskets of vegetables, bread, or other goods. Others herded goats or sheep. One woman pulled a handcart loaded with crates of chickens. Two men led a pair of oxen whose backs bore sacks of grain. The people were attired much as Jack was—in crude peasant garb stitched from leather and homespun cloth—and their appearance prompted him to feel more comfortable than he'd expected.

As crowded as Callitti looked from beyond its walls, it was even more so within. It teemed with people—more people than a country boy like Jack had ever seen before. People walking through the streets, the alleyways, and the open squares. People selling pots, scarves, knives, candles, food, and books. People shopping for all these items. People standing about and gossiping. People telling fortunes. People singing or playing instruments. People everywhere.

Though dizzied by the crowds, Jack was thrilled to be among them. "Just look!" he exclaimed as he and Loquasto eased their way through the city. "These folks will surely welcome a story." Like a man throwing a hook and line into a trout-filled stream, he felt sure that someone would take the bait. He found a corner that looked promising, then called out: "Once upon a time—"

"Louder," said Loquasto.

"Once upon a time—"

A few people turned toward Jack or backed off, making room for him.

"Here's a storyteller!" someone shouted.

More people drew near. Women toting baskets of vegetables. Men lugging bundles of firewood. Children carrying their own loads.

"So tell a story!" a woman's voice called out.

Jack had never addressed so many people before. "Once upon a time—" he blurted again. Then, bracing himself, he plunged into the first story that came to mind: how a farm boy distracted his hungry family with stories.

"Another!" someone shouted when he'd finished.

"They like you," said Loquasto. "Keep talking."

Jack told them about a boy who got lost in a forest and met the Woman of the Woods, the long-vanquished queen of a distant realm.

"Another story!" a man yelled.

"Yes, another!" cried a woman.

Loquasto, squawking loudly, called back, "Pay the teller! Pay the teller!"

Jack couldn't believe his eyes when he saw five, six, eight, ten people reach out to him with coins.

"The least you can do," Loquasto told him, "is accept their money."

Removing his shapeless leather cap, Jack extended it, took what people offered, and marveled at the clink of the coins as they accumulated.

Now he began to tell a tale about a one-eyed highway robber.

"You!"

"Once upon a time an evil man named Garth Golden-Eye—"

"You there!"

Startled, Jack glanced around.

A guard standing at the crowd's edge had spoken. Massive, stocky, and clad in armor, this man now strode over to him. "Who are you?" the guard demanded, "and by what right are you telling stories?"

"My name is Jack Storyteller."

"This isn't good," Loquasto whispered.

"If you tell stories," said the guard, "you must come with me." He motioned to a squadron of soldiers.

"Not good at all," the bird told Jack.

"The crow stays here," the guard commanded.

Jack protested at once: "He's not a crow—he's my friend."

The guard nudged Loquasto off Jack's shoulder. "Shoo! Shoo, I say!"

Loquasto veered upward, perched on a balcony overlooking the square, and arched his wings in alarm.

"Wait! No!" Jack shouted, close to panic.

The squadron surrounded Jack and marched him off.

❦ 13 ❦

You can imagine how Jack, led away like that, might have expected the worst. He wondered: Had he offended someone? The market master, perhaps, or the lord mayor? Perhaps even King Alphonse himself? Jack couldn't guess. But he knew that six armed men wouldn't be marching him through Callitti if he weren't in trouble.

In trouble for what, though? He'd only told a few stories. Was there a law against that? Maybe so. Perhaps the king had banned all storytelling. Perhaps storytellers needed a permit. Being escorted through the streets, Jack felt his spirits sink. What a fool he'd been to seek his fortune, to try to prove himself to his family. Hah! Within a short while, he'd end up in prison—or dead.

"Where are we going?" he asked fearfully.

The guards didn't even glance at him, much less answer.

To Jack's amazement, he didn't end up lying in a dungeon or kneeling before an executioner. Instead, he found himself standing in a huge room whose walls, painted with forest scenes, bewildered him with their beauty. Not one but three hearth fires warmed the room. The furniture seemed sufficient to seat fifteen or twenty guests. Yet once the guards had deposited Jack and departed, he waited there alone. How he wished that Loquasto could have accompanied him!

A plump man entered. He wore a red robe embroidered with gold. His face was as round, pale, and doughy as a half-baked pie, and a wig swirled atop his head like meringue.

"Are you indeed a storyteller?" the man asked.

"My name is Jack Storyteller," Jack replied.

"Then we have need of your services."

Jack felt confused. "Services?"

"I am the lord high chamberlain," the pie-faced man announced, "and I'm here to inform you that His Majesty King Alphonse faces a terrible problem." He paced back and forth. "The king's youngest child, Prince Yoss, has suffered a great misfortune."

"Is he ill?" asked Jack. "Did he injure himself?"

The chamberlain drew close. Clearing his throat, he whispered into Jack's ear: "Prince Yoss stuck a ruby up his nose."

"He did *what?*" said Jack, unable to contain his amazement. Was this what royal offspring did to amuse themselves?

"The prince's behavior isn't yours to judge," the chamberlain scolded. "He may do whatever he wishes."

"Apparently so."

"Silence! You will simply assist Prince Yoss to the greatest degree possible."

"*Assist* him? But I'm a storyteller. What the prince needs is a physician."

"A physician has already been summoned. Several of them, in fact."

"They'll help the boy."

"They've employed every available medicine, but nothing has helped."

"Couldn't they use some sort of pincers to extract the jewel?"

"They tried that, too, but without success. If anything, their attempts made the situation far worse. The pincers not only failed to remove the gem, they pushed it farther up the prince's nose."

Jack felt more and more convinced that the lord chamberlain's request, far from offering him an opportunity, presented a terrible threat. "I regret to learn of the prince's affliction," he said gravely. "It's a hardship that no child should suffer. But—"

"He doesn't need your sympathy," the chamberlain interrupted. "Only your help."

"I have no help to offer!" Jack shouted. "If the royal physicians have failed, how can a mere storyteller succeed?"

The chamberlain said, "That's your problem to solve, isn't it? Otherwise, your fate will be the same as the physicians'."

Alarmed, Jack asked, "Fate? What fate?"

The chamberlain didn't answer.

Before Jack could press the point, the door swung open. Six guards marched in and stopped short, thumping their battle-axes against the floor as they announced: "Step forth, Jack Storyteller!"

☙ 14 ❧

As Jack followed the guards, he expected to find himself in a room containing just a small audience—the king, the prince, and some attendants, perhaps—for this command performance. He now realized his mistake.

This room was the largest Jack had ever seen—a great high-beamed hall whose ceiling could have accommodated tall trees—and in it he saw more people than lived in the entire village of Yorrow. All of them appeared to be nobles, for no one else would wear such elegant attire—so much velvet, silk, and fur. Despite the number of people present, however, the hall was nearly silent. Men, women, and children alike waited quietly as Jack strode from the back of the Great Hall to the front.

Straight ahead, a large bearded man sat on a lavishly carved throne. Surrounding him were four children of various ages. Three were daughters—one about fourteen years of age, another perhaps fifteen, the third seventeen or eighteen—all of them tall, long haired, and lovely. The fourth child was a son: perhaps twelve or thirteen years old, handsome in appearance, with wavy golden hair and clear blue eyes. All five members of the royal family gazed at him somberly as he approached.

Jack couldn't have felt more awkward. Surely he shouldn't have been there in the first place. To make matters worse, he stood before them in his dirty village clothes—his muddy boots, his rough home-spun pants, his deerskin tunic, his woolen cloak. The contrast between the nobles' fine attire and his own crude garb left him dizzy with shame. Yet he felt angry, too. King Alphonse and his children! This was the family that sucked the life out of Sundar as greedily as a leech drinks blood from a fish! Yet despite his embarrassment and rage, Jack did what he knew he must: he knelt and bowed his head.

"You are Jack Storyteller?"

Jack looked up.

King Alphonse had spoken. Strong in appearances and sporting a sandy brown beard, he wore a dark blue fur-trimmed robe and a jewel-studded crown. He gazed down at Jack with an expression of surprising hopefulness.

"I am, Majesty," Jack answered.

"You are a master of the storyteller's art?"

He shrugged. "I tell stories."

"Arise."

Jack stood tall again.

"Tell stories, then," the king commanded. "I have great faith in the arts—in their power to diminish suffering. Chief among the arts is storytelling. Tell stories, then, to relieve my son, Yoss, of the burden that he has so foolishly—"

"*No!*"

Jack turned to face the person who had uttered this word: the prince himself.

"I don't *want* stories!" Prince Yoss stated in a nasal voice. "I *don't!*"

King Alphonse made a brushing motion with his hand as if shooing flies from a piece of cake. "Jack Storyteller," the king commanded, "tell a story."

"No *stories!*" whined Yoss. "I *hate* stories!"

Torn between these two contrary commands, Jack hesitated. The king was the king, however, and even the prince followed his father's command. And although Jack feared that granting the king's request would inevitably lead to failure and an unknown fate, silence would lead to trouble even faster.

Jack thought quickly. *Tell stories that make people laugh or cry,* the Woman of the Woods had urged him, *or even sneeze.*

Was it possible that a story could make someone sneeze?

"Once upon a time," Jack began, "there was a kingdom called Archooie—a kingdom known far and wide for the spiciness of its peppers. The peppers of Archooie were, in fact, so peppery that the farmers growing them feared harvest time much as soldiers fear going off to battle. Many of these farmers, climbing high into the pepper trees to pick their crop, would sneeze so hard that they'd tumble to the ground."

Silence. Everyone in the Great Hall appeared to be listening.

Prince Yoss stared at Jack with an expression of mixed boredom and contempt.

"There's also the land of Kachá," Jack continued, "where the peppers exceed the pepperiness of those from Archooie. In fact, these peppers are so peppery that birds flying over the orchards often sneeze until they knock all their feathers off."

Jack faltered. His efforts were going nowhere. The king gazed at him with great perplexity. The princesses' faces revealed slight bemusement but nothing more. Prince Yoss smirked in contempt.

"Far from Archooie and Kachá, in a land called Hablishoo," Jack went on, "peppers grow with such alarming pepperiness that, when ripe, they are as dangerous as bombs. The soldiers in Hablishoo use them as weapons. Shot from cannons, the peppers explode, showering the enemy with peppery particles and leaving the hapless soldiers to sneeze and sneeze until they have no choice but to surrender."

No response—not even the tiniest sniffle from the crowd.

Suddenly, Jack realized that he'd taken the wrong approach. He needed his stories to hit closer to home. "Once upon a time," he said abruptly, "there was a prince who loved flowers."

The audience stirred. The king leaned forward. Even Prince Yoss watched Jack with sharp, hostile attention.

"This prince—Prince Kersplat by name—loved flowers more than anything. He loved their shapes, their colors, their textures, and most of all their magnificent aromas. Prince Kersplat loved to wander through the royal gardens sniffing flowers."

Prince Yoss glared at Jack as if to say: *I dare you to make me sneeze.*

"One day," Jack went on, "Prince Kersplat went about his business sniffing flowers. Life was full. Better yet, his *nose* was full—full of the lovely perfumes he adored. Sniffing one flower, though, Prince Kersplat realized that he'd sniffed more than he'd bargained for. He had sniffed an Aroozuppian pepper flower. Now, what you must know is that the Aroozuppian pepper flower attracts the notorious pepper bee. Prince Kersplat had, to his great dismay, inhaled a bee. A bee! A bee right up his nose! Worse yet, an Aroozuppian pepper bee!"

At that moment, a startling sound reached Jack's ears: a sneeze.

Who, though, had sneezed? He couldn't tell. Maybe one of the courtiers.

"You have to understand," Jack continued, "that inhaling a pepper bee would be itchier than the peppers from Archooie—"

Another sneeze echoed through the hall: "*Ka-choo!*"

"Itchier even than the peppers from Kachá—"

Now two people sneezed together: one high and shrill— "*Eeeeesh!*"—the other lower and louder—"*Ha-thpppp!*"

"And itchier even than the peppers from Hablishoo," said Jack.

At least five or six people sneezed, one after another.

Jack raised his voice: "Imagine how *you* would feel to have an Aroozuppian pepper bee mistake your nose for a flower—"

Soon the whole court erupted in a skirmish of sneezes. Like a tavern brawl, in which one man's ill temper kindles a flame of rage among the others in the room, this free-for-all of sneezes now spread among the courtiers. The king himself sneezed once, twice, thrice. The princesses sneezed. The councilors as well. No one could avoid catching this plague of sneezes. No one except Jack—and the prince.

Prince Yoss stared at Jack with an amused, arrogant gaze that said, *You, Storyteller, will never make me sneeze. You have failed. And because you have failed, you will die.*

Jack stared back, exhausted but unwilling to admit defeat. "Imagine that bee flying around inside *your* nose," he said, "buzzing about, nuzzling inside your nostrils."

"Ah—!"

At first Jack thought Prince Yoss was calling out to him.

"Ah—! Ahhh—"

All the people in the Great Hall fell silent. Everyone stared at the prince.

"Ah—! Ahhh—! Ahhhhhh—!"

With his head tilted back and both hands clutching the sides of his head, Yoss stared at the distant ceiling.

Jack saw his chance and grabbed it. "The bee flies around,

attempting to escape!" he exclaimed. "Imagine the beating of its wings! The buzzing of its body! The savage tickle of the tiny creature as it bounces about inside your nose!"

"Ah—! Ahhh—! Ahhhhhh—! Ahhhhhhhhhh—!"

"What could be worse," Jack went on relentlessly, "than to have a bee trapped there! What could itch more wildly than the throbbing of those tiny wings! What could prickle more terribly than the bee's stinger! It's enough to drive you totally, complete, absolutely—"

"*Hachxfthrqqnkthtutha!*"

Despite the monstrosity of Prince Yoss's sneeze, the people in the Great Hall heard another sound a moment later, a much smaller sound, a sound that somehow stood out because of its precision: a sound of something small and hard hitting the stone floor and skittering away.

❧ 15 ❧

At that moment Jack reached an insight, one he never forgot: a bee in a story could tickle worse than a real bee. He realized, too, that a story peach could be sweeter than a real peach, a story flower more fragrant than a real flower, a story song more melodious than a real song. What existed in a story could be more real than what existed in the world. And by reaching this insight, Jack understood the true power of his art.

He wasn't the only one.

"Jack Storyteller has performed a noble deed," King Alphonse declared to the assembled courtiers, "and we are grateful indeed for his efforts." The king stood before his throne and beckoned for the boy to come forward.

Jack knelt and bowed his head. Something touched his left shoulder: the royal scepter.

"You have saved Prince Yoss from a foolish and hazardous mistake," said the king. "In appreciation of this meritorious deed, we bestow upon you this token of our thanks."

Then the lord high chamberlain approached and deposited a small leather bag into Jack's palm. The weight and clinking of its contents told Jack that he had just received more gold coins than he had ever seen, much less owned, in his entire life.

"Majesty," Jack said, "I've done nothing to deserve your praise and thanks."

"What I offer now is only the beginning," said the king.

Jack felt confused. Only the beginning?

King Alphonse turned to the courtiers. "So extraordinary are this young man's abilities," he said, "that I hereby appoint Jack Storyteller to the King's Artists."

A great roar greeted this proclamation.

Jack's confusion deepened. The King's Artists? Who were the King's Artists? He bowed again. "I thank you, Majesty."

"The pleasure is ours. Now go in peace."

Thus dismissed, Jack walked out of the Great Hall—walked calmly, though he could have leaped for joy. Courtiers smiled and applauded politely as he left.

Jack understood, however, that not everyone in the hall shared the king's gratitude and the courtiers' admiration. As he departed, he caught a glimpse of Prince Yoss. The boy gazed at him with barely concealed rage and hatred.

Why? More than anyone else present, the prince should have felt grateful to Jack for rescuing him. If the ruby had remained stuck up his nose, the boy would have suffered infection, fever, and eventual death. Why, then, should the prince be so furious? *Ah, yes, Jack* realized. Although he'd rescued Yoss, the prince had paid for this service with the coin of public humiliation. No wonder the boy resented him.

So Jack left the palace—escorted this time not by guards but by an elegantly attired servant—and he pondered the results of his story-telling. Yes, his story had allowed him to exercise great power. He had rescued the stupid prince and had earned the king's admiration and gratitude. Yes, he had impressed the whole court. He had accomplished what even the royal physicians had failed to do. Power indeed!

But power is a sword with two edges. He had attained his goal, but he had also risked getting slashed by his own blade. What would have happened if his efforts had failed? How would the king have treated a storyteller who let him down? And how would Yoss have responded if he hadn't been just a boy but a young man capable of revenge?

Jack felt too weary to ponder his fate. For now, he wanted nothing more than to stop thinking about the day's strange events. A chunk of bread, a slab of cheese, a mug of cold water, and a place to sit alone and eat—these were the only rewards that Jack Storyteller craved.

THREE

Did Jack become rich and famous?

Well, listen to me, and you'll find out.

Did he become the world's best storyteller?

One thing at a time. He'd only just arrived in the Royal City. All he wanted at the moment was to settle in, catch his breath, and rest.

He went there to tell stories, didn't he?

Of course. But even a storyteller must do more than just tell stories.

☜ 16 ☞

Jack had never imagined achieving so much so easily and so fast. Yet the signs of his new status were unmistakable. Upon leaving the palace, Jack followed the king's servant across a courtyard and from there into a nearby building that housed Jack's new room. And what a room: it was larger than his family's entire cottage! It contained a huge bed, several chairs, two tables, a mirror, some chests for storage, several candlesticks, and a fireplace. Large windows looked out toward a courtyard below and the palace.

That room soon became the setting for further satisfactions.

First, a tailor arrived to measure Jack for new clothes.

"A member of the King's Artists must dress properly," the tailor stated. "We can't have you presenting yourself before Majesty in your filthy old clothes."

By day's end the new finery arrived: breeches, tunics, cloaks, hats, boots, and gloves, all made from velvet, satin, and fine leather.

A parade of serving boys showed up, too, each bringing Jack some tasty delights. A savory stew. Roasted meat. Cake, custard, and candied fruits. Jack stared at the food as if watching a magician's act. Would these wonders disappear if he touched them? He reached out, took a small pastry, and ate it. Delicious! And altogether real.

Only one aspect of his new situation troubled him: where was Loquasto? Jack worried that he'd never see his new friend again. "Is there a bird somewhere in the vicinity?" he asked one of the servants.

"Many birds dwell in the royal gardens," replied the servant, looking puzzled.

"I'm referring to the one who accompanied me to the Royal City. The one who . . . *talks*."

A look of awareness dawned on the boy's face. "Ah, yes. I know just the one. The guards caught him not long ago when he tried to enter the palace. I'll go fetch him at once."

A short while later, the boy returned with an angry-looking Loquasto in a gilded cage. The bird waited for the boy to leave, then started squawking. "Never in my life have I felt so humiliated! Me, a rare midnight mynah, locked up like a common canary!"

Jack opened the door to the cage and released his friend. "I'm sorry," Jack said, "but it's been worth the trouble."

"That's easy for *you* to say."

Jack motioned toward his new quarters. "See for yourself. I've gained us a fine place to stay—and plenty of food, too."

Loquasto fluttered about as he surveyed the room. "Hmm," he said, calming down. "Maybe so. But I won't tolerate such treatment again."

"Shh! Not so loud!"

"Why are you hushing me?"

"You're going to get us both in trouble."

"I'm going to get us *in* trouble?" Loquasto said, astonished. "Tell me if I'm mistaken, but didn't I recently get you *out* of trouble? Does the name Garth Golden-Eye ring a bell?"

"Of course," Jack admitted, "but that's not what I meant. It's how people react to you. Can't you pretend to be like other birds?"

"I'd die of boredom."

"Just talk less. You can chatter on and on when we're alone, I promise."

The bird fidgeted impatiently. "What must I do, precisely?"

"Just use a few choice phrases when we're out and about. The sorts of things I've heard you say already—'Once upon a time!'—that sort of thing."

The bird gazed at Jack. "Well," he said at last, "I'll consider your request."

So Jack and Loquasto settled in, both of them relieved to be out of danger but unsure what would happen next.

❧ 17 ❧

For all Jack's delight in his change of fortune, a hundred doubts nagged at him. Who, exactly, were the King's Artists? How difficult would Jack's duties be, and would he prove able to fulfill them? Would he find favor in the Royal City? Or would his good luck run out?

Jack and Loquasto kept their own company through the following day. The next evening, though, Jack received a summons to present himself before the chief of the Artists, a man named Geoffrey Jester. Elderly, pink-faced, and plump, Geoffrey had a nimbus of soft white hair that surrounded his otherwise bald head like a cloud clinging to a mountaintop. "So what do you do?" Geoffrey asked Jack.

"I tell stories," Jack replied.

"Very good," Geoffrey said. "We've never had a storyteller in our troupe, but clearly some aspect of your act caught the king's fancy."

Jack shrugged. "All I know is that I tell stories, and the king asked me to join the Artists."

"If that's what Majesty wants," said Geoffrey, "that's what we'll give him."

Geoffrey then explained that the King's Artists were practitioners of many different arts. Some played musical instruments. Others danced. Some created sculptures, paintings, or drawings to beautify the palace. Still others sang. No matter what the king's whims, the Artists stood ready to amuse, console, or humor him.

Now Jack stood ready to join them.

"Heed me well, young man," said Geoffrey. "You are now the king's servant, so you must serve Majesty whenever he calls for you."

Jack nodded curtly. "I'm ready."

"If he wants a story in the middle of the night, you'll get up and tell him one."

"Of course."

"If he wants a sad story—"

"I'll leave him weeping."

"If he wants a scary story—"

"I'll leave him trembling."

"Whatever Majesty wants, you'll give him."

"Indeed I shall."

"This above all," said the chief of the Artists. "Try to make him laugh. Majesty hasn't laughed in a long, long time."

❧ 18 ❧

The Artists' Hall was a large room, complete with tables, benches, and a hearth. Few Artists spent much time there, since their practice and performance schedules allowed only limited opportunities for social visits. Jack, settling in among them, crossed paths with them only during their two main meals—the first early in the morning; the other, midafternoon.

"My name is Jack Storyteller," he said one day, reaching out to shake hands with the people seated at his table.

"Edwin Flutist," said a balding, bearded man.

"Mog Dancer," said a slim young woman.

"Ned Painter," stated a long-haired boy.

All of them were cordial. Following these introductions, however, they turned to their food—barley soup, roast lamb, and big slabs of bread—rather than conversing.

Perplexed by their silence, Jack tried to draw them out. "So tell me, how often do you perform before the king?"

"Whenever he calls for us," Ned answered.

"Which could be never," Edwin noted, "or it could be every day. No matter what, you have to be ready."

Beyond these few comments, the Artists said little. Soon everyone finished eating and departed, leaving Jack and Loquasto alone in the hall.

"Well, I guess either the king will call us," Jack told the bird, "or else he won't."

Little did he know how quickly the call would come.

"You, Storyteller," said Geoffrey, entering the room a few moments later. "The king has asked to see you."

Jack stood. "To see *me?*"

"Right now," the chief of the Artists told him. "Don't keep him waiting."

A short while later, Jack and Loquasto found themselves in the Great Hall. King Alphonse, flanked by several councilors in gray robes, sat on his massive throne. "Tell me your name again, lad," he said.

Jack bowed. "Jack Storyteller, at your service," he said.

The king nodded. "Service indeed. You have already done far more, certainly, than the royal physicians."

"Has the prince recovered, Majesty?"

At these words King Alphonse frowned. "Your stories cured Yoss of the ruby afflicting him," he said. "Whether a story can cure his greater malady, though, I'm not so sure."

Jack ignored this last comment. He couldn't say that only a fool would stick a ruby up his nose. As he recalled Yoss's fury, however, he said, "I apologize for any dismay that my stories may have caused the prince."

King Alphonse looked uncertain. "Dismay?"

"Because of my telling those stories in public."

The king still showed no sign of comprehension. A great cloak of sadness shrouded him and seemed to shield him from so obvious an insight.

At this point the lord high chamberlain—the pie-faced man with the creamy-looking wig—intruded: "What the storyteller means," he said, "is that he believes Prince Yoss felt humiliated."

"Humiliated!" exclaimed King Alphonse, his perplexity turned to anger. "Well, then, let him feel humiliated! That's what he ought to feel, committing such a foolish act. He's twelve years old, not two. But a ruby up his nose is hardly the worst of Yoss's problems. If you have other stories capable of knocking sense into the boy's head, tell them all!" Then, before Jack could respond, King Alphonse spoke again. "Something else."

"Majesty?"

"I want you to tell *me* stories as well."

This request struck Jack as a gift, not as a demand. "With pleasure, Majesty. Whenever Majesty wishes."

A smile flickered across the king's lips. "All right, then—go," he said. "Prepare yourself for the great deeds ahead."

Jack bowed again and left, his spirits soaring. Yet he soon felt a more complex mix of emotions. King Alphonse had complimented his skill, thanked him, and invited him to visit. He had implied that Jack's future among the Artists would be promising indeed. Yet despite these compliments, Jack felt unsettled. Why? Because the situation with Prince Yoss still concerned him. Jack dreaded even the possibility of crossing paths with the prince.

Something else, too, troubled him. Why was King Alphonse so sad? Why did such a pall of grief surround the man? He was sovereign of the Realm. He commanded the army, controlled the treasury, and taxed the kingdom's people. He possessed great wealth. He lived in luxury. He headed a handsome family. True, his children were a sullen lot, and at least one of them was a fool. So perhaps it was these odd children that burdened their father's mood. Even so, Jack wondered if family life alone could account for the king's sadness. He couldn't help feeling that something else must surely explain the royal gloom.

Jack struggled to restrain his curiosity. He discussed the situation with Loquasto, but the bird offered no insight. Finally, he decided to seek information from his fellow Artists. While eating in the hall one afternoon, Jack nodded toward the rain thrashing the windows. "Compared to Majesty's mood," he said, "today is a bright, sunny day."

"Enough of that," said Geoffrey, reaching toward a platter with his knife to skewer a chunk of roasted chicken. "We're not here to criticize the king's spirits but to raise them."

Jack understood that he'd spoken too boldly. "I wasn't criticizing, only noting."

One of the musicians—a lean, black-haired youth—spoke up. "You've only noted what everyone knows."

"*I* didn't know it," Jack said.

"Well, now you do," stated Eliza, a gray-haired singer who sat across from him.

"And you'd best leave it at that," added Hildegard, a young harpist.

Why the king's low mood inspired such wariness, Jack couldn't guess. But of course everyone's reluctance to speak of it made him even more curious.

That evening, once the other Artists had gone off to bed, Jack stood before the hearth in the Artists' Hall to soak up a little more heat before he and Loquasto retired to their room.

"I'll answer your questions now."

Startled, Jack looked around. "Who is it?" he asked, feeling a twinge of alarm.

A plump figure stepped out of the darkness. It was Geoffrey Jester. He shuffled over to Jack, seated himself beside the hearth, and warmed his hands before the fire.

"Make yourself comfortable," the old man said. "I wish to explain a few things."

"But earlier you said—"

"We can speak privately now."

With Loquasto perched on his wrist, Jack sat nearby. "Why would you bother?"

Geoffrey shrugged. "Because you'll find out anyway. You may as well hear the truth early instead of late."

And so the chief of the Artists told Jack the story of King Alphonse.

☙ 19 ❧

You are so newly arrived among us (Geoffrey began) that you understand little of the Royal City and its people. You know even less about King Alphonse. Oh, you think you know him, for you've heard a thousand tales about this harsh king, but you don't know half the story. No matter what some people claim, Majesty isn't evil. I won't say that he bears no responsibility for the state of his kingdom. Quite the contrary. But our suffering springs from a deeper source than bad intentions.

What source, you ask? Why is the Realm such an unhappy place? Well, lad, listen to me and then decide for yourself.

Once upon a time there lived a prince named Alphonse, born into a royal family but destined never to be king. He had six brothers and sisters, each of whom stood ahead of him in the line of succession. In many hearts this situation would have bred great bitterness, but Prince Alphonse felt delight rather than dismay. In fact, nothing pleased him more than knowing that he would never inherit his father's throne.

Why? Because this young man loved the arts, not power. While his oldest sister, Zoë, prepared to become queen and rule over Sundar, Alphonse could go about his own activities. He learned to play many musical instruments. He mastered the arts of painting and sculpture. He perfected his skills in dancing. He honed his ability to write poetry. In short, Alphonse grew accomplished in the arts.

Then, during his twenty-eighth year, a plague swept through the Realm. Thousands of commoners perished. Hundreds of nobles did, too. Even members of the royal family succumbed in great numbers. Both of Alphonse's parents—the king and queen—fell victim to the plague. Then his oldest sister. Then two brothers. Then a second sister and a third brother. Alphonse found consolation only in the survival of his sole remaining sister. Then she, too, sickened and died.

No king ever ascended more reluctantly to his throne. In fact, Alphonse hated being king. You may imagine a king's life to be one of freedom, delight, and joyful exercise of power, but the truth is far different. Alphonse spent all day and half of each night attending councils. His advisers presented problems to solve, disputes to settle, and projects to fund. Courtiers demanded his time, attention, and financial support. Everyone *wanted* something. Alphonse had little opportunity to enjoy the arts he loved. He would gladly have renounced the throne, but that was impossible. All the other members of the royal family had perished. Had Alphonse abdicated, the Realm would have burst into flames like a forest in dry weather. He was the rain that kept the garden of his kingdom a vital, growing place.

If only his burden had been limited to the weight of the government! Yet that load was just one of many. When he decided to marry, for instance, Alphonse felt pressured by his councilors to make a strategic match. He resisted this notion, then capitulated; he agreed to marry not for love but for political advantage. A neighboring kingdom, Navatte, had long been in conflict with the Realm of Sundar. To end this smoldering strife, Alphonse chose Princess Mercuria of Navatte to be his bride, thus forging an alliance between her kingdom and Sundar. The royal councilors applauded this match. One problem, though: Princess Mercuria was, by all candid accounts, as lovely to look at as a dove but roughly as intelligent as one, too. She laughed with a high-pitched giggle; she enjoyed eating whipped cream with her hands; she scratched her feet in public. She was often irritable and always impatient. Alphonse despaired of conversing with her. He dreaded keeping her company. He joked publicly of preferring to battle the kingdom of Navatte over battling his wife-to-be.

But every kingdom needs an heir, and Alphonse resigned himself to marrying Princess Mercuria. Representatives from both realms met to arrange the ceremony. The councilors set the wedding date. Preparations quickly took shape.

Then lightning struck—gentle lightning, if you can imagine such a thing.

While selecting musicians to play at the royal wedding, Alphonse met a musician, Mattie Lutenist by name, who caught his fancy. King Alphonse himself was an accomplished player of the lute, and this young woman delighted the prince with her musical skill, her warmth, her intelligence, and her beauty. Thus Mattie soon inspired the king's affections.

You can imagine what transpired. Alphonse fell in love with Mattie, and Mattie with him. The king called off his wedding to Princess Mercuria and insisted on marrying the commoner instead. This decision nearly triggered a war between the kingdoms of Sundar and Navatte. Somehow the wiser councilors in both countries prevailed, however, and their armies held off from mutual attack. It was a tense time for everyone. Oddly, the risk of warfare may have worked to Alphonse and Mattie's advantage: the whole Realm, having suffered so many recent losses, was desperate to keep the new king on the throne. The crisis eased within a few months.

Better yet, everyone within the government could see that their monarch was now a happy king with a happy queen. Alphonse and Mattie were, in fact, the most blissfully wedded couple ever to rule the land. Their delight in each other spread throughout the Realm, and they ruled with fairness, justice, and warmth. The common good flourished—and the arts as well. A golden age dawned in Sundar.

To everyone's further delight, Queen Mattie gave birth to an heir, the Princess Stelinda, and then to two more daughters, Giselle and Mythunia, over the ensuing years. Yet one of the royal couple's greatest joys—creating such a fine family—led as well to the king's greatest grief. Queen Mattie died while giving birth to her fourth child—a son named Yoss. King Alphonse abruptly found himself a widower and sank into deep grief. So profoundly did he feel the loss of his beloved wife that although he continued to carry on his royal duties, he did so without joy, care, or wisdom. Outwardly, he kept on living, but inwardly, the king had died.

I should add that the royal children didn't make the situation any easier. With their mother dead and their father lost in sorrow, three of the four went astray. The firstborn, Stelinda, was the exception. The others were unpleasant children—impatient, demanding, and irritable. Giselle and Mythunia were selfish and spoiled, and Yoss proved to be the most exasperating child of all. Moody, restless, and hostile, he did everything within his power to infuriate his father. King Alphonse withdrew even deeper into melancholy.

This, Jack, is the situation we face. Our monarch is a good man driven to a bad state of mind. I pity him, but I find him hard to please, for I'm a jester employed by a king who never laughs. Thus I must deliver this news: you, too, will face difficulties, for you are a storyteller employed by a man who refuses to be entertained.

❧ 20 ☙

Jack felt at once troubled and reassured by Geoffrey's story. Troubled, because he wondered what, if anything, he could offer the grief-stricken king. Reassured, because he now understood the root of the king's problems. Suddenly, much more of his own situation—and, indeed, the situation facing the whole Realm—made sense.

"So what this means," Jack told Loquasto the next morning in their apartment, "is that we have to cheer up King Alphonse."

The bird chuckled. "Cheer him up? We're as likely to teach a stone to sing."

"We *must*," Jack stated firmly.

"Sorry—that's not our problem," said Loquasto.

Jack paced the room. "It *is* our problem. It's mine, anyway, because I'm supposed to tell him stories."

"Aren't you taking your obligations too seriously?"

"The king's grief burdens not just Majesty but all of us," Jack said. "King Alphonse isn't a bad man—he's just a heartbroken widower who's neglecting the Realm out of sadness and confusion."

"All the more reason to keep our distance."

Jack suddenly stopped pacing. "On the contrary, we must draw close to him. We must pull him out of the sadness that's swamping him."

Loquasto peered warily at Jack. "I do believe you've lost your mind."

"Not at all," Jack protested. "I've only just now found it."

"How, exactly, do you propose to cheer up the king?"

"By doing what I always do—by telling stories."

"I see. And precisely *which* stories?"

"I don't know yet."

"When will you know?"

"When they exist."

"Ah, now I understand. You'll tell him nonexistent stories," Loquasto said flatly. Then he began to preen his feathers.

"They don't exist *yet*," Jack declared, "but they will. And you'll help me invent them—"

"What!" Loquasto squawked.

"And you'll help me tell them—"

"Now, just a moment!"

"—so we can transform the king's mood from gloom to delight."

"Listen, you succeeded in expelling a ruby from the prince's nose," Loquasto stated ominously, "but grief will be much harder to dislodge from the king's heart."

"I agree," Jack said at once. "The task will indeed be difficult. Still, we must rise to the challenge. We must do everything within our powers to accomplish this goal—not just to win the king's favor, but also to ease the burden on the Realm."

And so, with Loquasto's grudging assistance, Jack proceeded to create stories that he hoped would amuse, distract, and delight King Alphonse.

He made up a story about three young wolves who built their houses—one made of straw, one of sticks, and one of bricks—to protect themselves from a big bad pig that roamed the forest.

He dreamed up a story about a young woman, Rose Briar, who pricked her finger on a witch's spinning wheel, fell asleep, and slept for years until a young prince arrived and kissed her; whereupon Rose Briar awoke, conversed briefly with the prince, and found him so tedious and smug that she pulled up the covers and went right back to sleep.

Jack also invented a story about a poor shoemaker who discovered that elves were manufacturing shoes in his workshop all night long. This free labor saved the shoemaker and his wife from hunger but led to problems when the elves demanded higher wages, regular hours, and better conditions in the shop.

Working constantly, Jack and Loquasto created all kinds of stories—stories that would leave the king trembling in amazement, stunned with delight, dizzy with disbelief, and giddy with amusement. Soon Jack had accumulated twice as many stories as he'd ever told before. He felt ready. He felt strong. He felt brave. Like a soldier ready for battle, Jack now felt sure of his ability to fight valiantly and win the battle ahead.

❧ 21 ❧

A few days later, Jack received a summons to appear at the Great Hall. "Come with me," said Geoffrey.

"King Alphonse wishes to hear my stories?" Jack inquired.

"Perhaps he does."

"And if not?"

"Then you'll wait meekly and observe the other Artists."

With Loquasto on his shoulder, Jack followed Geoffrey at once.

"Sit," said the old jester when they arrived at the Great Hall.

Jack tried not to stumble in the dim light. Spotting a bench, he eased onto it. His eyes adjusted until he became aware of other Artists, among them Hildegard Harpist and Ned Painter, all of whom watched the drama unfolding a short distance away in the only well-lit area of the hall. For at that moment, an aristocratic-looking man stood on a raised platform before the throne and entertained the king, the royal family, and the whole court.

"Who's that?" Jack asked Hildegard.

"Zephyrio the illusionist," she whispered.

Jack had never seen this man before. That in itself was surprising, for he thought he'd already met all the other people who entertained the king. He certainly would have remembered the illusionist, for Zephyrio's appearance was striking. Though average in height, Zephyrio moved with the confidence and prowess of a larger, more powerful man. His attire intensified the effect. His dark blue satin doublet was broad at the shoulders and narrow at the waist. His black silk leggings and knee-high black leather boots emphasized the muscular shape of his legs. And his gold-embroidered blue cape gave him an air of great elegance. His sleek, well-combed hair and his neatly trimmed beard accentuated the handsome features of his face.

This man now went about his act. As Jack watched, Zephyrio poured tea from a teapot into a china cup, took a sip, and made a sour face—the tea wasn't sweet enough! When he tipped the teacup, though, what fell out wasn't tea but snow, sparkling and sifting to the floor. A second serving from the pot once again displeased Zephyrio. This time three white mice tumbled from the cup. Now exasperated, Zephyrio tried once again. He poured the tea, added a spoonful of sugar, and stirred his beverage carefully. He took a sip. He smiled. He swallowed. Then, sputtering, he spewed forth a burst of gold sparks that left his audience gasping.

Jack felt astonished, too, as Zephyrio performed one startling feat after another. He transformed a squirrel into a lizard, the lizard into a dove. He chopped an apple into tiny bits, placed the bits in a basket, shook it, and dumped out a perfectly formed rose. He swallowed a live sparrow only to remove the same bird from his left ear. He poured lamp oil into the palm of his left hand, lit the oil with a candle flame, and walked sedately among his spectators carrying a handful of fire.

All the while, Zephyrio maintained an air of calm bemusement that heightened rather than diminished the remarkable nature of his deeds. A faint smile graced his lips. Otherwise, he betrayed no emotion as he performed his act.

Jack soon felt that this man couldn't possibly do anything more impressive than what he had done already. He was mistaken.

Bowing deeply to the royal family, Zephyrio asked, "Would one of the lovely princesses honor me with a brief moment of collaboration?"

The two younger sisters giggled when they heard this request. The oldest made no response. Prince Yoss simply stared at them with an expression of mixed envy and contempt.

"Giselle? Mythunia?" asked Zephyrio. "Won't you help me practice my trade?"

More giggles ensued, but neither girl moved from her seat.

"And *you?*" said the illusionist, suddenly focusing his attention on Alphonse's oldest daughter. "Princess Stelinda, I hardly recognize your lovely face, transformed, it seems, into such a somber mask."

Stelinda said nothing.

Zephyrio persisted. "Perhaps you'll assist me in entertaining your noble family."

"Perhaps not in our entertainment," Stelinda said, "so much as our enlightenment."

The illusionist shrugged. "*Enlightenment. Entertainment.* The words are almost identical."

"But their meanings, sir, notably diverge—as fully as a love song from a dirge."

Now Zephyrio laughed. "Well, I say the entertainment *is* enlightenment. And the lighter the entertainment, the better."

Jack pondered the odd scene taking place before him: the remarkable performer and his inexplicable tricks; the somber, defiant princess; and the gathered courtiers awaiting the outcome of their contest of wills. Then King Alphonse roused himself from his habitual sorrow and cut the knot binding everyone together in this awkward impasse.

"Good daughter," said the king, "do as the gentleman requests."

Stelinda shook her head. "I've heard no request from Lord Zephyrio—only taunts that cause me grief and woe."

Alphonse took offense at these words. "No request? Well, then, hear my command: assist the good gentleman."

The merest nod was Stelinda's answer. She stepped forth, halting an arm's length from Zephyrio.

The audience cheered warmly—acclaim that Stelinda noted only with another nod.

Jack stared at Stelinda, stunned not only by her lovely appearance but also by her poise and calm. He admired this young woman, yet he hoped, too, that Zephyrio might somehow thaw the chilly mood encasing her like ice. If Yoss's flaw was foolishness, then surely Stelinda's flaw was gloomy solitude.

Before Zephyrio could speak, however, the princess addressed him: "I stand before you in humility. Pray tell me, then, good sir, what you ask of me."

He gestured quizzically with both hands. "The greatest marvel I could perform tonight would be to coax a smile from Princess Stelinda."

She nodded again, saying, "In truth, sir, I would eagerly comply, if by doing so I might bid you all good-bye."

"Now, now—"

"I mean no disrespect, believe me. But staying here will deeply grieve me."

"Now I understand," Zephyrio told her. "You're not just a princess; you're a poet. A poet who chants clever, gloomy couplets."

"Good sir, I would prefer—"

The illusionist winked at King Alphonse. "Let's add a little spice to this dull soup. We'll find a giggle in you yet."

With these words, Zephyrio pulled off his left boot, inverted it, and dumped three toads onto the carpet. They hopped away at once, croaking loudly.

The audience roared its approval, and the king's younger children clapped and shouted loudly, but Stelinda gazed about with an expression of great tedium.

"Not sufficiently amusing?" Zephyrio inquired. He pulled off his other boot, tipped it, and poured out enough water to fill a good-sized jug.

Again the audience cheered.

Again Stelinda showed no reaction.

"This girl's heart is frozen solid," quipped the illusionist.

To which she responded: "Perhaps it is—but no warmth *you* impart could ever melt the ice within my heart."

Zephyrio smiled. "No?" he said. "Well, then, let's see what kind of heat I have in me." The illusionist pulled a handkerchief out of his right sleeve, whirled it around, and tossed it into the air. At once it erupted into flames that darted about in the air—blue-white, hot, and wild. The audience recoiled, gasping and shouting, yet no sooner did this vision appear than it diminished harmlessly, the fire changed at once into a cloud of feathers sifting to the floor.

Jack applauded, cheered, and laughed. Everyone else did, too, except the king and Stelinda.

Zephyrio ignored the king, but he stared in exasperation at the princess. Removing the blue and gold cloak from his shoulders, he announced: "I won't insist on a laugh, a chuckle, or a giggle. All I ask is the merest smile."

To which Stelinda replied, "But why, good sir, should I consent to smile when you strive so harshly to beguile?"

"I pity you," said the illusionist, whirling his cape through the air. "For in your youthful body dwells a dry, old spirit." He draped Stelinda in his cape, then yanked it off at once, revealing in the maiden's place a skeleton. Stark white now, the princess tottered where she stood, her legs on the verge of buckling, her hands grasping at the air.

Jack felt faint. He'd never seen such an appalling sight in his life—a lovely maiden reduced in the blink of an eye to mere bones!

All around him people gasped, moaned, and shrieked in dismay. Some of the courtiers backed off. Others fell to their knees and began to pray.

This terrible vision broke the king's silence: "Stelinda!" he shouted, stepping down from his throne and striding toward his eldest daughter.

Even before the king reached her, though, Zephyrio whirled his cloak once more, engulfed Stelinda within it, and yanked it off again. Where the skeleton had teetered a moment earlier, Stelinda—as beautiful and young as before—now gazed about in bewilderment.

The king stopped short. He, too, gazed in confusion. "My daughter . . ."

The princess and the king stared at each other; then Alphonse turned to Zephyrio, faltered a moment, nodded curtly, and told him, "Most impressive."

Stelinda turned and strode out of the hall.

King Alphonse called out to her—"Come back at once!"—but she ignored him.

As if to ease the lingering tension, Zephyrio bowed deeply, first to the king, then to the assembled courtiers.

Their applause swelled until it pounded the Great Hall like surf against the seashore.

☙ 22 ❧

That night, Jack lay sleepless in bed for hours. He couldn't empty his mind of the sights he'd seen: a man who could transform a squirrel into a lizard and a lizard into a dove. Who could swallow a bird and extract it, alive and chittering, from his ear. Who could wither a lovely maiden into the image of death, then restore her beauty and her youth. Jack felt so dizzy as he recalled these sights that he clung to his bed like a wave-tossed sailor clinging to a slab of wood after his ship has sunk.

Three aspects of Zephyrio's performance troubled him.

The first was simply that Jack didn't understand what he had witnessed. Were these marvels the work of a wizard? Jack had long believed that such people didn't exist. He noted, too, that Zephyrio made no claims to supernatural powers; he presented himself only as an illusionist, an entertainer whose act derived from cleverly tricking people's senses. But if Zephyrio's marvels weren't magic, how did he create such spectacular illusions?

The second aspect was the awareness of how fully this man had captivated his audience. Jack had long ago grown accustomed to his listeners' strong responses to the stories he told: expressions of wonder, delight, fear, alarm, and longing. Yet what he'd witnessed in the Great Hall that night had exceeded any reactions to his storytelling.

The third aspect was Jack's greatest concern: if Zephyrio himself couldn't prompt King Alphonse to cheer, laugh, or even smile, then how could Jack ever hope to entertain the king? How could he do anything but humiliate himself before Majesty?

Jack felt plagued by these thoughts. Something else, too. . . . Just as he fell asleep, a most unsettling image came to him: Stelinda, resolute in refusing to play a game even though her refusal shoved her beyond the grave, before yanking her back again.

❧ 23 ❧

With so many strange new experiences filling each day, Jack often distracted himself by wandering through Callitti. As a village boy, he found the Royal City's size and complexity a source of great fascination. The marketplaces teemed with people selling and purchasing merchandise. The military garrisons resounded with soldiers' shouts as they marched and drilled in the yard. Callitti was so big that Jack sometimes ended up lost even within the palace at the city's center. The maze of corridors . . . the courtyards, chambers, chapels, and banquet halls. . . . Wandering through this labyrinth, Jack felt simultaneously drawn forth and contained by the Royal City.

He responded to this dilemma by seeking solace in the palace gardens. There, Loquasto could fly about while Jack wandered the paths—a great relief to them both, following such long hours indoors.

Jack loved these gardens because they reminded him of his family's farm back in Yorrow. Not that the cultivated flowerbeds in Callitti bore much resemblance to a humble farm. But in both places he could see plants, flowers, and trees, and the birds and squirrels that lived among them. This setting left him wistful yet also reassured. He missed his parents. He missed his brothers and sisters. He missed his home, his village, and the countryside he'd left behind. At the same time, he felt pleased to leave the smoky Artists' Hall and to find himself once again in the natural world.

In the royal gardens Jack discovered many remarkable places.

One, called the Gallery, was a collection of trees and bushes so precisely trimmed that they resembled statues of kings, queens, and other famous people from Sundar's history: two warriors engaged in hand-to-hand combat; a woman battling a gigantic eagle; three children riding a huge horned beast. Among these leafy statues Jack now walked and enjoyed the gardeners' art, the fine weather, and Loquasto's companionship as the bird bobbed on his shoulder.

Suddenly, Loquasto squawked in pain.

"What the matter?" Jack inquired.

"Something hit me."

Jack glanced around. Maybe an acorn? But no large oaks grew nearby.

"Ow!" yelled Loquasto suddenly. "Another one!"

Jack looked to and fro, increasingly puzzled. Suddenly, he felt a sting on his neck. And he heard something, too: a little click right after. Gazing around, he saw something glint on the walkway underfoot. He stooped to pick it up. Green, clear, and hard as a pebble . . .

"An emerald."

Jack caught sight of someone ducking behind one of the tree-statues—a boy with curly blond hair.

At once Loquasto exclaimed, "It's *him!* The royal brat!"

"Yoss?" asked Jack in disbelief. "Surely even Yoss wouldn't—" Another sting cut him short. Once again he heard a clicking noise, but this time he spotted a dark blue sapphire on the ground.

Jack didn't know what to think. On the one hand, he was shocked by the prince's attack. On the other hand, he now had two jewels in his pocket, a fortune no matter how rude their delivery.

Loquasto said, "Let's leave at once."

"Not yet," Jack replied. "I want to speak with him."

"Speak with the little tyrant? He's nothing but trouble."

"Perhaps we can reach an understanding."

At that moment, Yoss poked his head out from behind a tree and, blowing abruptly into a short tube, let fly with another projectile.

Which struck Jack in the forehead.

Now Jack didn't know what to do. His first impulse was to drop to his knees and locate this third gem for his collection. His second was to catch hold of the prince and teach him a lesson he'd never forget.

"Hey!" Jack called out. "Your Highness! Come out and talk with me!"

The only answer was series of projectiles, all of which missed Jack.

"I mean no harm!"

"Nonsense," said Loquasto. "You'd like to harm the royal brat as much as I would." And with those words, he sprang from Jack's shoulder, shot through the air, and started swooping and diving at Yoss's head.

The prince dodged his assailant and swatted at him with his weapon.

"Loquasto, stop!" Jack shouted.

Again and again the bird attacked, jabbing at the boy with his beak.

Jack ran over, took several swipes at Loquasto, and even shielded the prince with his own body. At last the bird gave up.

Yoss, suddenly aware of Jack's touch, shouted, "Get your filthy hands off me!"

"Your Highness—"

"Don't you ever touch me again—or let that vile crow come *near* me!"

"Crow! Crow!" cawed Loquasto harshly.

"He was only defending me," Jack said.

"Silence!"

Jack stood still. Aware of how much trouble could come of this incident, he restrained his words.

Glaring at the storyteller, Prince Yoss reached into his front pocket, removed another gemstone, and placed it in the wooden tube. He raised the tube to his mouth and blew hard. A ruby struck Jack on the cheek. Then Yoss turned and walked away.

☙ 24 ❧

Why, Jack wondered, did the prince hate him so much? Perhaps Yoss envied Jack's contact with his father. Perhaps he envied the gifts that King Alphonse had bestowed on Jack. Perhaps he simply resented how Jack had rescued him from his own foolishness. Jack wasn't sure. All he knew was that Yoss hated him. Hated him intensely.

Pondering these questions, Jack understood that a practical matter required an immediate response: what to do about the jewels. In the aftermath of the prince's attacks, he had collected five of Yoss's projectiles. Now, seated at the table in his room, he stared in astonishment at the precious stones resting before him.

"If you ask me," said Loquasto from his perch on the chair, "you should take those gems, stick them back in your pocket, and leave."

"Leave?"

"Leave Callitti. Leave the Realm of Sundar, even. You came here to seek your fortune, right? Well, now you've found it."

Jack sighed. In one sense the bird was right. Owning one of these gems would make him rich. Owning *five* . . . He couldn't even start to calculate the wealth.

Yet he balked at keeping them. "They aren't mine," he stated.

Loquasto chittered in derision. "Not yours? You must be joking!"

"They belong to Prince Yoss—"

"Who values them so much that he shot them at you like dried peas!"

Jack shrugged. "He may be foolish, but these jewels still belong to him."

"Come to your senses!" squawked Loquasto. "Take the gems. Flee this sorry place. Go live in splendor."

"It's not splendor I crave," Jack said. "Just a chance to tell my stories."

"So here's your chance. You're a wealthy man now. Go tell stories for the rest of your days."

Jack shook his head. "I'd have to live like an outlaw. I'd be no better than Garth Golden-Eye."

Loquasto shrugged in frustration. "All right, all right. So what will you do, then?"

"I'm not sure yet."

Loquasto settled down for a nap, but Jack wanted to solve this problem as soon as possible. He decided to request an audience with the king, hand over the jewels, and be done with the whole business. Thus he set off, working his way through the maze of corridors to the palace itself.

But his efforts proved fruitless. None of the palace guards would let Jack approach the king, the chamberlain wouldn't see him, and the councilors, too, were unavailable. Was it possible, he asked, to speak with one of Majesty's valets? This request, too, was denied. Tired and discouraged, Jack decided to head back to the Artists' House.

On his way, though, he passed a courtyard, and hearing music, he peered around a pillar to watch and listen.

A young woman, seated on the edge of a stone fountain, sang a song while accompanying herself on a lute.

> "I'll sail the sea in a boat made of water—
> Spray my canvas, bubbles my keel—
> I'll put back the fish that fishermen slaughter
> With a net, a trap, a line, and a reel."

"Stelinda," Jack whispered.

> "I'll furrow the fields with an artichoke thorn,
> Sow the soil with shadows and snow—
> I'll harvest the darkness like cabbage and corn
> While icicles hiss in the earth as they grow."

The princess was uncommonly beautiful, and her fine features gave her an air of grace and refinement. Yet Jack's fascination went far beyond his delight in her appearance. The beauty of her voice so entranced him that he wanted nothing more than to stand there and listen. The notes she sang became both the source of his longing and its fulfillment.

> "I'll sing you a song without words or a tune—
> My tongue is silent, my voice is mute—
> I'll play you music on a tree in bloom:
> Bees the melody, blossoms the lute."

What struck Jack just then wasn't the perfection of her voice but the desperation of her lyrics. *My tongue is silent, my voice is mute—* She wasn't singing in delight but in despair.

Drawn like a hummingbird to a flower, Jack approached the princess.

Stelinda looked up, her expression showing more puzzlement than alarm. "Sir? Do I know you?" Lightly grasping her lute, she stood, the silk of her gown whispering as she moved. Then a look of recognition crossed her face. "You are the storyteller."

"I am, Your Highness. Jack Storyteller."

Although she didn't smile, her face relaxed in a way that pleased him.

Almost belatedly, Jack remembered his mission. "I wish to return something to your family," he said, stepping closer.

Looking uncertain, she asked, "Return something?"

Jack reached into his pocket, pulled out the jewels, and revealed them in his palm. "Your brother—" He faltered. He wanted to explain that Yoss had shot these gemstones at him and Loquasto. He wanted to say, *Here is further evidence of your brother's foolishness.* But he didn't. Instead, he simply said, "Your brother dropped these."

Stelinda gazed at Jack's outstretched palm. "Rubies, emeralds, and a sapphire," she said with a touch of amusement.

"Please take them."

Stelinda reached out and let Jack pour the gems, clicking, into her right hand. "You are an honest man," she told him.

"The jewels belong to the prince," Jack said, "not to me."

"My brother is careless."

"All boys are careless."

"Few work so hard at carelessness as my brother Yoss," Stelinda said. She held Jack's gaze as if reading his thoughts.

Suddenly uncomfortable, Jack said, "I must go."

"To practice your art," said Stelinda.

"I must imagine new stories," he told her.

Stelinda nodded almost imperceptibly. "Go, then. Go imagine new stories."

Jack bowed deeply.

As he backed away, she added, "Imagine one for me."

If Yoss's hatred can lead me to this young woman, Jack thought as he left the palace, *let him hate me forever. If his attacks allow me to speak with Stelinda, let him attack with every weapon in his arsenal.*

❧ 25 ❧

Jack returned to the Artists' House in a state of dizzy agitation. Of all the events he had experienced in the Royal City, none had confused him more than his brief conversation with Stelinda. She was the most beguiling woman he had ever met. But he was a commoner; Stelinda was a princess. No matter how entranced he felt, Jack faced her across a chasm that he could never bridge.

Loquasto was awake now. "Out and about, I see," the bird commented as Jack walked into the room.

"Just running an errand," Jack told him. "I returned the jewels to their rightful owner."

"Not Yoss, surely."

"His family."

"You spoke with the king?"

"I tried to," Jack said, stretching out on his bed, "but I couldn't obtain an audience with Majesty, so I almost gave up. Then, on my way back, I ran into one of his daughters."

"A silly princess?" asked Loquasto with a hoot.

"No, the somber one, Stelinda."

"Ah, yes. Proof that a pretty pastry can be sour indeed."

Jack took immediate offense. "She's not like that!"

"No? I say she's a bitter morsel."

"You'd be bitter, too, if your father's despair poisoned the whole kingdom. If your sisters were giggly dunderheads. If your brother—"

"Very well, then," the bird concurred. "She has a right to her bitterness."

Jack reclined dreamily. "There's much more to her than you'd imagine," he stated. "She sings more sweetly than any nightingale. She plays the lute. She's intelligent and thoughtful—"

"Well, now! I believe you fancy this fine young woman."

Jack protested at once: "I admire the princess, that's all."

"I see more than admiration in your eyes."

Jack sat up suddenly. He needed to distract himself. He needed to avoid thinking of Stelinda by any means possible. "Enough chatter!" he said. "We have work to do—stories to imagine, lines to memorize. We must get ready for the king's summons."

Although he and Loquasto spent several hours planning stories, Jack found his mind straying from the room and seeking out the courtyard where Stelinda played and sang.

I'll sing you a song without words or a tune—
My tongue is silent, my voice is mute—

What a shame that the king's gloom so heavily burdened his daughter, and that his melancholy encased her like a coffin. Not that the king meant to do anything so heartless—he probably wasn't even aware of his actions or their consequences. Yet intended or not, the results were identical—and the entire Realm shared Stelinda's fate.

Jack felt more convinced than ever that by means of his storytelling art he could coax King Alphonse back into the land of the living. Jack would tell stories so mysterious that they would crack the walls of stony grief surrounding the king. He would tell stories so funny that the king's laughter would shatter those walls to pieces. He would tell stories so moving that Alphonse would kick past the rubble and emerge a changed man. Then Alphonse would resume a normal life. He would free his subjects from their captivity. The Realm would flourish anew. All the king's subjects—even those in faraway Yorrow—would thrive and prosper.

Stelinda, too, would come alive again.

❧ 26 ❧

Jack's opportunity to act on his plan arrived just a few days later. Geoffrey informed him that King Alphonse had requested his presence, and a guard escorted him and Loquasto to the Great Hall.

King Alphonse looked weary and irritable. Dark circles ringed his eyes, and his hair was disheveled. "Storyteller," he snapped, "tell me a story."

"With pleasure, Majesty," Jack responded.

"Make it a jolly one," the king added, "for I'm in foul spirits."

"Jolly! Jolly!" cried Loquasto.

Intent on cheering the king, Jack started in at once. He told him the story of the three little wolves and the big bad pig, which left Majesty looking confused. He told him the story about Rose Briar and the smug, tedious prince, which prompted no response at all from King Alphonse. He told him the story of the elves who demanded higher wages, regular working hours, and better conditions in the workshop—a story that made the king visibly squirm on his throne.

"Well?" huffed the king. "Where's the jolly tale you promised?"

"I'm trying, Majesty."

"Promise! Promise!" shrieked Loquasto. "Who's kept his promise?"

"If you're trying to cheer me, spare me such jolliness," the king said. "I have far greater weight on my shoulders than this puny effort can dislodge. Have you any notion of the hardships I've suffered? Of the burdens I carry?"

"Burden, burden," hooted Loquasto. "Who's got the burden?"

"Answer me, storyteller—and silence that crow!" the king shouted.

Outraged, Loquasto began to squawk: "Crow? Crow? Who's a crow?"

"What did he say?"

Jack reached over and held Loquasto's beak shut. "My friend takes offense when called a crow. He's actually—"

"*Silence!* Are you a storyteller?" bellowed King Alphonse.

"I am, Majesty."

"Are you in my employ?"

"Indeed, Majesty."

"Then tell me a story powerful enough to thaw the wintry mood that has frozen my heart," growled King Alphonse.

Jack thought a moment. Every story so far had bored, annoyed, or infuriated the king; none had brightened his dark spirits. Jack perceived his error: he had attempted to accomplish his task by feeble means. Now he understood how to proceed. If King Alphonse's heart was a city layered over with a hundred winters' snows, Jack's story would be a bonfire so intense that its heat would thaw the ice once and for all.

Suddenly, Jack felt a story come to him, *become* him, until there was no difference between the teller and the tale.

Once upon a time (Jack began) a king named Alfortis ruled Ftora, the most beautiful kingdom in the land. He was a good king, and he treated his subjects well. His queen, Matusia, was the most beautiful queen in the world. Alfortis and Matusia worked for the good of their people, and their people loved them deeply in return.

The king and queen had three daughters. But in laboring to give birth to a fourth child—a baby boy—Matusia died.

Alfortis wailed for days. "Why has this fate befallen me?" he asked his councilors. "Why has my whole life turned to dust?"

"We understand your grief at the queen's death," said the first councilor, "but take comfort: you yourself remain as rich and vital as a young tree."

"Silence!" shouted King Alfortis.

"You have three lovely daughters," the second councilor told him.

"Enough of this impudence!"

"You have a newborn son," the third stated.

"Be silent!"

"Your people love you," said the fourth, "and your kingdom is a place of great beauty."

King Alfortis would hear none of it. "Beauty! Beauty, you say? Well, it's beauty that has betrayed me. I loved the queen because her beauty seemed perfect and changeless, and now look what has come of it! I'll hear nothing more of beauty."

The king's grief drove him mad. In his rage, King Alfortis struck out against Ftora so that its beauty could never betray him. He ordered his army to cut down the forests, poison the lakes, burn the orchards, and sow the farmlands with salt and ashes.

"Enough of this beauty!" screamed the king.

Yet even as he finished transforming Ftora from the most beautiful kingdom in the world into the ugliest, he learned that his task was far from over. A visiting monarch, unaware of the actions that King Alfortis had taken, told him, "What a shame that your kingdom has suffered such harm. What was once a lovely land is now ugly. Even so, your subjects remain the most beautiful anywhere."

In response to this comment, King Alfortis ordered his army to round up all the people in Ftora—men, women, and children alike. Then he had the royal witch cast spells to make everyone ugly. The more beautiful the person had been, the uglier he or she became. With faces twisted, limbs deformed, and skin marred, all the king's subjects relinquished their beauty. The soldiers did. Even the councilors did. Soon there was no human beauty left in Ftora.

Then one night, as he walked along the ash-strewn shore of a once-beautiful lake surrounded by the ruins of his once-beautiful city, King Alfortis saw the sparkle of cinders on the shore, saw the glimmer of light on the greasy water, saw the subtle hue of the feathers on a dead bird lying in his path. He smelled the fragrance of wood smoke on the wind and the scent of rain falling over his kingdom. He heard the lullabies of mothers putting their children to sleep in the ruins of their huts nearby. Even the wreckage of his kingdom taunted him with beauty.

King Alfortis cried, "Enough! Is there no end to this plague of beauty?"

A voice answered quietly: "Perhaps you should put out your eyes, Majesty."

King Alfortis turned to see who had spoken. A woman sat near him, half hidden by some rubble and burnt timbers. Although her shape suggested a girl of sixteen or seventeen, her wrinkles and white hair were that of a woman at least five times older: skin weathered, eyes gone bad, hands gnarled like old roots.

"What are you telling me?" King Alfortis demanded. "How dare you speak to your king?"

"I only want to help you," said the woman. "If you wish this plague of beauty to end, perhaps you should cure yourself."

Enraged, the king stormed off. Yet he soon realized that the woman had spoken the truth. King Alfortis commanded the royal witch to blind his eyes, deafen his ears, stop up his nose, wither his hands. Then he could no longer see, hear, smell, or touch any beauty.

Over the next few days, as he lay ill in bed, Alfortis discovered that the loss of his senses had done nothing to cure the malady that afflicted him. Memories of sights, sounds, smells, and textures came and went within his mind. The sound of his mother's voice. The scent of plum blossoms in his father's orchard. The softness of his cat's fur. The aroma of baking bread. The mutter of wind in the trees. The smoothness of a pebble in his hand. The shuffle of shadows across a wheat field. The ripple of his children's laughter. And this above all: the steady, clear gaze of his beloved wife.

Desperate to escape even the memory of beauty, King Alfortis toppled out of bed. Before his servants could stop him, he stumbled across the floor to a great stone stairway beyond his bedroom. He eased himself onto the first step—and tumbled down all the rest.

As he died, King Alfortis saw a cloud of clear white light swelling before him, brighter than any light he'd ever seen, more beautiful than anything could be, simple yet complete, at once overwhelming and gentle. And as the light engulfed him, King Alfortis squinted to avoid it.

There was no escape.

Jack looked around like someone waking from a dream. King Alfortis? . . . He couldn't recall how that character had entered his mind or why he had spoken about him at such length. King Alfortis . . . But it wasn't King Alfortis, it was King Alphonse who faced him now.

Suddenly, Jack realized that for him, too, there was no escape.

King Alphonse glared at the storyteller. His hands trembled. *"Why have you told me this story?"* he asked through gritted teeth.

Jack motioned awkwardly. "I—I don't know."

"You don't *know?*"

"Perhaps you needed to hear it," Jack said.

"Go!" King Alphonse ordered. "Go to your quarters and await your fate."

☜ 27 ☞

N ow you've done it," Loquasto lamented as he and Jack rushed back to the Artists' House.

"I tried my best," Jack told him.

"You offered the king a consoling hand, then punched him instead."

"I didn't punch him."

"No? Then you kicked him—kicked the poor man right in the belly."

Jack gestured awkwardly. "Sometimes it's hard to know what's the best story for the occasion—"

"But it's easy to know that some stories are wrong for *all* occasions," said Loquasto.

They remained in Jack's room all that night and throughout the next day. No one locked them in, but Jack opened his door and peered into the hallway several times, and he always spotted an armed guard standing watch. A servant brought food three times that day. Nothing about their captivity was harsh, yet it was captivity all the same.

Seated beside the window, which allowed a clear view of the Royal City and the countryside beyond, Jack turned to Loquasto. "You should fly away," he said. "Fly away and leave this sorry place."

"I won't," said Loquasto.

"If you go right now, you'll be safe. If you stay, you'll probably end up dead and stuffed and roosting on a branch in the king's trophy room."

"I'll take my chances."

"Loquasto, this is all my fault. I was too intent on dragging the king out of his melancholy. You tried to dissuade me."

"True. But I went along with you, and I'd be a coward to leave now."

"A *live* coward."

"Perhaps, but a coward all the same."

Jack made one last effort: "Listen, go now and you'll have another chance to find Artemisia. To invent a way for a bird to live with a fish. To be together."

Hearing these words, Loquasto grew pensive.

"This may be your last opportunity," Jack told him.

"I chose to join you on your quest," the bird stated firmly. "I'll remain no matter where the path takes us."

How was it possible, Jack wondered, that he could have made such a foolish mistake? Why had he chosen to tell that particular story? He hadn't intended to tell a cautionary tale of this sort—a fable that would rub salt into the wound of Majesty's grief. King Alfortis of Ftora? Jack had never heard of him before. In fact, Jack didn't know where this story had come from, and he hadn't been fully aware of his own words even as he'd spoken them. It was less a tale he'd told than a dream he'd dreamed. Yet its consequences were plain enough.

Storyteller indeed! Now his final bow wouldn't be to acknowledge applause for his storytelling art; it would be to place his neck on the king's execution block.

The sun sank beyond the hills. Night fell. Stars drenched the sky.

Jack sat up almost all night, pondering his fate and wondering what he could have done differently. His life was a story that he should have told more skillfully. What a shame for it to end before he'd had a chance to develop the plot and flesh out the characters.

❧ ——————————————————————————— ❧

So did the king execute Jack?
What do you think?
I think he wanted to.
You're right.
But did he go ahead and kill him?

❧ 28 ❧

As you can imagine, Jack, too, wondered if he was about to die. He spent the next three days waiting for word of his fate. He continued to receive brief visits from servants bearing trays of food, but no members of the King's Artists came to see him. Even Geoffrey kept his distance. When Jack asked the servants if they'd learned of any developments, they always stated: "The chief of the Artists will contact you when he hears the news."

When he hears the news . . . Jack couldn't help assuming that the longer this silence continued, the more terrible his punishment would be. Even now King Alphonse was probably ranting at his councilors about Jack's impudence. To humiliate the king with an absurd story! To imply that Alphonse bore a resemblance to that imaginary King Alfortis! To suggest that the queen's death might in-spire rage so intense as to destroy an entire kingdom!

On the third day, Jack heard a knock at the door. He looked up in alarm.

"Don't answer it," said Loquasto.

"How would that help us?" Jack asked. "They know I'm here." He crossed the room and pulled open the door.

He expected one of the Artists' servants to be standing in the hallway, or Geoffrey, or else a squadron of guards. But the person be-fore him was Zephyrio. As when performing before the king, the illusionist wore elegant attire—a ruffled silk shirt, a dark green vel-vet jacket, black leggings, and black boots. A black velvet cape swirled around him when he turned.

"You've brought a message?" Jack asked.

"I bring no messages," said the illusionist. "Only my consola-tion."

"Consolation . . ." Hearing this word, Jack felt intense alarm. Was it possible that King Alphonse had already sentenced him—to prison, to hard labor, to the chopping block—but Jack simply hadn't gotten the word?

As if reading Jack's mind, Zephyrio told him, "I regret to say that I know nothing of your fate. I'm certainly aware that the other Artists have been avoiding you, and they may be correct in assuming a dismal outcome. Still, it seems premature to treat you like someone who's lying in his coffin."

Jack shuddered at this description.

"May I come in?"

Impressed by the man's willingness to risk a visit, Jack motioned for him to enter.

Zephyrio flung his cape over one shoulder, strode into the room, and took a seat. He glanced around. Noting Loquasto perched on the back of a nearby chair, he said, "That's a handsome crow you've got."

"Crow! Crow!" squawked Loquasto. "I'm no crow!"

"Clever lad," Zephyrio told Jack, "throwing your voice like that."

"I'm not throwing it," Jack replied.

"Throwing it, throwing it!" exclaimed Loquasto with a huff.

The illusionist laughed cordially. "I studied the art of voice-throwing years ago, but I'm not half as accomplished as you are. I can do it well enough to fool my audience, though, which is all that counts."

"I don't mean to fool anyone," Jack protested.

"I can talk," Loquasto insisted. "Talk and talk!"

Once again Zephyrio smiled with admiration. "Yes indeed," he told the bird. "You talk and talk. Clever lad—especially how you speak exactly when the crow's beak moves."

"Look," Jack said, changing the subject. "I appreciate your visit. I'm in a bad way, though—very bad."

Zephyrio nodded sympathetically. "Yes, I hear there's been a terrible misunderstanding."

"I tried to do something to benefit Majesty," Jack said, "but somehow my efforts failed. When I tried to boost his spirits, I only dragged him down."

"Despite your best intentions," Zephyrio noted with warmth in his eyes.

"You understand what I'm saying, don't you?"

"I do indeed."

Jack felt a flicker of hope for the first time in days. "Can you help me?"

"I wish I could. The sad truth, however, is that I have no influence over the king. I'm just a humble illusionist."

"So . . . there's nothing you can do?"

"Listen, lad," said Zephyrio. "I don't know if you'll escape Majesty's wrath. The odds aren't good."

"I wish you wouldn't say that—"

"But I'm here to tell you that I perceive your actions as an honest mistake." The illusionist stood and walked over to the hearth. Unattended during this conversation, the fire had flickered and gone out; the logs now merely smoldered. But then Zephyrio snapped his fingers twice and flames sprang forth, filling the room with light and heat. The illusionist warmed his hands before the blaze.

"How did you do that!" Jack exclaimed.

Zephyrio smiled. "A cheap trick," he said. "Nothing worth explaining. What matters far more is what I just told you: your actions were a mistake."

Jack drew his attention away from the hearth. *"Mistake?"*

"Of course. I know you meant no harm. You intended no insult. You're just too young to know what serves as true entertainment. The truth is, people are foolish. The reason they enjoy my act is that they *like* being foolish."

Jack shook his head in dismay. "I don't see it that way," he said. "I don't think people are foolish at all. Oh, maybe a few of them. But most are capable of wisdom. I believe that's true for King Alphonse as well."

"My good man!" exclaimed Zephyrio. "You are a generous soul indeed! Wisdom—what a lofty thought! In my experience, what people want is a chance to forget their troubles. What they want is *amusement.*"

"I believe you're wrong," Jack said calmly.

"Believe anything you wish. The truth remains: people will always prefer my act to yours because mine lifts their burden—the burden of having to think. All I do is indulge them. That's why my act will always draw a bigger crowd, and greater applause, than yours."

"I'm not talking about a crowd," Jack said. "Only the king."

"Draw your own conclusions." Zephyrio continued to warm his hands.

Jack felt confused. What was Zephyrio telling him, exactly?

"Here's why I've come to you," said the illusionist. He turned slowly, putting his back to the fire, and Jack saw that his fingers were glowing—bright yellow-orange at the tips fading to dull red where the fingers joined the hand.

Zephyrio showed no interest in their radiance. He noticed Jack's astonishment, however, and said, "Clever, isn't it? Someday I'll show you the proper technique. It's really quite simple." He flexed his fingers; the glow diminished. Then he continued speaking. "Perhaps you'll survive this little mishap. Perhaps not. If you do, here's my advice: don't try to foster wisdom. Just amuse your listeners. Entertain them—nobles and commoners alike."

Jack was crestfallen. So much for Zephyrio's assistance! "I appreciate your advice," he replied. "I'll certainly consider what you suggest—if I have the chance."

"Please do," said Zephyrio. He bowed and moved toward the doorway. "Who knows? Maybe you *will* have a chance. I'll ask around. Someone among the courtiers may prove helpful. One never knows what's possible here in the Royal City."

❧ 29 ❧

Jack felt no surprise when, just after dawn, someone pounded on the door. He opened it and found a squadron of six guards before him in the hallway. Why should he have expected anything else? He had insulted the king; no such offense would go unpunished. The only question in Jack's mind was how King Alphonse would deliver the punishment.

"Here we go," said Loquasto quietly.

"Here *I* go," Jack told him. "If you have even a speck of sense, you'll fly away *now*."

The bird didn't reply.

"Jack Storyteller!" bellowed one of the guards. "Come along!"

Loquasto hopped onto Jack's shoulder, and the prisoner and his escorts headed off on what Jack was sure would be his last walk anywhere.

What surprised him wasn't the route they took—the long sequence of corridors and staircases—but their destination. For it wasn't the executioner's block that awaited Jack; it was the Great Hall.

The chamberlain called out: "Step forth, Jack Storyteller!"

Without hesitating, Jack obeyed.

King Alphonse sat on his throne and watched Jack warily as he approached. The prime councilor stood on the king's right; the other councilors stood on his left. Several dozen courtiers lingered here and there throughout the hall.

"*Not a jolly mood*," whispered Loquasto as they entered.

King Alphonse eased off his throne and walked slowly over to where Jack stood.

"*Here's your chance*," Loquasto whispered to Jack. "*Talk your way out.*"

"Shhh!"

King Alphonse said, "You are a storyteller?"

"I am, Majesty," Jack answered.

"In whose employ?"

"Yours, Majesty."

"And your duty, tell me, is what?"

"To entertain you, Majesty."

"I see," the king said sternly. "So why, then, did you tell me that story? That least entertaining of stories? That most troubling, disturbing, and insulting of stories?"

"*Here's your chance!*" Loquasto repeated. "*Beg the king for mercy!*"

"Shhh!"

"Are you shushing me?" asked King Alphonse, outraged. "Would you humiliate me first—and now silence me?"

"No, Majesty," Jack replied. "I was only clearing my throat."

"Answer me, then: why did you tell me that story?"

Jack pondered the situation. Perhaps Zephyrio was right; he should dismiss the story about Alfortis as a mistake.

Loquasto whispered again: "*Beg for mercy!*"

Yet Jack decided he could speak nothing but the truth. "I told the story," he said, his voice trembling, "because you needed to hear it."

King Alphonse looked startled. "*Needed* to?"

"Because it speaks to your condition. Because it's not too late, Majesty, for you to come to your senses."

Jack suddenly grew aware that everyone was staring at him. The chancellor, the councilors, the courtiers, and especially the king.

"Do you make these claims even at the risk of your life?" asked the king.

Jack nodded. "At the risk of my life. For the story needed to be told. The story is the medicine I offer you, Majesty, and nothing I can do will remove its bitter taste."

Perched on Jack's shoulder, Loquasto drooped in despair.

King Alphonse rose and took two steps forward, standing so close now that Jack could have reached out and touched his face. Would the king strike him? Spit on him?

"Your stubbornness is what I have assumed," said King

Alphonse. "Your claims are what I have anticipated." He raised his club-like scepter. "For this reason," he stated, "I see no alternative—"

Jack winced, waiting for the blow.

"—but to appoint you my royal storyteller."

Blinking, Jack opened his eyes wide. "Majesty?"

"You alone have told me not what you believe I *want* to hear but what I *must* hear." With these words, King Alphonse looked about angrily, scowling at the councilors and courtiers. "It seems that no one else was willing to tell me the truth. Everyone tried instead to humor me with sickly sweet candies." He turned back to Jack. "Everyone but you. Your medicine is bitter indeed, but it's the cure I need."

Jack couldn't believe what he was hearing.

"I've sickened the whole kingdom with my grief," said King Alphonse. "But with your help, perhaps I'll recover—and the kingdom will, too."

Jack glanced around. Most of the courtiers were staring in astonishment. A few backed off and left the hall to spread the news.

"When," asked King Alphonse, "can you tell me another story?"

Jack gestured with open hands. "Whenever it pleases you, Majesty."

The king smiled. "Good. Please kneel." When Jack obeyed, Alphonse stated: "By the power of the crown I wear and the scepter I wield, I hereby appoint you royal storyteller." He reached out and touched Jack on the head with his scepter.

A cheer rose from the assembled courtiers.

❧ 30 ❧

The changes in Jack's outward circumstances were now as great as those that had occurred following his cure of Prince Yoss many days earlier. After ascending to the rank of royal storyteller, Jack gained new privileges. Before, he had lived among the King's Artists; now he and Loquasto moved to their own apartment. Before, he had answered to the chief of the Artists; now he reported directly to the king. Before, he had lived comfortably; now he lived in luxury.

"I'll admit it," Loquasto said grudgingly once he and Jack had settled into their new quarters. "I was wrong and you were right."

"I just told him what I believe," Jack said. He took a pastry from a plate on the table and started eating.

"Though I might add that if Majesty had reacted more angrily," the bird went on, "you'd be lying with your head disconnected from your body, and I'd be mounted on the king's trophy wall."

"You're always convinced we're on the verge of execution."

"Well—we *are*."

"Thus far we've avoided that fate."

"Maybe so," said Loquasto, snapping up a grape from a bowl of fruit, "but I'm not sure how. I just hope our luck holds."

Jack understood that the most recent crisis had been a particularly close call, and its happy resolution had taken him by surprise. But the king's enthusiasm for his storytelling art now convinced him that he'd chosen the right course. All would be well.

What would happen next? Jack couldn't even imagine. Once again his life had become a story he couldn't predict, with a plot he could follow only by letting it unfold.

"My, my—isn't *this* a well-feathered nest."

Jack looked up to see a tall figure standing in the doorway. "Zephyrio!" he exclaimed. "Do come in."

"Zephyrio! Zephyrio!" cawed Loquasto.

"With great delight," said the illusionist. He flung his cape over his left shoulder, entered, and sat near Jack.

"How are you?" Jack inquired.

"Very well indeed, thank you—though not in nearly so fine a state as you are." Zephyrio gestured toward the splendid furnishings all around them.

Jack shrugged. "Oh, the new apartment. It's nice. The truth is, though—I don't really care. I'd be just as happy with the plainest room. All I want is a chance to tell my stories."

"Which, if I hear correctly, you've gained."

Jack couldn't restrain his delight. "I'll tell the king all kinds of stories," he said, smiling.

Loquasto bobbed his head. "Once upon a time!" he shrieked. "Once upon a time!"

Zephyrio nodded cordially. "Indeed," he said. "But listen." He leaned forward as if to confide in Jack. "I need to repeat what I told you just a few days past."

Jack knew at once what to expect. "You want me to entertain Majesty, not enlighten him."

The illusionist gazed thoughtfully at Jack. "You told the king that you'd dosed him with bitter medicine. Perhaps you have. And perhaps you've done the Realm a great service in trying to cure his ills. But don't dose Majesty so severely that the cure does more damage than the sickness. I've presented illusions to the king for many years, and I know there's a limit to what he can tolerate." With those words he walked calmly to the door. "If I can help you again, I'll gladly do so."

⚛ 31 ⚛

Jack didn't know what to make of Zephyrio's remark. He felt confused by the illusionist's hint that he had intervened on Jack's behalf. Zephyrio had claimed earlier that he had no special influence over King Alphonse. Did that modest claim disguise the truth? Perhaps the man possessed more power than he cared to reveal. After all, he was one of the king's favorite performers. Was it possible that Zephyrio had spoken with Majesty and somehow eased the royal rage toward Jack? But if Zephyrio *had* intervened to help him, Jack couldn't imagine why. The illusionist seemed to disapprove of Jack's art. Why, then, should he have acted as Jack's defender?

After a while, Jack grew weary and stopped trying to figure it out. All he knew was that when he reached up to rub his neck, he felt both surprised and delighted to find his head still firmly connected to his shoulders.

Something else struck him hard: he wanted to see Stelinda—and soon. But how? His earlier encounter with the princess had occurred by accident. He didn't know where in the palace she lived. He worried that looking for her might draw too much attention. Yet he craved Stelinda's presence with such intensity that he couldn't simply wait for a chance encounter.

Then Jack thought up a plan. "Loquasto," he said to the bird one morning, "I need your assistance."

The bird eyed him warily. "Assistance?"

"I need you to deliver a message for me."

"A message!" exclaimed Loquasto, clearly displeased. "Of course. I'm a regular carrier pigeon."

"I need you to contact Stelinda."

"That's even better! You'll have me find the princess and drop her a love note."

"It's not asking much," Jack said.

"It's more than you've done for *me*."

"True, but I'll make it up to you. Please?"

Loquasto grudgingly agreed to this request. Jack wrote a brief note to the princess; the bird took it in his beak, and he launched himself outward, upward, and over the palace rooftops.

Loquasto's mission left Jack alone for the first time in many days. He felt both relieved and anxious in his solitude. He sat for a long time, wondering what would come of the bird's errand. Then he got up, paced for a while, and abruptly lay down on his bed. His head spun. His hands tingled. His ears buzzed with strange voices. Odd visions flashed before his eyes.

It took him a long time to realize what anyone else would have already understood.

He'd fallen in love with the princess?

Precisely.

But wouldn't that be—

Risky? Of course. Yet Princess Stelinda had so beguiled Jack that there seemed no choice in the matter.

He wasn't really thinking.

Right. Or at least, not thinking clearly. This was an event that Jack, given all his knowledge of storytelling, should have expected. But he hadn't. He'd never seen it coming. And he didn't understand that falling in love with Stelinda would change his life in every imaginable way.

❧ 32 ❧

Over the next several days a new routine took shape. King Alphonse would summon Jack. Jack would present himself at the Great Hall. King Alphonse would say, "Storyteller—tell me a story." And, standing before an audience of the king, his daughters, Prince Yoss, and a scattering of councilors and courtiers, he would comply.

Jack told stories that Majesty found puzzling and confusing. He told him about a boy who comforted his hungry family with tales of abundant food. He spun a yarn about Garth Golden-Eye: how a storyteller once made up directions for locating the robber's treasure, then learned that villagers had dug up a real chest full of Garth's jewels and gold. He told him a story about the Woman of the Woods: how a young storyteller, fearful of falling prey to a witch in the forest, discovered that she was, in fact, a deposed queen who'd sought refuge there.

"How is it possible," the king asked, "that a queen might leave her throne only to rule over mice, birds, and weasels in the forest?"

"I don't know," Jack admitted. "That's just what happened in the story."

"What a stupid tale," Yoss muttered.

"Be silent," Alphonse ordered his son. Then, speaking to Jack, he asked, "Is this a story that you yourself made up?"

"No," Jack said, "one that an old woman told me."

"An old woman hiding in the woods?"

"Yes, Majesty."

Yoss guffawed. "Such a pile of nonsense!"

"Let the storyteller speak," Princess Stelinda said abruptly.

The king ignored his squabbling children and addressed Jack

instead. "Do you believe that she was, in fact, a deposed queen?"

"That's what she claimed to be," said Jack.

King Alphonse was perplexed. "An odd story—so odd that I wonder why you've told it to me."

Jack shrugged. "I don't know, Majesty."

"That makes no sense!" the king said, raising his voice. "How can you tell me such a story if you can't even explain its purpose?"

Prince Yoss grinned as he listened to his father's exclamation, the smug look on his face suggesting that he had somehow beaten Jack in a fight.

Stelinda's expression suggested curiosity and concern.

"Sometimes, Majesty, the story itself reveals its purpose," said Jack plainly. And with those words, he suddenly started to tell yet another.

Once upon a time (Jack began) King Alfurzo hired a stonemason to pave the palace courtyard. The king wanted his courtyard to be beautiful and free of mud. The stonemason, Colm, set to work performing his task. He dug up the muddy courtyard, leveled it, and laid a foundation of sand. Then he brought in thousands of paving stones and, working carefully, set the stones in place. Finally, the courtyard surface was smooth and even.

"How do you like it now, Majesty?" asked the stonemason.

King Alfurzo surveyed the finished project. In many ways he liked it greatly. The courtyard looked much better now, and there was no mud. But one thing disturbed him: a peculiar rock that jutted up above the others. The king examined it. Sparkly and pointier than the surrounding cobblestones, this rock was beautiful, yet it bothered the king because it looked out of place.

"What's the purpose of this one?" he asked Colm.

"Purpose?" inquired the stonemason.

"Why is it here—and what good is it, sticking out like that?"

Colm Stonemason shrugged. "I don't know."

"Then remove it."

"It's best to leave it there."

"I order you to remove it."

"Majesty, I humbly urge you to leave it."

Outraged, King Alfurzo dismissed the stonemason, refused to pay his wages, and asked his groundskeepers to remove the offending stone.

Somehow the task was never done. Perhaps the groundskeepers tried to pry out the stone and failed. Perhaps they forgot to perform the task. In any case, that odd, beautiful, obstructive stone remained in the courtyard—and continued to trouble King Alfurzo. It bothered him that the stone marred the perfect order of the new courtyard. It angered him that no one had corrected the situation. Most of all, it disturbed him that the stone served no purpose.

Not long afterward, King Alfurzo stood on the palace steps and addressed the nobility. Lords and ladies stood before him in the courtyard. Certain royal decisions had not been popular, so the king wanted to explain himself. Most of his courtiers listened politely. A few looked disgruntled. One, Lord Foxtooth, watched the king with obvious hatred.

Lord Foxtooth was, in fact, the most dangerous man in the kingdom, someone whom the king suspected of plotting against him.

Suddenly, Lord Foxtooth drew his sword, raised it high, and sprinted toward the king.

King Alfurzo knew at once that his life was over. Lord Foxtooth was huge, powerful, and accomplished in the art of swordsmanship. No one among the other courtiers could move fast enough to prevent his attack.

Yet he never reached his intended victim. Not five paces from King Alfurzo, Lord Foxtooth tripped on the protruding stone and fell hard on the courtyard, which made him an easy target for the many courtiers who rushed forth to restrain him.

Thus ended King Alfurzo's close encounter with death.

As you can imagine, the king made no further efforts to remove the odd, sparkling rock that protruded from his courtyard. Now grasping the wisdom of Colm's refusal to remove it, King Alfurzo not only paid him his wages—he appointed him royal stonemason.

"A strange story," said King Alphonse once Jack had finished.

"A *worthless* story!" Yoss exclaimed with an unpleasant laugh.

"I didn't intend it to be strange," Jack replied, ignoring the prince. "Maybe the story is an explanation—or a warning."

The king looked uncertain. "An explanation of what? A warning of what?"

"Perhaps my stories are like that stone," Jack said. "They seem to serve no purpose, but they actually do."

Stelinda now spoke up: "They seem merely to lie there and sparkle, but they protect you."

King Alphonse sat for a moment without speaking. Then he stood, paced for a short while, and seated himself again. Before Yoss could interrupt, he said, "Protect me? Well, so be it. Tell me another story."

So Jack did. One after another.

❦ 33 ❦

King Alphonse didn't always understand the stories that Jack told him, but he didn't tire of them, either. Soon Jack was spending more time with the king than all the senior councilors.

Late one morning, after he'd finished telling a new sequence of stories to Alphonse, Jack walked across the councilors' meeting hall on his way out of the palace. The hall stood empty, and Jack was aware only of his footsteps and their echoes in the hall. Then, abruptly, he heard other footsteps. He slowed and turned.

Stelinda stood in a doorway off to one side. Her sky-blue gown provided the perfect complement to her wheat-colored hair.

Jack paused for a moment, his mind racing. Did he dare to approach? Would he risk offending her? He had to take the chance. Without thinking further, he stepped closer. "Your Highness," he said, bowing low.

"That title is supposed to elevate my soul," she told him, "but it burdens me like a massive stone."

"I'm sorry."

"Don't apologize. Your eyes show what you think of me."

"I would do anything to gaze at you longer."

"So I read in the message that your bird delivered."

"I am a fool and a storyteller."

"But only half a liar."

"Should I take my leave and never seek you again?"

"Take your leave—but seek me."

"When?"

"Tonight, at midnight. In the Cherry Courtyard. Come tell me a story."

Jubilant, Jack left at once and returned to his chambers. He tried to nap but failed. At dinnertime he tried to eat but couldn't. Finally, incapable of sitting still, he ventured out into the evening air to walk off his restlessness. He would stroll through the palace. He would walk laps around the castle. He would do anything to hasten the night's arrival.

Within a short while, however, Jack crossed paths with the person he was most eager to avoid.

"A word with you, boy," Prince Yoss said when he encountered Jack in a corridor.

"Highness?" Jack could scarcely force himself to speak the word.

"I've noticed something. Something that displeases me."

"Yes?"

"You like my sister Stelinda."

"She is a member of the royal family," Jack told him, "and thus I feel great fondness for her."

"You like her far too much." Prince Yoss pinned Jack with an unwavering gaze.

Jack gestured uncertainly. "No affection is too great when a subject looks with admiration and gratitude on the royal family."

Yoss continued gazing until Jack felt like an insect squashed beneath a child's thumb. "True," Yoss said at last. "But we're not talking about admiration and gratitude, are we? There's something else. Something not so pure-hearted. You *stare* at her."

"The princess is beautiful."

"You stare like a filthy dog drooling at the sight of a dove."

"Not at all," Jack said.

"You have no reason to look at her, do you? No reason to speak with her."

"I am a storyteller," Jack stated. "I would tell her a story if she wishes."

"No one cares a whit about your stories."

"Princess Stelinda does."

"That's a lie!" shouted the prince.

"Your father does, too."

"Another lie!"

"Why, then, did your father appoint me royal storyteller?"

"Silence! *I'll* ask the questions!" Prince Yoss cried. "And you'll cease this insolence!"

Jack restrained himself. At this rate, he'd end up getting not only himself in trouble but the princess as well. Better to fall silent.

"Be warned. I'm watching you. And I have other eyes watching you, too, when mine are busy. Stay away from Stelinda."

"Yes, Highness."

"Do you hear me?"

"I do indeed, Highness."

"Stay away from my sister."

Jack returned hastily to his room. No matter how restless he felt, he couldn't risk another encounter with Prince Yoss. It was bad enough that the prince hated him as a result of their past conflicts; it was still worse that Jack's love for Stelinda might now feed the flames of Yoss's rage. But should he stifle what he felt for Stelinda just because her brother hated him? Wasn't his love good in its own right?

He made his decision. Nothing—not even the prince's resentment—would prevent him from meeting Stelinda that same night.

❦ 34 ❧

The next few hours passed like a feverish dream. Moody, restless, and aching with eagerness, Jack went about his business almost unaware of his own actions.

Stelinda . . . Stelinda in the courtyard . . . Stelinda in the court-yard at midnight . . .

Loquasto noticed Jack's strange mood. "Are you ill?" he asked.

"Never better," Jack responded.

"You don't look well."

"If this is sickness," Jack replied, "it's far better than health."

When the bird persisted, Jack brushed aside his questions. He was tempted to confide in Loquasto, but he didn't; he was sure that his friend would attempt to dissuade him from meeting Stelinda. Better to keep the secret to himself.

But his decision not to leave the apartment increased the tension with Loquasto. Trapped together yet unable to talk openly, they soon started to bicker. They squabbled over food. They argued about whether to open or close the windows. They sniped back and forth about stories they'd been working on.

Then, abruptly, Loquasto stated: "I just don't understand what's bothering you!"

At this point Jack was so desperate to reassure his friend, he said the first thing that came to mind: "I shouldn't tell you this, but there's a good reason for my restless mood. It concerns you and the fish princess."

The bird grew alert. "Artemisia?"

"Indeed. I've been thinking about your problem, and I believe I've found someone who can help you and your beloved."

This wasn't true at all; Jack hadn't given Artemisia a moment's thought. But he'd think about her shortly, he told himself. He'd ask around at court. He'd help his friend as soon as he could.

At once Loquasto looked both calmer and sadder. "How is that possible?" he asked. "How can anyone help a bird live with a fish?"

Jack gestured vaguely. "I don't rightly know. But I've located someone who claims to understand such things." Surely *someone* in the Royal City, Jack thought, would know what to do.

"Who?"

"I can't tell you."

"You must!"

"Loquasto, this is a complex situation. Please don't make it even more so."

"My happiness—and Artemisia's—is at stake."

"Precisely. Which is why we must proceed with great caution." Jack could feel his words rolling out of control like stones he had accidentally dislodged from a hillside. Yet still he went on. "If I could tell you what's happening, I'd do so. But I can't. You simply have to trust me. It's our secret."

"Our secret!" exclaimed Loquasto.

As night deepened, the bird fell asleep.

Jack felt uneasy about misleading his friend, but he assured himself that his intentions were good and that sooner or later he'd keep his promise. Putting on his boots, his cloak, and his best feathered hat, he set off just before midnight to meet Stelinda.

❧ 35 ❧

Jack reached the Cherry Courtyard without difficulty. Encountering guards at several doors and archways, he managed to talk his way past them or evade notice altogether. At midnight he arrived at his destination and stepped out into the moonlight—alone.

"Stelinda!" Jack whispered.

Only the muttering fountain answered him.

He glanced about. The courtyard couldn't have been emptier. Other than the fountain, Jack saw only a cherry tree planted in each corner and the ivy on the walls.

His spirits sank. Why had Stelinda failed to show up? He struggled to understand her absence. Had she been unable to leave the royal quarters? Had her brother accosted her and reported her to their father? Or had she simply lost interest in meeting him?

Jack waited in the courtyard, alone, for a long time. A distant bell tolled one. Crestfallen, he saw no alternative but to leave.

"Jack Storyteller!"

The whispered name jolted him. Jack glanced about. "Who is it?"

"Jack!"

He couldn't see who spoke. "Stelinda?"

"Up here!"

Once again he looked around. Where—? Then, abruptly, he caught sight of a pale hand waving to him from among the limbs of one of the cherry trees.

"Stelinda!" Jack rushed over to the tree. To his astonishment, the princess was perched like a songbird among the branches. "What are you doing up there?"

She laughed. "Waiting for you."

"Couldn't you have found a more comfortable resting place?"

"Of course—but none safer," she said. "Although I can see anyone who ventures into this courtyard, no one can see me."

Jack's delight soon turned to dismay. "Why did you hide for so long?"

"To watch you."

"To *watch* me."

"To watch, wait, and see how long you'd linger."

"What a dull pastime."

"Patience, too, tells a story." Stelinda eased herself off of her perch and dropped to the courtyard. Dressed in a black velvet robe studded with pearls, the princess was more beautiful than the starry sky above.

They stared at each other as if bewitched.

"We have so little time," Jack noted at last. "I worry that the prince will find us."

"Yoss would have trouble finding the ground he's standing on," Stelinda said with a laugh.

"He hates me."

"Much to your credit."

"He'll try to keep us apart."

She touched Jack on the cheek. "He'll fail."

"He has already failed," Jack noted.

They walked over to the fountain in the middle of the courtyard and settled together on the stone rim. Moonlight twisted and shifted in the pool.

Jack took Stelinda's hands. "I want to know everything about you."

"And I about you."

"You tell me first."

"No, you first."

"*You!*"

"No, *you!*"

They squabbled amiably until their protests turned to laughter.

"*You* are the storyteller," the princess announced, "so *you* tell the story."

"I've told too many," Jack countered. "Now it's your turn."

"I didn't bring my lute."

"Your lute?" Jack failed to grasp her meaning.

"I tell my stories in song," she said. "I need my lute to accompany myself."

"Let the fountain be your accompanist," Jack told her, gesturing to the water as it spilled into the pool.

Stelinda hesitated. "Do you truly wish to hear my tale?" she asked. "If so, be warned, for it's a feast of disappointments."

"All I ask is to hear about you," Jack told her.

"Well, then—you'll hear more than anyone should know."

Once upon a time (Stelinda said) a princess lived in a palace. She was a perfect princess—high-born, beautiful, intelligent, blessed with great artistic gifts—and she lived in perfect bliss. Residing in a perfect palace, eating perfect food, sleeping in a perfect bed, attending perfect banquets, and fulfilling perfect duties, she could find no flaws in her existence. She had two perfect sisters, a perfect brother, and a perfect father who was the perfect king to reign over this family's perfect kingdom. Everything about her life was perfect.

Is this the story you'd have me tell? Is this the tale you want to hear? Most people assume that the royal life resembles a plate of pastries—sweet, rich, delicate, delightful—and they're offended if told otherwise. Are you willing to hear the truth?

Well, then, let me tell you.

For if my life consists of pastries, what I taste on eating them is chalk, dust, and ashes. Now, I imagine you're thinking: *Poor little princess! What deprivation she endures. What pain she tolerates. What a struggle she makes to survive in a cold, cruel world. What a hard life she lives, crushed beneath a burden of nobility, wealth, power, and beauty.* Well, I know I'm spoiled. I know my life is easy. I know my complaints sound foolish, given what most people face in life.

But I have my own reasons for complaint. I never sought an empty life. Yet I find myself trapped in one, and I feel no qualms about searching for a way out.

Is noble birth a cage surrounding me? Is this elegant dungeon the fate of all persons born to high estate? Perhaps so—or perhaps not. Sometimes I believe that being a princess isn't really the problem after all. If I could put my riches and advantages to good purpose, I'd be the happiest princess alive. I could feed the hungry. I could help cure the sick and heal the wounded. I could assist the lost in finding their way, the ignorant in finding knowledge, the sad in finding joy. But it's not just the burden of royalty that afflicts me—it's the woe that has befallen my family.

No doubt you've heard about my mother. Here's what I recall about her.

I recall that she was beautiful. I remember a game we played during my early years, in which Mother would lean forward and let her long hair dangle to the floor, creating a room for me to sit in—a room with the most delicate, radiant walls.

I recall that she was indifferent to her beauty. When people praised her looks, she couldn't always restrain her laughter. And when she laughed, it wasn't a ladylike titter but a sudden belly laugh, for she thought it preposterous that anyone should care about her appearance.

I recall that she played the lute—that her fingers plucked the strings as precisely as a weaver grasping threads, that she wove a cloth of music, and that instead of singing lullabies at night, she played for me, covering me with the warm blanket of her tunes.

She died just before I turned six. What had been a joyous day—the occasion of my brother's birth—became a day of mourning. I recall the proclamation, my father's screams, the courtiers' lamentations. I remember feeling that this event made no sense. How was it possible that someone so thoroughly alive could now be dead? That someone so warm could now be cold? That someone so present could now be forever absent?

My life, and that of the whole Realm, changed overnight. My father withdrew so completely that he, too, might as well have died. He ignored his family—me, my sisters, and our new brother. He ignored the councilors, the courtiers, the commoners. He ignored the entire Realm. And when he didn't ignore us all, he lashed out at us, berated us, and punished us for being everyone but the one person whose company he craved above all others. The Realm and everything within it has withered under his touch—or from the lack of it.

What grieves me most is knowing that despite my father's actions, he loves me. His heart is true; his intentions are good. No matter what you may believe, he isn't a cruel man. What afflicts him isn't evil but grief.

And my brother, Yoss? Who knows what accounts for his ill humor. Perhaps it's simply his nature. Perhaps it's his way of dealing with the difficulties we've faced as a family. Perhaps it's the guilt he feels, for he believes that he caused our mother's death. My response—quite beyond my own choice, mind you—has been sadness. Yoss's response has been anger. He loathes the world and everyone in it. Some people inspire his loathing more than others, but few escape his contempt and rage. In a way I pity him; he's like a scorpion whose tail lashes out here, there, everywhere, stinging without aim or mercy. No doubt someday he'll sting himself as hard as he stings everyone else.

As for what will come of all this loss and pain—I can't even imagine. Perhaps my whole family will sink under the weight of our failings. Perhaps we'll learn, somehow, to throw them off, start anew, and live full lives again.

I hope so. I hope so deeply.

Surely we could be more than a sour, angry family.

Surely I could be more than just a spoiled, gloomy princess.

⚜ 36 ⚜

Jack looked around in a daze. The fountain beside him . . . the courtyard walls . . . None of these things had existed a few moments earlier; the world had consisted only of Stelinda and her story.

"I regret having bored you," said the princess.

Jack impulsively reached out, took her hand, and told her, "Nothing could have pleased me more than to have listened."

"I went on and on."

"I would have listened forever."

"I would have run out of words long before that."

"You could tell me a story made of silence, then."

"Sometimes I believe that's the story I should be telling."

"Don't say that."

"The world has no need for my story."

"*I* do," Jack declared. "*I* want to hear it."

Stelinda smiled at him weakly.

"You have a right to tell your story," Jack said. "Believe me, your story isn't just the words you're saying, it's the life you're living."

"A grim story, then. I've done nothing. I've *been* nothing. All I do is live my rich, empty life and sing my rich, empty songs."

"Maybe that's where the plot will twist."

Stelinda looked uncertain. "I beg your pardon?"

"Perhaps your songs will change your life and, in turn, change others' lives as well. You said your songs are like stories—stories told by singing."

"That is my intention."

"And, like stories, your songs are powerful. Perhaps they will be what sparks a change—a change in yourself and perhaps in the Realm as well."

Stelinda gazed at him with an expression that mixed confusion and hope. "So you believe I'll escape from my cage?"

"You'll sing your way out of it."

Unaware of the moon's passage overhead, Jack and Stelinda paid heed only to each other. They talked half the night away, sharing stories about the past: he about his life as a farm boy in Yorrow, she about her upbringing as a princess in the Royal City. With amusement and amazement they pondered the differences between their lives. They asked each other questions. They listened to the answers. They speculated about what the future might bring. With each of them caught in the other's web—or rather, with both of them caught in a web they spun together—they entangled themselves in threads more complex than what even the cleverest spider could have woven.

Together, Jack decided, they could overcome all the hardships facing them. Together they could right all the wrongs inflicted on the Realm. Together they could live happily—

Jack suddenly turned to Stelinda and asked, "Will you marry me?"

Stelinda stared as if awakened from a dream. "I beg your pardon?"

At once Jack came to his senses. Had he really just proposed marriage to a princess? Never mind that she was the most wonderful person he had ever met. The audacity of his proposal shocked him. "Forgive me," he said. "I have no right to ask." Then he added: "But . . . would you marry me?"

"*Marry* you," she repeated.

"That's what I said," Jack told her, now speaking hesitantly.

"*You*, a commoner, marry *me*, a princess?"

Jack gestured in confusion. "I'm sorry—"

"How sorry?"

"Well—not very," Jack admitted. "Actually, I'm not sorry at all."

"Good," she declared. "I'm glad of it. You have nothing to be sorry about. Of *course* I'll marry you."

They'd scarcely met!

True. But it's also true that Jack and Stelinda understood the love in their hearts. Why shouldn't they have wanted to marry?

But they were so young!

Jack was seventeen. Stelinda had just turned eighteen. In those days they would have been considered of marriageable age.

Did they go ahead, then?

Well, that's certainly how they wanted the story to develop. But sometimes a plot twists in ways that startle even the storyteller.

⁓37⁓

Jack half sprinted, half danced back to his quarters. He moved with such haste that he stumbled time after time, scaring cats that hissed and dogs that barked as he pranced through the alleyways. More than once, irate courtiers opened their windows and shouted down at him: "Silence!" or "Stop that racket!" Jack ignored them. He quickly reached his apartment, raced up the staircase, and dashed into the sitting room.

"Wake up!" he shouted to Loquasto, who was asleep on his perch.

The bird sputtered in alarm: "What! Where! Once upon a time!"

"I'm back!"

"Back . . . ," said Loquasto, looking rather dazed. "What news of Artemisia?"

Jack blurted, "I'm getting married!"

"Who? Who is?"

"You're not an owl—talk to me!"

"It's not even daylight yet," groaned Loquasto. "Why are you shouting?"

Jack declared: "Because I'm getting married!"

"What are you talking about?"

"The princess." Jack puffed out his chest in triumph. "The princess Stelinda."

A long silence followed. Loquasto only stared at him.

"*Say* something!"

"You're out of your mind."

"Why shouldn't I marry her?" Jack asked defiantly.

"Because it's foolish!" squawked Loquasto.

"What's so foolish about two people who understand each other?"

"When one is a princess and the other a mere storyteller," the bird replied, "it's ridiculous!"

"What's so ridiculous about two people who love each other?"

"It's impossible!" Loquasto screeched. "As impossible as a bird marrying a fish."

Jack stopped short. Loquasto was right. The situation *was* impossible. How could he marry Stelinda? She was a princess. He was a commoner. King Alphonse would throw him into a dungeon simply for asking. Suddenly, Jack couldn't recall what had bewitched him into making such a foolish request. He—Jack Storyteller—had asked for Princess Stelinda's hand in marriage! "So what should I do?" Jack inquired, now despondent. "Just give up?"

"Precisely. Give up."

"That's pathetic."

"Accept the true nature of things."

Jack grew angry at the bird's eagerness to capitulate. "And will *you* give up, too? Give up seeking Artemisia?" he demanded.

"I have no choice," Loquasto said, drooping on his perch.

"But you *do* have a choice."

"There's no point," sighed Loquasto. "I'm a bird. She's a fish. What's the solution to a problem like that? The only worse match would be a princess and a storyteller."

"Well, *you're* a big help!" Jack huffed.

"I'm trying to make you face the truth."

"I can do just fine without you, thanks very much."

"Jack, come to your senses. There's no point in striving for what's impossible."

But the more Jack listened to Loquasto, the more he rejected such a hopeless attitude. Let the bird give up, if that was what he wanted. Jack himself would never relent.

"I'm going to marry Stelinda," Jack announced, walking over to the window and gazing outward. Off to the east, in the direction of the palace, the sky had begun to lighten. "I don't care if she's a princess and I'm a commoner. I'm going to marry her."

But how could Jack do that?

Well, he wasn't sure. It's difficult enough to marry a princess if you're a nobleman. And if you're a commoner . . .

So what did he do?

Jack realized that the obstacle he'd face would be to win the royal blessing. The king's opposition would doom the marriage, while his backing would make it possible. Jack also felt that since King Alphonse himself had married a commoner—Mattie Lutenist—he might be favorably inclined toward Jack and Stelinda's union.

He'd understand their love.

Precisely. He'd feel sympathetic toward their plight.

But how would Jack win over the king?

Jack understood that his challenge would be to push past the icy crust of the king's grief to reach the still-warm heart beating within. And he would accomplish that task, Jack decided, by telling a story.

✥ 38 ✥

The more Jack contemplated the situation, the more he believed that a story would win over King Alphonse. So when a royal summons arrived just a few days later, Jack was ready. He and Loquasto went at once to the Great Hall. There he found himself standing before the king, the councilors, a group of courtiers, and Stelinda herself.

"Storyteller, tell me a story," King Alphonse commanded.

"With pleasure, Majesty," Jack answered. "Is there any particular one you'd like?"

"Something strange and wonderful."

"As you wish," Jack said. Then, as everyone settled in to listen, he addressed King Alphonse.

Once upon a time (Jack began) a common crow made his way through the world by telling stories. Crow was a good storyteller, and all the other creatures in the forest liked the tales he told. Crow went happily about his business. Only one thing troubled him: Crow was lonely. Affectionate by nature, he wanted to find a mate, settle down, and raise a family. But Crow found no wife among the other birds, so he grew lonelier and lonelier as the years passed.

Then something happened that changed his life forever.

Picking berries down by the lake one afternoon, Crow spotted the loveliest creature he'd ever seen. Her feathers glistened orange-yellow in the sunlight. Her wings, though small, moved with grace. Her tail was languid and lush, fuller than any that Crow had ever seen. And her eyes were the largest, saddest eyes in the world. Just watching her filled Crow with longing. He'd found his soul mate. He wanted nothing more—and nothing less—than to spend the rest of his life with her.

There was only one problem.

She was a fish. And not just any fish. Her name was Stelicia, and she was the daughter of the fish king and queen who ruled the lake.

As Jack told this story, he made sure that King Alphonse was deeply moved by what happened to Crow and Stelicia. He described how they fell in love. How they discovered that neither of them could live in the other's realm. How they despaired of being together. How they reluctantly decided that, despite their love, they would have to live apart.

"I will always love you," said Stelicia. And with those words, she swam away.

Crestfallen, Crow withdrew. What could be worse, he asked himself, than to find a soul mate but to end up separated from her forever?

Then, suddenly, Crow heard a voice call out to him: "Do not despair!"

He looked around but saw no other creature along the shore. "Who is it that speaks to me?" Crow asked.

"It is I," said a voice coming from the lake. "The fish king."

Crow peered into the water and saw a huge fish—silvery in hue and muscular in appearance.

"Majesty?"

"I am Stelicia's father."

Crow bowed his head.

"Do you love my daughter?" asked the fish king.

"More than life itself."

"Then come and join us in the lake."

"I'll drown," Crow protested.

"You said you love her more than life itself."

Crow hesitated. Was the king's request a trick to get rid of a pesky suitor? Crow decided it didn't matter. He'd risk anything for his beloved.

He leaped into the lake. Though sputtering at first, he soon realized that he could breathe underwater. Thrashing about, he realized that he could swim. And he rejoiced as he saw the princess swimming toward him.

"What has happened to me?" asked Crow as he and Stelicia swam together, around and around, in the lake.

"My father is a magic fish," answered the princess, "and because you love me, he has granted you the gift of living both on dry land and in the water."

"But why?"

Swimming close, Stelicia exclaimed, "So we can be together!"

As indeed they were.

And as a result of the king's wisdom and generosity, Stelicia and Crow soon married, and they lived happily ever after.

Finishing, Jack saw King Alphonse gaze at him in silence, his expression as serious as ever. "A strange story, Jack Storyteller."

"Strange! Strange!" squawked Loquasto loudly.

"Not so strange," Jack said.

"What does it mean?" asked the king.

"It means that I wish to marry your daughter."

King Alphonse was stunned. "My daughter!"

"The princess Stelinda."

"But she's a princess!" the king exclaimed. "You are a commoner."

"Commoner!" shrieked Loquasto.

Jack hesitated for a moment; then, looking King Alphonse in the eye, he said, "Majesty—you, too, married a commoner."

A gasp of shock and consternation rose from the assembled courtiers.

"What did you say?" demanded the king. "What are you telling me?"

"You loved Mattie Lutenist and she loved you, and it was right that nothing kept you apart."

"How dare you—"

"So, too, should it be for Stelinda and me."

"Silence!" shouted King Alphonse.

Jack winced as he understood how intensely his words had angered King Alphonse—and opened all his old wounds of loss and grief.

The king said nothing for a long time.

Everyone watched and waited.

Then at last he said, "Listen to me, Jack Storyteller. The tale is well told, the moral clear. But none of that makes any difference. What matters is what *Stelinda* wants."

All eyes shifted to the princess.

Stelinda reached out and took Jack's hand. "What I want," she told her father, "is to marry Jack."

King Alphonse gazed at her. "If indeed you love each other," said the king, "I can only rejoice in your decision to marry."

Some of the councilors stared at him in bewilderment. Courtiers began to whisper intently among themselves.

"Does this mean you'll allow us to proceed?" asked Stelinda, clearly not yet confident of her good fortune.

King Alphonse stood and embraced his daughter. "Not only will I allow you," he said, "I will assist you in any way possible."

Jack could scarcely restrain himself. He felt like leaping into the air and shouting in delight. Instead, he knelt abruptly, bowed low, and placed his forehead on the king's feet.

"Now, now," said King Alphonse. "That's no way to treat your future father-in-law."

"Thank you, Majesty. Thank you!" Jack exclaimed.

"Up with you, lad. We have a wedding to plan."

Jack forced himself to his feet.

Joining hands with Jack and Stelinda, the king turned to the gathered courtiers and said, "Listen, all of you. I hereby decree that Sunday next will be the wedding, and everyone in the Royal City is invited."

At once great cheers went up from the assembled courtiers:

"Long live the king!"

"Long live Princess Stelinda!"

"Long live Jack Storyteller!"

ᴧ 39 ᴧ

We did it!" Jack exclaimed as he and Loquasto left the Great Hall. "We got what we wanted."

"*You* got what *you* wanted," Loquasto stated, gripping Jack's shoulder tightly with his claws.

Jack didn't seem to hear. "Princess Stelinda and I will soon be married."

"At my expense, I might add."

Now Jack stopped short. "What do you mean, 'At my expense'?"

"You used my story," said Loquasto.

"So?"

"It was the bait that caught your fish."

"What bait?" Jack asked. "What fish?"

"You're the storyteller, Jack. Don't you even listen to yourself?"

"I don't know what you're talking about."

Loquasto pecked him hard. "You told the king *my* story to catch *your* princess."

"Does my gain harm you?" Jack inquired, feeling baffled and hurt.

"I suppose not," the bird admitted, "but it does me no good, either. And you haven't done anything yet to help me and Artemisia."

"I promise I'll do so."

"When, though? *When?* So far, what you've done serves only your own interests."

Jack grasped his friend's complaint. Yet his mind was so caught up in dreams of Stelinda that he couldn't spare any thoughts for Loquasto's plight. "I promise to help you as soon as possible," he said.

"*How* soon?"

"After the wedding."

Loquasto ruffled his feathers, then suddenly sprang off Jack's shoulder and flew up to their apartment's open window.

Jack regretted the dilemma he had created. It *was* unfair that he'd used Loquasto's story to his own advantage; he could understand why the bird felt angry. Still, he'd had no choice. And his strategy had worked.

Stelinda . . . Jack would soon marry the princess Stelinda.

So they got married and lived happily ever after.

Well—

And that's the end of the story. That's always the end of the story, isn't it?

Just listen a while longer—

Why? What happened?

More than you can imagine, believe me.

❧ 40 ❧

The truth is, neither Jack's plans nor anyone else's came to pass in the manner they'd anticipated.

Jack himself half expected something odd to happen. Although he could think only of Stelinda and of their wedding, worries bled him like leeches fastening onto the ankle of someone crossing a stream.

Yoss. Prince Yoss, Jack realized, would oppose the match. Not that the prince had any good reason to object, but he would oppose it anyway. The prince hated Jack under the best of circumstances; now Yoss would hate him even more. Over the next few days, with preparations for the wedding under way and the ceremony fast approaching, Jack grew more and more concerned about Yoss's likely reaction.

"What should I do about the prince?" Jack asked Loquasto one afternoon.

"Do?" inquired the bird in response. "Do anything you like."

"What do *you* think I should do?"

"It makes no difference what I think."

"I take your opinion seriously."

"Oh?" asked Loquasto. "I see no evidence of that."

Jack, shocked by these words, confronted his friend. "Are you still angry about what happened the other day?"

"It wasn't *I* who lit the fire beneath this pot."

Further efforts to solve their differences got nowhere. Jack soon gave up and decided to seek assistance elsewhere.

"Perhaps you can help me," Jack said to Zephyrio when he visited the illusionist's apartment in the palace.

"Of course," Zephyrio answered. "I'll do anything within my powers. Though, frankly, I can't imagine why a lad who's lucky enough to marry the princess Stelinda will need any help."

Jack was surprised. "You've heard of our betrothal?"

Zephyrio laughed heartily. "Heard? It's the only news anyone is discussing!"

"I love her deeply."

"So I gather," said the illusionist. "Well, then—please make yourself comfortable."

Jack looked around the apartment before he took his seat. It was spacious and elegantly appointed. Its dark walls displayed several portraits of Zephyrio. A rack of swords stood near the door. A set of shelves across the room housed six cages containing small creatures: a rabbit, a weasel, a pair of quail, a parrot, a dove, and a coiled snake. Other shelves held objects that perplexed Jack: strange mechanical devices, bottles of colored liquids, and a small glowing sphere.

"I'm concerned about Stelinda's brother," he said.

Zephyrio smiled. "Ah, yes—young Prince Yoss."

"I worry that my marriage will anger him," Jack went on, "and that he'll try to prevent it by any means possible."

The illusionist raised his left eyebrow. "By *any* means?" he inquired. "I doubt it. The prince lacks the influence to do so. He lacks the power. Above all, Prince Yoss lacks the wit. He's not a clever lad like you. If you handed him a dagger dipped in honey, he wouldn't think twice before licking the blade."

Jack winced at the thought but felt reassured by the illusionist's opinion.

Zephyrio continued. "He's not one to scheme and plot. That's much too demanding for him. No, you have little to fear from Prince Yoss. He'll huff and puff. He'll spit a few jewels at you. Yet little more will come of his protestations than from a child's tantrums."

"You think so?" Jack asked.

"I'm sure of it. He's a storm full of thunder yet empty of lightning. But look—if you're concerned, let me size up the situation. I've performed many times before the prince, and I've gained his confidence. I can approach him as few others can. Shall I have a word with him?"

"I wish you would," Jack said.

"I'll find out what you're up against."

"That would be helpful."

"Better safe than sorry, eh?" Zephyrio clapped a hand on Jack's shoulder. "Don't worry; we'll keep the situation well under control."

Thus Jack Storyteller moved quickly to prevent Prince Yoss from ruining the plans that he and Stelinda had made. He was reassured by Zephyrio's offer of assistance, and—pleased to have contained the risks—he did everything necessary to prepare for the wedding itself.

He had the royal tailors sew him a splendid suit of clothes for the ceremony. He visited a barber to have his hair cut. He purchased new boots and a fine feathered hat. In short, Jack readied himself for what he knew would be the happiest day of his life.

⊰ 41 ⊱

Then a series of events took place that changed not only Jack's life but everyone else's throughout the Realm.

The situation started quietly enough. Having set a time to discuss wedding plans with Stelinda and Jack, the king sent a messenger to announce that he had canceled the appointment.

"Canceled?" Jack asked the messenger. "But why?"

"He didn't say."

At first Jack suspected outside intervention. Perhaps Yoss had committed some new mischief against him and Stelinda. Then Jack worried that King Alphonse had suffered a change of heart.

Consulting with Stelinda put these worries to rest—though not without raising a new cause for concern. "Father sends you his regrets," the princess told Jack. "He urges you not to misunderstand his decision. The truth is, he simply feels too tired."

"*Tired?*" Jack said.

"I've never seen him so exhausted."

"Is he ill?"

Stelinda shook her head. "He said nothing of illness—only deep fatigue."

Yet the next day Jack learned from Geoffrey that King Alphonse now seemed ill indeed.

That same day confronted Jack with further events. Like clouds accumulating on the horizon—just a few at first, then bigger, darker ones as the day passed—these events arrived so gradually as to avoid alerting Jack to any danger. He was concerned but not alarmed. Perhaps the king had simply caught a cold. Surely the crisis would pass.

Then, late that afternoon, the princess requested that he visit the king's private chambers. Jack hastened there at once.

On arriving, Jack found King Alphonse propped up in a bed so large that it dwarfed the man nestled among the quilts and pillows. Several paces from the bed stood the chamberlain, some of the councilors, and a scattering of nobles. The king's younger daughters sat on chairs near the bed. Looking wary, Prince Yoss stood behind them. Princess Stelinda, seated close to the bed, looked up as Jack entered the room. The mood couldn't have been gloomier. With good reason, too, for the king looked deathly pale.

Jack approached slowly and stood beside Stelinda. He expected her to reach out for his hand, but she didn't. She only sat motionless and gazed at her father.

At some point Jack realized that King Alphonse had focused his gaze. His eyes, like tiny, frightened creatures peering out from their refuge inside a hollow log, now sought out the storyteller.

Jack knelt, bowing until his forehead rested on the quilt. Then a noise distracted him—a noise that wasn't quite speech. He glanced about, trying to determine who or what had produced the sound: half hiss, half click. Turning to Stelinda, Jack saw her nod in her father's direction. Only then did he realize that the king himself had spoken. "Majesty?" he said.

"T—," the king said. "Tell—"

"Forgive me," Jack told him, "but I don't understand—"

"Tell me—"

Just then Yoss interrupted: "Leave him alone. Leave my father *alone!*"

"*You* leave him alone!" Stelinda yelled at her brother.

"Get that commoner out of this room!" shouted Yoss.

Guards stepped forth to expel Jack from the royal chambers.

Stelinda stood abruptly. "He stays," she told them. "Father himself has summoned Jack. The storyteller belongs *here.*"

At once the guards retreated.

Again King Alphonse uttered those half-choked words: "Tell me—"

"This boy is the source of Father's illness!" Yoss bellowed. "*He's* the one who sickened the king! *He's* the one who has pushed him to death's door! *He's* the one—"

"Stop it!" cried Stelinda. "*You're* the sickness that's afflicting him."

"No, *you* are!"

"*Silence!*"

It was King Alphonse who had spoken. "Storyteller," he said in a weak but intelligible voice, "tell me a story."

Once upon a time (Jack began) there lived a king named Alphonse. He was a good man but not a happy one, for he had always wanted to be an artist, never a king. Having become the monarch of Sundar, though, he had no choice but to rule that kingdom rather than the realms of music, poetry, sculpture, dance, and painting. He cared nothing for the edicts, proclamations, and judgments that are a king's creations, and burdened by his duties, he lashed out against his people. Years of great suffering followed. The Realm sank into despair.

Late in his life, however, King Alphonse reached an understanding that changed him. He withdrew his harsh edicts. He lifted the burdens that had been placed on his subjects. The effects on the Realm were almost immediate. People began to create once again. They started to live free of fear. They attended to one another, not just to themselves. The Realm became a place of hope and delight rather than one of dread and suffering.

In this sense, King Alphonse fulfilled his destiny as an artist after all. The Realm became the material he shaped. His subjects' health and happiness became the art he practiced. Of course he didn't accomplish everything he strove to do. He did, however, do much more than he imagined, for King Alphonse sought what all artists seek but don't necessarily attain: the craft mastered, the form realized.

Later that night, Jack left the king's chamber and returned to his room. He sat there feeling desolate, eating little, and sleeping not at all. Then, just before dawn, as he prepared to venture out and see if anyone in the palace knew the king's fate, a messenger arrived with the news that he dreaded most.

King Alphonse was dead.

❧ 42 ❧

Jack felt a vast hollowness in his soul. He had lost the monarch to whom he owed allegiance. Worse, he had lost the employer who had treated him so well, who had allowed his art to grow, to bloom, to bear fruit.

What troubled Jack most of all was seeing how this event affected Stelinda. He visited her that afternoon and found her incapable of speaking. She gazed at him, she embraced him, but she refused to answer his urgent questions. Sad under the best of circumstances, Stelinda had now become even more withdrawn. Jack could only hold her and keep her company.

It was obvious that he and Stelinda would have to postpone their wedding. Mourning would come first, rejoicing later. Fair enough. His future bride's well-being—and the well-being of the entire Realm—required honoring the loss that Sundar had suffered.

Thus they did. The funeral took place just two days later.

Jack observed this solemn occasion as it unfolded: how the king's body lay in state in a glass coffin; how the pallbearers carried the coffin through the palace and through the Royal City; and how, after much ceremony, the gathered family members, courtiers, councilors, court officials, artists, and attendants placed King Alphonse to rest in a tomb within one of the royal gardens. Yet none of these rituals made any impression on Jack. He was too worried about Stelinda to pay much attention. He knew that as frustrating as the princess had found her father, she had always loved him. As much as she lamented his failures as king, she mourned him.

Jack understood something else as well: Alphonse's death would at least have one fortunate consequence in the Realm. Alphonse had been a widower. By law, his oldest child, whether male or female, would inherit the throne. Princess Stelinda was Alphonse's oldest child.

Stelinda would be queen.

⚘ 43 ⚘

S o what does that mean, exactly?" Loquasto asked when Jack returned to their apartment and explained the situation.

"Just that," Jack said. "She'll be queen."

"Of course. But what does that mean for *you?*"

Puzzled, Jack gestured awkwardly. "For me?"

"Wake up, lad. If she becomes the queen and you marry her, what
happens?"

"Hmm," Jack said. "I hadn't thought about that."

"You hadn't *thought* about it!"

"Truly."

"I find that difficult to believe."

"Loquasto, it's true."

"So the pure-hearted lad who stole *my* story to catch *his* princess
never considered that by marrying Stelinda he'd end up king of the
Realm."

Jolted by these words, Jack understood at last. How could he
have been so foolish? "You're right," he said, half dazed.

Loquasto hooted with derision. "You're a good storyteller but
a bad actor, Jack. Don't imagine for a moment that I find you convincing."

"You think I've planned this whole thing, don't you? You think
I've planned to wed the princess only to reach the throne!"

"Well, not *only*—"

"Loquasto, I'm offended."

"You love her, that's obvious enough."

"I'm *deeply* offended—"

"But it's convenient, isn't it, that she's next in the line of succession and that—"

Jack stormed out of the apartment before Loquasto could finish the sentence.

Half the day passed before he found Stelinda. Seated in her favorite garden, she strummed her lute without much interest and sang a wistful song.

"My dreams are flowers that bloomed all night.
Now, cut and dried, they're pressed within the book of sleep.
And when I go to bed this evening, light
Will fade and dreams will bloom for me to pluck and keep."

"I dread what happens next," she told Jack as he sat down beside her.

"What's there to dread about becoming queen?" he asked.

"Everything."

"You will rule the kingdom brilliantly."

"I don't wish to rule the kingdom," said Stelinda. "I want to write poems and sing songs."

"Write and sing, then, as well as rule."

She shook her head. "You know what happened to my father. The burden of the crown crushed his spirit. Once he ascended to the throne, he never again found the time or inspiration to pursue the arts."

"You will be different."

"I don't see how."

Jack wouldn't let her win this argument. "You'll be different by not succumbing to despair. You'll make poetry and song into torches that light up your subjects' lives."

"And you?" Stelinda asked. "Will you withstand the burden of the crown?"

"I have no interest in becoming king," Jack told her. "But if my marriage to you requires it, then I'll do so without complaint, and I'll do everything to rule with you as wisely as possible."

She strummed a harsh chord on her lute. "Then we have no choice. The Realm will be the instrument, and the people's benefit our melody."

That's how they made their decision. Not pleased but resolute, Jack and Stelinda sought the prime councilor, communicated their wishes to him, and sent messengers to alert everyone that a proclamation about Stelinda's ascension to the throne would be read the next morning.

☙ 44 ❧

The following day, Jack and Stelinda entered the Great Hall together. Jack felt strange walking at her side—a mere storyteller next to a princess—yet he was proud to accompany her. They strode into the hall to a burst of sound—not just from the drums and trumpets proclaiming Stelinda's arrival but also from the crowd's lively cheers: "Long live Queen Stelinda!" "All hail Queen Stelinda!" "Praised be Queen Stelinda!"

The princess nodded, smiling just a little, clearly uneasy at being addressed as the monarch.

"They're happy to see you," Jack told her, "and with good reason."

"I only hope I can live up to their expectations."

They reached the platform on which the royal thrones—draped now in black cloth—awaited. Stelinda's sisters, Giselle and Mythunia, stood to the left of the thrones; Yoss stood to the right. The councilors lined up behind the royal offspring. Stelinda walked forward until she stood before the empty thrones, then turned and faced the crowd.

Jack, having no official place in these proceedings, bowed deeply before the princess, and moved to one side.

Once the commotion subsided, the prime councilor stepped forth to address the court. This man, Jeremy the Younger, was so ancient that people often joked that they couldn't imagine someone old enough to be Jeremy the Elder. Standing perhaps five feet tall, he wore his beard so long that with each step he risked tripping on it. Thin, dazed, and wobbly on his feet, Jeremy the Younger now tottered before his audience.

"A proclamation," he said at last in a reedy voice.

One of the lesser councilors approached with a scroll that unrolled so abruptly that one end dropped clear to the floor.

Jeremy mistook his beard for the scroll, raised it to his face, and tried to read what he believed to be its text.

Shouts erupted from the courtiers: "The scroll, Lord Jeremy! The scroll!"

"Oh, my!" he exclaimed. "Quite so. The scroll indeed." Taking the document from the councilor waiting patiently at his side, Jeremy now began to read. "'Be it known to friend and foe alike that by the Realm's law the line of royal succession shall pass from the king or queen to his or her lawfully wedded spouse, *unless*,'" Jeremy said as he raised a twig-like finger, "'the king or queen has been widowed, in which case the scepter shall pass to whichever of their children is eldest—'"

New shouts arose: "Long live Queen Stelinda!"

"'—and of sound mind.'"

A moment of silence reigned. Courtiers glanced at one another, baffled. Jack looked about, too. *Of sound mind?*

Commotion burst forth again: "Long live the Queen!"

Jack, caught up in the court's excitement, shouted, too. Stelinda would be queen!

Yet Jeremy the Younger, reaching out to silence the crowd, continued to read. "'And because Princess Stelinda, though indeed King Alphonse's oldest child, has nevertheless preoccupied herself with the arts—squandering untold hours writing poems, singing songs, playing lutes, and pursuing other frivolities, all unbefitting of a sovereign's dignity and gravity—for these reasons, the princess has proved herself to be of *unsound mind*; indeed, of such unsound mind as to threaten the safety and well-being of the Realm.'"

"What!" someone shouted.

"Who makes these claims?" asked a woman near Jack.

"Nonsense!" a man yelled.

Jack looked over at Stelinda. Suddenly aware of his attention, she turned abruptly and stared, stricken, into his eyes.

"'Moreover, because the princesses Giselle and Mythunia, though indeed the second- and third-oldest offspring of the late King Alphonse, are silly girls who spend all their time gossiping and playing foolish games, all unbefitting of a sovereign's dignity and gravity—for these reasons, these princesses, too, have proved themselves to be of *unsound mind*; indeed, of such unsound mind as to threaten the safety and well-being of the Realm.'"

"What!" cried out several people.

"'Therefore,'" the prime councilor continued, "'be it known that from this day forth, the crown, the scepter of the Realm, and all the power that resides within them shall pass to Prince Yoss—'"

More shouts: "What!" "Prince Yoss?" "That's an outrage!"

"'—who shall in one day's time be crowned king of Sundar.'"

More shouts: "Usurper!" "Pretender to the throne!" "Down with Prince Yoss!" "Long live Queen Stelinda!"

Alarmed, Jack watched as the assembled courtiers, who had

already began to mill about in the crowded hall, now pressed forward. Surely this gathering would turn violent soon. Jack pushed his way over to Stelinda's side. No matter what happened, he was determined to stand by her.

Before the tinder of the courtiers' wrath could erupt into flames, a squadron of armed guards wielding swords, maces, and battle-axes entered the Great Hall. At once they spread out, encircling the crowd.

Then Yoss strode forth. "I, Prince Yoss, am heir to the throne of Sundar," he announced. "My coronation is tomorrow."

FOUR

❧ 45 ❧

After Yoss dismissed everyone—"All depart!"—the Royal Guard escorted the courtiers from the Great Hall.

Jack watched them leave, then turned to Stelinda. "There must be some mistake."

"Oh, there's no mistake," she replied, her face tinged red from anger. "He told us exactly what he means to do."

"But surely the councilors won't allow—"

"*Shhh!*" Stelinda nudged Jack and nodded to her left.

Yoss, still standing beside the throne, was staring directly at them.

"We must part company," she said. "Farewell." Without another word, she walked off.

Jack left the palace at once and wandered the streets. Other residents of Callitti milled about, too, seeking information and solace, and in a short while the entire Royal City churned with rumor. Many people blurted their sentiments. "*Yoss* will be our king?" "Yoss, of all people!" "How is this possible?" "He thinks he'll get away with it." "But *Stelinda* should be our monarch!" "Yes, Stelinda is the true heir to the throne."

But all public doubts vanished over the next few hours. Yoss would indeed be king. Why? Because some of the councilors, many of the nobles, and most members of the Royal Guard decided to back him. No one felt any affection for Yoss, but everyone feared his sheer audacity, and fear prompted them to accept the prince as their future king. Thus people reluctantly prepared for the coronation and resigned themselves to serving a mere boy.

Alarmed and exhausted, Jack retreated to his apartment. He

bolted the door, staggered over to a chair, and sat down abruptly. Yoss—king! As if the Realm hadn't suffered enough during the reign of Alphonse, now the people would face this new calamity! "We're doomed," Jack said under his breath.

"Doomed?" Loquasto repeated from his perch.

"A terrible event has befallen us."

"Tell me, then," Loquasto demanded. "Let's not play guessing games."

"Although Stelinda is the rightful heir, Prince Yoss proclaimed himself king."

"A fine legacy to us all from good King Alphonse," Loquasto noted tartly.

"It's Stelinda I'm most concerned about."

"Of course, the princess. Always the center of your attention."

"She's at great risk," Jack said. "Yoss distrusts and fears her. She needs our assistance."

"*Our* assistance?"

"Well . . . I hope you'll join me in helping her."

"So far," Loquasto said coldly, "all the help has flowed only in one direction."

Jack held up his hands in surrender. "I know you're angry with me, and you have good cause for anger. But even if you feel no confidence in me, please help Stelinda!"

Loquasto balanced on one foot and scratched the back of his head with the other. "Well," he said at last, "what would you have me do?"

"Deliver a message."

"Ah, yes—I'm the messenger service."

"I'd contact her myself, but that would put us both in danger."

"I suppose it would."

"Please?"

"Write the message," Loquasto said wearily. "I'll take it."

❧ 46 ❧

Loquasto was gone the rest of the day. Jack remained in his apartment, alternately sitting, pacing, and staring out the window. His fears deepened. Had his friend been captured? Had his message fallen into the wrong hands? If so, then surely both Stelinda and he were in great danger.

Finally, just as the sun set, Loquasto flew in through the window and alit on the back of a chair. "I delivered your message," he said.

"Did she read it?" Jack inquired desperately.

"As eagerly as a beggar devours a morsel of food."

"Well, then? What is her response?"

Loquasto hopped over to a bowl of fruit resting on the table. He plucked a grape and gobbled it. Then he took another grape, another, and another.

Jack grew exasperated as the bird's first few bites became an entire meal. He reached over, grabbed the bowl, and cried, "Why do you torture me like this?"

Using his beak, the bird snapped a thread binding a tiny coil of paper to his left leg, then nudged the coil in Jack's direction. "Here."

Jack snatched it away. Stelinda's message read: *The Cherry Courtyard at midnight.*

Hours later, Jack found Stelinda awaiting him as she had before, high among the branches of a cherry tree. This time, however, she whispered to him: *"Join me here!"*

Jack scrambled up into the tree. Soon he and Stelinda were perched like doves on a limb. She embraced him. "Oh, what's to become of us?" she moaned. "My brother will be king!" She wept in his arms.

Jack, too, was despondent. "Perhaps we should leave," he said quietly.

Stelinda pulled away. "Leave?" she said. "Where would we go?"

Jack shrugged. "Somewhere. Anywhere. The provinces, perhaps."

"But the provinces are part of Sundar, so we would remain under Yoss's dominion."

"We could leave the country," Jack suggested.

Stelinda shook her head sorrowfully. "I'd like nothing better," she said, "but I mustn't. I can't simply surrender the Realm to Yoss."

Jack tried to offer her reasons for hope. "Perhaps he won't be such a terrible king," he suggested. "Perhaps he'll prove less foolish than we imagine. Perhaps—"

"Jack, it's not just that he's foolish. He's cruel. He's . . . *harsh*. That's what frightens me."

Chastened, Jack fell silent. Fear seeped into his flesh like a chill.

"What, then, shall we do?"

"We have to stop him," replied Stelinda.

"Stop him? But how?"

"Perhaps *disrupt* is a better word. Oh, he'll become king, that's certain. We can't stop Yoss from ascending the throne. But perhaps we can prevent him from sitting there for long."

He took her hand. "I swear I'll do everything within my power to aid you in this task."

❦ 47 ❦

I'll describe the coronation as briefly as possible. Heralds blew trumpets, children threw flower petals, singers sang anthems, and soldiers marched in formation. Yoss strutted into the Great Hall. The prayers that followed his arrival sounded absurd and contemptible. So did the vows that the prime councilor administered to the prince. But whether absurd or not, this ritual made Yoss the king of Sundar. His head now wore the crown. His right hand now held the scepter. The power of the monarchy now resided in his person.

Concluding the ceremony, Yoss raised the royal scepter like a club. "Now I'm the king! I make all the decisions!" he bellowed. "And you, *all of you,* must do what I say!" He stared at the crowd, alert to any signs of treachery.

The people waited. Surely their new ruler would explain their fate. He would clarify his plans. He would describe his aspirations. He would offer promises.

Yet no other words came forth.

Somewhere came the abrupt sound of someone sneezing.

At once Yoss's glare became a furious scowl. He scanned the crowd as if to spot a hidden assassin.

The moment passed.

Then at last Yoss spoke again: "That is all. Go, now, all of you. Go!"

Everyone obeyed, and none more eagerly than Jack.

⚘ 48 ⚘

Within hours, King Yoss started to wield his power by issuing a series of royal edicts. One of them banned anyone else from having a name that started with the letter Y. Another required everyone to shout "Long live the king!" right before sneezing. Still another made mocking the king a crime punishable by death. Yet another taxed the sale of turnips on Monday, candles on Tuesday, carrots on Wednesday, bricks on Thursday, and wool on Friday. Still another outlawed singing without a permit.

The new king issued edicts of every sort for every purpose. The only pattern was that none of them made sense. Worse yet, they were vast in number. Yoss issued thirty-two edicts on his first day as king, eighteen the next, twenty-three the next—dozens and dozens within the week. Like mushrooms growing on a log, these edicts fastened themselves on the Realm and devoured their host.

What concerned Jack, however, wasn't merely the sheer number of these edicts, but two of them in particular.

The first disbanded the King's Artists. Yoss disliked music, dance, painting, and poetry, so he dissolved the troupe and cast its members out of the palace. Worse yet, he banned their activities everywhere else. *Henceforth,* read the proclamation, *all those persons formerly appointed to the King's Artists shall no longer practice their squalid, useless, time-wasting arts anywhere within the Realm.*

"Is it true?" Jack asked Geoffrey shortly after he heard the news.

"Aye, it is," replied the old jester as he watched his servants packing up his clothes, books, and other belongings. "True indeed."

"But where will the Artists go?"

"Elsewhere. Anyplace but here."

"All of you?"

"Every last one of us."

Jack was dismayed by his friends' plight. As he spoke with Geoffrey, he saw other Artists departing: Ned Painter, Edwin Flutist, Mog Dancer, and Brynne Singer, each person following a servant and a cart loaded with his or her belongings. At once a new concern struck him: "What will they do?" he asked. "I mean, if they're unable to practice their arts, how will they earn a livelihood? Will the king find them work?"

Geoffrey nodded sadly. "Work indeed! Mog Dancer has been ordered to dig coal in a mine. Edwin Flutist has been ordered to pour molten copper in a foundry. Brynne Singer has been ordered to load salt into sacks—"

Jack recoiled from these words. "They're being forced to do hard labor?"

"Oh, *forced* is too strong a word. They can refuse the work. . . . But they'd better accept it if they want their children to have food to eat and clothes to wear."

The sight of these people leaving the palace oppressed Jack unbearably. He wasn't one of the King's Artists—he was the royal storyteller. He was, however, an artist. His role within the kingdom was to practice his art. If Yoss felt so hostile to the Artists that he'd force them into hard labor, wouldn't he condemn Jack to an equally terrible fate?

The second edict troubled Jack even more than the first. *Henceforth*, read this new proclamation, which Jack found posted on every wall and door in the palace, *no commoner shall marry any person of royal blood, and he who violates this prohibition shall be put to death.*

Jack had never read anything that caused him such despair.

"What shall become of us?" he inquired when he met Stelinda that night in the Cherry Courtyard.

"That's obvious enough," she answered gloomily, stroking his cheek. "I can't marry you, Jack. Our wedding vows would be your doom."

"I'll take those vows," he stated brashly, "and I'll risk that fate."

"I know you would, but I won't have it. Can't you see what he's doing? He knows our love is more powerful than his hatred, so he'll wield it against us like a weapon. He'll set a trap for us and use our love as bait."

"I don't care!" Jack shouted. "I'll marry you anyway!"

"That," said Stelinda, "is the sound of the trap's jaws snapping shut."

"All I want is to marry you."

"Then you must deny yourself precisely what you want. For only in so doing will you help me defeat my brother."

❧ 49 ❧

Jack felt helpless and hopeless. How could he escape the dilemma that he and Stelinda now faced? Who would help them thwart the king? Whom could they trust? Geoffrey had departed from the Royal City; so had all the other Artists. And Loquasto had been acting more and more remote.

For this reason, Jack turned to the one person who seemed both well meaning and well connected: Zephyrio.

"I need your assistance," Jack said when he visited the illusionist in his quarters. "I'm so confused."

"I'm always happy to help," replied Zephyrio. "Please have a seat and join me for a spot of tea."

Jack didn't know how to begin. "This is all so complicated," he said.

The illusionist smiled. He took a sip of tea, set down his crystal cup, laced his fingers, and spoke. "Let me see if I can fathom the depths of your anguish. You worry that with King Alphonse's death, you've lost your great benefactor. Now that Yoss is king, the whole game has changed. The young monarch resents you because of your—let's call it your *affection*—for his sister. Worse yet, you're an artist, and Majesty has little patience for the arts. As the darkness follows sunset, great gloom follows the decline of your status here. Am I describing the situation well enough?"

"Better than I could myself."

"Well, then," continued Zephyrio, "we must find a way to make the sun rise again, mustn't we? To let the light shine once more on the landscape of your life."

"How is it that *you* have succeeded?" Jack inquired abruptly. "You've kept your post. You've clearly thrived." He gestured at the illusionist's fine attire. "What's your secret?"

Zephyrio exhaled in amusement. "Secret?"

"You're the one Artist that King Yoss hasn't thrown out."

The illusionist smiled as he heard these words. "Here's the secret, lad: I'm no artist. I've never claimed to be. I'm a mere entertainer, and that works to my advantage."

"But I *am* an artist! I'm a storyteller!" Jack exclaimed. "I can't *not* be who I am. How can I possibly—"

"There's only one course of action worth pursuing," said Zephyrio firmly. "King Yoss has all the power. He'll determine our fates—yours, mine, everyone's. We don't have to like it; we just have to accept it. I see no alternative but cooperation."

"Cooperation!"

"If I were you, lad, I'd do everything possible to avoid incurring Majesty's wrath. In fact, I'd curry favor with the king to the greatest degree possible."

Later, brooding in his apartment, Jack considered Zephyrio's advice: *I'd curry favor with the king. . . .* But how? Jack wanted nothing more than to flee from the new king's presence—flee the Royal City, flee Sundar, even. Yet he couldn't. Not without Stelinda. And, as the princess had noted, there could be no escape anyway, not with Yoss holding sway over the whole kingdom. Thus, no matter how eagerly Jack wished to leave, he felt compelled to stay.

"What I can't figure out," he told Loquasto, "is how the princess will take action against her brother. He's king now. Yoss claimed the throne specifically to control her—to leave her helpless—so how can she possibly fight him?"

Perched on his usual chair, Loquasto gazed back silently.

Jack said, "She's smart, though. She'll think of something."

The bird arched a wing and poked among his feathers with his beak.

"Of course, she knows her brother well, and this knowledge will help her find his weaknesses. Yes, I daresay it will!" Jack said with a laugh. Then he caught himself short. Loquasto hadn't said a word all morning. "Are you all right?" he asked the bird.

"If I weren't, I can't imagine *you* caring."

"Why wouldn't I care?"

"Because you're so absorbed in your own troubles, you have no time for mine."

Jack saw the truth of Loquasto's accusation, and he felt ashamed. "Look," he said, "I'm sorry. I've been selfish, I'll admit it. But I'll make it up to you. When I next see Zephyrio, I'll ask for his help regarding Artemisia. Surely he knows about this sort of thing."

Loquasto didn't look convinced.

"I promise."

No response.

Jack continued: "In the meantime, I have a little errand for you to run."

"Another errand!" the bird cawed in outrage.

"I want you to visit the palace, linger about the king's quarters, and tell me what you see and hear."

"Now you'll use me as your spy?"

Jack shrugged. "Why not? It'll serve us well—"

"*Us?*"

"—and it'll give you something to do while we solve the problem of Artemisia."

The bird didn't speak.

"Well?" Jack asked.

"I suppose I'd best be going," said Loquasto. Without further comment, he hopped over to the windowsill, then flew out into the cool blue morning.

Hours passed. Jack paced in his room, ate some food, stared out the window, and resumed pacing. Where was Loquasto? What intelligence had he gathered? Why, meanwhile, was there no word from Stelinda? Should he venture out, or was he safer in his own quarters? How oddly like a prison this apartment had become, with Jack's own worries restraining him as fully as bars on the windows or locks on the door.

Then, in the midafternoon, he heard footsteps in the courtyard. Peering out the window, he saw six armed guards approach and enter the house. The tramp of boots on the stairway grew louder. Then came loud thumps at the door.

Though terrified, Jack saw no alternative but to throw the bolt and open up.

Soldiers clad in armor and wielding battle-axes stood before him.

"Jack Storyteller!" declared the officer in charge. "By orders of King Yoss, present yourself at once to His Majesty!"

❧50❧

The scene greeting Jack in the Great Hall was what he'd feared: a scattering of nervous courtiers and unsmiling councilors, and, dwarfed by the throne he sat upon, King Yoss smirking as Jack approached.

Jack bowed.

"That's not deep enough," Yoss noted. "Do it again."

Jack obeyed, although his actions brought a sour taste to his mouth.

"That's better." The fair-haired boy stared at Jack for a few moments, leaving him time to ponder his fate. Then he said, "So—you're a storyteller."

"As you say, Majesty."

"Who granted you permission to be one?"

"It's my work, Majesty," Jack said. "As cooks cook, as weavers weave, as singers sing, I tell stories."

King Yoss, clearly dissatisfied with this answer, asked, "But who allowed you to tell these stories? Who granted you permission?"

Shrugging, Jack said, "It's just what I do." Then, concerned that this comment might sound impudent, he added, "And, too, your father appointed me the royal storyteller." At once Jack realized that mentioning Alphonse was a mistake.

"Who cares what my father did?" Yoss asked, raising his voice. "He had a foolish weakness for the arts. What a waste of money! We may as well dump gold in a latrine as waste it on the arts."

"Then I shall resign my post, Majesty," Jack said.

Yoss chuckled at this remark. "I'd never let you *resign!*" he exclaimed. "That would deprive me of the pleasure of *dismissing* you!"

Disheartened, Jack said, "Well, then—feel free to dismiss me."

The king's eyes narrowed. "Feel free, you say? Don't you *ever* tell me what I'm free to do."

Jack felt more and more alarmed by this conversation. His every word was making the situation worse. He glanced around. Where was Stelinda? He wished she were present—her closeness would have given him courage—and he worried that her absence boded ill for her safety. Yet in one respect he was grateful that she wasn't in attendance: she wouldn't witness his humiliation. He said, "I would never presume to tell Majesty anything."

"Good," said Yoss. He sat back in his throne. "All right—if you're such a splendid storyteller, tell me a story."

"Pardon me?" Jack asked in bewilderment.

"Just what I said: tell me a story. No, tell me *lots* of stories."

Jack couldn't believe his ears. King Yoss, requesting a story? Was this a trap? Since Yoss had proclaimed that artists could no longer practice the arts, wouldn't telling stories lead directly to punishment? Yet he realized that this situation also provided an opportunity. If he could impress the king, perhaps he could—as Zephyrio had suggested—curry favor. Yes, he'd sway him. He'd win him over.

At once Jack started to search his mind for a story capable of pleasing King Yoss. But despite every good intention, Jack quickly found his hatred for this vile boy welling up fast. He tried to contain it; he failed, and he found that he could tell only the least pleasing, most insulting story possible.

"Once upon a time," Jack said, "a bored and restless king demanded that the royal storyteller entertain him.

"'Storyteller!' the king bellowed. 'Tell me a story!'

"'With pleasure, Majesty,' answered the storyteller.

"'Better yet, tell me a *dozen* stories!'

"'With great satisfaction—'

"'No, a *score* of stories!'

"'With delight—'

"'A *hundred* stories! *Two* hundred!'

"'But Majesty,' the storyteller protested, 'I'm not sure I know that many.'

"The king snorted in contempt. 'What? You don't know that many?'

"'A hundred, surely, but not twice that number.'

"'That's not my problem!' shouted the king. 'Tell me all you know, then submit yourself to the executioner for failing at your duty.'

"Alarmed by these words, the storyteller wanted nothing more than to serve the king to the best of his abilities. Maybe he'd manage to save himself; maybe not. But, hastening to try, he began at once:

"'Once upon a time, a bored and restless king demanded that his seven royal storytellers entertain him. "Storytellers!" the king bellowed. "Tell me stories! Lots of stories!"

"'"With pleasure, Majesty," answered each of the seven storytellers, whose names were Bumblenose, Stookoopoochie, Dull, Puttycake, Lord Raindrop, Peck-a-stick, and Cinderwallop. They bowed.

"'Then Bumblenose, the first of these seven storytellers, started to tell his story.

"'"Once upon a time, a bored and restless king demanded that his seven royal storytellers entertain him. 'Storytellers!' the king bellowed. 'Tell me stories! ! Lots of stories!'

"'"With pleasure, Majesty,' answered each of the seven storytellers, whose names were Jerry the Berry, Parsnip, Leatherface, Belcher, Lady Velvet, Jackaroe, and Mathilda. They bowed.

"'"Then Jerry the Berry, the first of these seven storytellers, started to tell his story.

""""Once upon a time, a bored and restless king demanded that his seven royal storytellers entertain him. "Storytellers!" the king bellowed. "Tell me stories!"

""""With pleasure, Majesty," answered each of the seven storytellers, whose names were Sorrysnoop, Whosiematoosie, the Earl of Swirls, Jan the Loser, Tweedle Ears, Thuggo, and Erminio. They bowed.

""""Then Sorrysnoop, the first of these seven storytellers, started to tell his story.

"""""Once upon a time, a bored and restless king demanded that his seven royal storytellers entertain him. 'Storytellers!' the king bellowed—"""""

"*Stop!*" King Yoss shouted, leaping up from the throne.

Jack Storyteller obeyed at once.

King Yoss stomped over to Jack and yelled, "What are you doing?"

"Telling a story," Jack said, "just as Majesty commanded."

"This story is *nonsense*."

"Majesty?"

"Your story is a maze, a jumble of hallways as confusing as the royal dungeon, only made of words instead of stone."

"With all due respect, Majesty, I beg to differ. These stories come forth in perfect order. My story is about a storyteller who tells a story about seven storytellers. Each storyteller tells a story about seven other storytellers. Each of these storytellers in turn tells a story about seven more storytellers . . ."

As Jack explained, King Yoss grew more and more agitated. He paced back and forth. He fidgeted with his fingers. "But *why?*" he asked, clearly confused. "Why?"

Jack said, "You asked for stories, Majesty. Lots of stories. I've simply obeyed your altogether reasonable command."

"Hmm," said King Yoss, calming down a bit. "How many stories?"

Thinking fast, Jack clarified the situation. "Since I told a story about a storyteller who told a story about seven storytellers, each of whom told a story about seven more storytellers, each of whom told a story about another seven storytellers—well, after a while there would be sixteen thousand eight hundred seven stories, and, if Majesty stays patient even longer, there would soon be one hundred seventeen thousand six hundred forty-nine stories, and then eight hundred twenty-three thousand five hundred forty-three stories, and if you add—"

"Stop! You're mocking me!"

"Mocking you, Majesty? I'd never do such a thing."

"You're doing it right now!" the king bellowed. "And the punishment for mocking the king is *death!*"

Jack bowed. "My intention has been solely to give Majesty what he requested, and what Majesty requested was a story. Thus, I told you a story."

Yet as the guards led him away to the dungeon, Jack realized his mistake. He'd let the story take over. Although he'd planned to curry favor and gain the king's support, he had enraged him instead. The story had vented the steam of Jack's contempt even as Jack himself struggled to win over King Yoss.

Now he was doomed.

☙ 51 ❧

Jack had been held under house arrest before, but Yoss now inflicted a far worse punishment on him. Hauled off by soldiers to the royal dungeon, he found himself in a cold, damp, dark cell infested with half-seen creatures that scurried and slithered underfoot and van-ished into cracks and crevices. He huddled against a wall and won-dered how long he could survive in such a place. The answer terrified him: he wouldn't *need* to survive. Yoss wouldn't give him a chance.

Jack sank into despair. He had ruined everything. Granted an opportunity to salve Yoss's fury, he had instead rubbed salt into the wound. Now he would never marry Stelinda or help her defeat the king.

And what about the princess? Had Jack's mocking story put her in danger? And Loquasto—was he, too, in trouble?

When the dungeon door suddenly swung open a short while later, Jack feared the worst. But it wasn't a squadron of guards he found in the doorway; it was Zephyrio, accompanied by a lone jailer.

The illusionist walked in, sweeping the folds of his cape around his chest to ward off the dampness and the chill.

"Zephyrio!" Jack exclaimed, springing up from the floor.

"Well, Jack," said the illusionist cordially, "I see you've gotten yourself into a rather tight spot."

The jailer left, closing and locking the door behind him, and the two men stood in the darkness for a while. Then a light flared. A can-dle? Jack saw with astonishment that a dazzling glow radiated from one of Zephyrio's fingers, which he raised before him to illuminate the cell. But Jack was too concerned about his situation to comment on this unexpected light. He said, "All I did was tell King Yoss a story."

"*Quite* a story, from what I hear. Not the best possible choice, eh?"

"I wanted to please him, but sometimes the story tells itself no matter what the teller intends. There's a truth to reveal. There's art to express."

Zephyrio shook his head in dismay. "That's where you go wrong.

Forget all this nonsense about truth and art. Just entertain your listener. Give him a rollicking good time. That was all King Yoss wanted, and you let him down."

"He's such a fool," Jack said, almost spitting as he spoke. "I hate him."

"Your hatred prompts you to miss an opportunity," Zephyrio said, smiling patiently. "As he told me recently, Majesty sees you as a man of considerable talent."

"He's never been impressed by my talents in the past."

"Oh, but you're wrong. He admires you."

"Is that why he compared funding me to dumping gold down a latrine?"

Zephyrio chuckled gently. "You misunderstand. Majesty holds your abilities in high regard," he said, raising a hand to forestall Jack's protest, "although he feels that you don't *apply* yourself."

Jack slapped his thigh. "Get to the point!" he blurted. "You're circling me as a cat circles a wounded mouse."

"The point, Jack, is that the king wants to hire you."

"*Hire* me!"

"So greatly does King Yoss admire your gifts," Zephyrio went on, "that nothing would please him more than to put these gifts to royal use."

"He wants me to be *his* storyteller?" Jack couldn't believe what he was hearing.

"Precisely."

"To entertain him? To tell him stories?"

"Well, not exactly. He wants you to entertain his subjects by telling stories *about* him."

Dumbfounded, Jack couldn't even speak.

"King Yoss would have you sing his praises throughout the Realm."

"That's madness," Jack told him. "I won't do it."

"You won't even consider it?"

"Never."

"Then there's nothing I can do to help you," Zephyrio said, bowing slightly. His glowing finger guttered out like a candle. He called to the guard, who, opening the massive door, let him walk out.

Alone again in the dark, Jack couldn't tell how long his solitude lasted. Light and sound had ceased to exist, midnight looked the same as noon, and his only clock was the tick-tock of his own worries. He might have sat in that dungeon for an hour or a day.

Abruptly, the door clanked open again and guards appeared. They bound Jack's hands behind him with coarse rope and marched him through corridors to an open courtyard. In the courtyard stood a low platform. On the platform rested a large wooden block, long as a bed, and, below one end of the block, a basket. A layer of straw surrounded the basket and the block. Standing near the platform was a huge man—pale pink like raw pork and attired in boots, rough wool pants, and a leather hood—who held the largest ax that Jack had ever seen. Other people were present, too, for Jack heard murmurs all around, but the shuttered windows on the surrounding walls obscured the identity of any onlookers.

"Git up," said the executioner.

Jack hesitantly climbed a short staircase to the platform.

"Sit."

Once again Jack obeyed.

"Lie down on the block."

A jolt of intense fear shot through Jack's body. How could he have reached this end? Surely someone would intervene. Stelinda would appear and dissuade Yoss from his madness. Loquasto would glide into view, carrying a message. Yoss himself would step forth, explaining that he didn't really intend to execute Jack after all.

"I said lie down on the bloomin' block!" the executioner shouted.

"Who *are* you?" inquired Jack impulsively.

"What difference does it make?" asked the executioner. "I'm just doin' me job. But if you need to know, the name's Young Moribundo."

"*Young* Moribundo!" Jack exclaimed. At once he recalled the story that the Woman of the Woods had told him—about how an executioner named Moribundo had rescued her in *her* time of danger. Jack asked, "Did your father—"

"Lie down," Young Moribundo ordered for the third time. "I don't want yer trouble."

Jack resisted. "Wait a moment—don't I get to say any last words?"

"No!" interrupted a youthful voice from somewhere nearby. "No last words! You've spoken far too much already."

Glancing up and to his left, Jack spotted King Yoss pulling away from a window in one of the palace buildings that faced the courtyard.

"No," echoed the executioner, his voice rumbling like distant thunder. "Git *down.*"

Jack now fully grasped his fate. Lying on the chopping block left little to his imagination. What sickened him most, however, was realizing that King Yoss would make him die face-up, which would force Jack to observe the ax as it descended toward his neck and would thus inspire the greatest dread possible. Dread was, in fact, exactly what Jack now felt. Sweating profusely and shaking hard, he squeezed his eyes shut; he couldn't bear to look. A moment later, though, he forced them open again, for he didn't want to miss even a moment of light before he was plunged into eternal darkness. But the sight before him only terrified him further: the huge, pink executioner picked up his ax, checked the blade gingerly with his forefinger, drew blood, and licked the wound, then grunted suddenly and hoisted the terrible weapon over his head.

Storytellers tell stories, of course, but they aren't alone in doing so. The dawn tells a story; so does the sun as it arcs across the sky; so does the sunset. The seasons tell a complex story. The fall of an acorn and the growth of an oak tree tell a story. A farmer's plow and the furrows in a field tell a story as well. Even the waves crashing on a beach tell a story. How easy to see, then, that an ax tells a story, too, at least while it hangs for a moment in the air just before descending onto your neck. That story is: *Now you die.*

It's also easy to imagine why Jack called out at that moment: "Wait!"

The executioner, still holding the ax overhead, peered down at him.

"I'll serve the king!" Jack shouted.

The ax hung in midair.

"*Talk* with him!" Jack pleaded. "I know he's watching! Explain to him! I'll serve the king!" He scanned the windows overlooking the courtyard. Something shifted there. "Majesty!" he yelled. "I'll tell your story! I'll do as you wish!"

What was the point of sacrificing his life if nothing came of the sacrifice? How would such a choice further his quest? How would it help Jack aid his family? How would it advance his goals? Agreeing to King Yoss's request would save his own skin—and probably Stelinda's, too. He'd buy some time. He'd gain another chance. Together he and Stelinda could determine how to defeat the person they both detested.

A voice called out from above: "All right—I'll spare you."

Slowly, carefully, the executioner lowered his ax.

"Thank you," Jack said. He raised himself slowly and sat dizzily on the edge of the long wooden block. He waited for his body to stop shaking.

Guards marched up to him and untied his bonds. "Follow me," said the captain.

❧ 52 ❧

Y ou've wasted my time," said King Yoss when Jack faced him again in the Great Hall.

"I'm sorry," Jack said, bowing in submission.

"You've mocked me."

"I beg Majesty's forgiveness."

"Silence!"

Jack made no further efforts to apologize, much less to explain himself. He would allow Yoss to humiliate him all day, if the king wished—anything to avoid a trip back to the chopping block. Even now Jack couldn't fully believe that he'd survived.

Perhaps the people around him couldn't, either. A scattering of councilors and courtiers stood in the Great Hall as the king berated the storyteller, but none seemed willing to watch or listen too closely, as though fearful of being stained by Jack's misdeeds. Jack realized that he was alone despite all the people present.

"I'll spare your life, but only on one condition," the king said, pointing a thin finger at Jack. "Make yourself useful! No more pointless storytelling! You must serve *me* and tell the story that matters. The *only* one that matters."

Zephyrio stepped forward from among the councilors and stood near Yoss. "Majesty, may I explain?" he asked.

"Do that," said the boy.

Zephyrio smiled patiently. "Storytellers tell stories. You are a storyteller, Jack, and you possess great gifts. Majesty has felt some hostility toward you in the past, but only because you haven't used your gifts to good purpose. Your role now is to tell stories about King Yoss. You will travel throughout the Realm, visit the common people in their towns and villages, and illuminate their lives with stories about their remarkable young king."

"But *what* stories?" Jack blurted. "He's been king for just a few weeks. He hasn't really done—" He cut himself short, aware that the wrong words would end his life.

The illusionist gestured calmly. "He *is* young. Majesty himself would be the first to say so. But that's all the more reason, isn't it, for us to celebrate the great deeds that lie ahead."

"I should tell stories about things that King Yoss hasn't done yet?"

"Precisely."

Jack had never heard anything more preposterous. "But that's totally—"

"Think of it," interrupted Zephyrio, "as *anticipatory truth*. You'll tell the stories first. The great deeds will follow once Majesty has had the opportunity to wield his full powers."

Jack couldn't respond. So this was what Yoss wanted: to have him serve as the royal liar! And the illusionist would encourage him to do so! Jack was surprised to find Zephyrio acting as the king's spokesman. Was this role a new step he'd taken, or had he held it for some time? Was that how he had intervened to benefit Jack in the past?

"Well?" Yoss demanded. "What is your choice?"

Jack had no choice. "I'll tell stories on Majesty's behalf," he said.

"Good lad—that's a wise decision," Zephyrio stated with a smile.

Jack ached to leave. He felt so sick that he feared he'd vomit.

"Something else," said King Yoss. "Stay away from my sister. You have no reason to be anywhere close to her."

"But he does," said a high, clear voice that Jack recognized at once. "He does indeed."

It was Princess Stelinda. She approached the throne and curtsied deeply before the king. "He has every reason to keep my company," she told her brother.

"Why would that be?" the king asked.

"Because Jack Storyteller's quest should be mine as well."

Yoss looked wary. "What are you saying?"

"You've granted Jack a mission to tell stories, Majesty, about your future glories. I ask permission now to go disperse the same delightful news—but told in verse."

"You'll recite *poems?*" the boy asked with a sneer.

"Of course—and every single poem will ring a bell to glorify you as the king."

Staring at her through squinty eyes, Yoss said, "You're serious?"

"Whatever disagreements we have amassed, I put behind me in the distant past. Although I'd hoped, of course, to rule the Realm, I'll celebrate you, Brother, at the helm. Feeling pride, delight, and wonder, I'll praise you everywhere in Sundar."

Jack himself could scarcely believe Stelinda's words, but *how* she spoke intrigued him. In the past, he had noticed that when angry, the princess declared her sentiments in rhymed couplets. Did Yoss notice? Probably not.

"You'll write poems about *me?*" asked Yoss.

"Indeed—poems both numerous and grand. I'll chant them everywhere throughout the land."

The boy looked suspicious. "You don't have to do that with *him,* though," he said, nodding toward Jack.

"What could be better, Majesty? A bard and a storyteller will sing your high regard. These two arts will become a school to teach the lessons of your rule."

Yoss considered these words. "Hmm," he said at last. "A school to teach the lessons of my rule. . . . I rather like that."

⚘53⚘

In this way Jack and Stelinda found an island of safety in the vast, hostile sea of Yoss's reign.

"You're brilliant!" Jack exclaimed after he and Stelinda left the Great Hall. He reached over to embrace her, but she held him off.

"Restrain yourself," she told him. "Yoss has spies everywhere."

"I don't care—"

"You *must* care."

"What are you telling me?" asked Jack.

"Simply what you already know. We must set our love aside while we forge your stories and my poems into the swords we'll use against him."

King Yoss wasted no time pressing Jack and Stelinda into service Within a few days, the king and his retinue visited Fibbleton, a village not far from the Royal City. Heralds announced the king's arrival, and soon a large crowd of men, women, and children gathered in the village square.

Looking out over his assembled subjects, King Yoss smiled gleefully. Then Zephyrio, who had come along, too, told Jack and Stelinda, "Do your duty. Tell a story and recite a poem about the great deeds the king will perform."

Jack stepped forward. At first, he felt odd not to have Loquasto perched on his shoulder. Perhaps it was better, though, that the bird didn't have to take part in this sham.

"Now listen, one and all!" Jack said. "I'll tell you a story about the grandest, greatest, most glorious king—good King Yoss—whose reign of peace and prosperity blesses our whole land. He may seem young. He may be lacking in experience. But King Yoss has, in fact, accomplished more in his first few weeks upon the throne than many monarchs achieve throughout long years in power.

"Consider, if you will, the battle of Thoragar. Surely you've all heard of Thoragar. No? Well, it's on the far side of the Realm, bordering the kingdom of Gar. A treacherous place, believe me. The Garians have long coveted our land, and for generations they've staged raids against the Realm. Many of our kings, even King Alphonse, did nothing to stop these invaders. But good King Yoss confronted the Garians and called their bluff."

Jack went on to describe the battle of Thoragar. How a vast Garian army confronted Sundar's much smaller force. How the Garian generals treacherously attacked in the middle of the night. How King Yoss rallied his men to prevail over the enemy. How the battle of Thoragar was an inspiring example of King Yoss's bravery and cunning and of his love for his subjects.

When Jack finished, there was a patter of applause from the audience. A few tepid cheers sounded as well: "Bravo," "Hurrah," "Long live the king." Most of the people in the crowd, however, merely watched and waited.

But King Yoss seemed delighted. "You're welcome!" he exclaimed. "I appreciate your gratitude! I'll do everything possible for you, my people!"

A long pause followed—dead silence. The gathered men, women, and children stared at their king. The king stared at his people. Then, before this situation could grow even more awkward, Zephyrio strode forth, raised both his hands, and announced, "Now the royal bard, Princess Stelinda, will recite a poem about our splendid monarch."

Jack watched Stelinda step onto the platform. Although her eyes looked fierce, her mouth wore a smile. Would she find a way to criticize the king? Would she humiliate Yoss before all these people? He waited with a growing sense of alarm.

Gesturing grandly toward her brother, Stelinda recited her first verse.

> "Here's a song of praise about good King Yoss,
> The monarch we all love because he's everybody's boss.
> He's young and he's intelligent,
> He's handsome and a total gent—
> He's full of great ideas and is never at a loss."

Stelinda then proceeded to recite verse after verse. The audience listened but made no response, and Jack watched with growing dismay. The peasants seemed restless, even annoyed. Of course, what he and Stelinda offered them *was* a waste of time. Jack worried Yoss would lash out at him and the princess for betraying his trust.

Finally, Stelinda finished her poem, shouting:

> "So trust my every word about good King Yoss—
> He can even work some wonders that are totally imposs!"

Once again the crowd seemed baffled. A few folks clapped, and a few called out halfhearted cheers. Jack could see many of them glancing about, trying to determine what King Yoss expected of them.

This time the king opened his arms as if to receive an affectionate embrace. "You are most welcome," he called out. "I will do anything for you, my people. And no doubt you'll do anything and everything for me!"

"That was a disaster," Jack told Stelinda once the royal entourage had set off again. "We made fools of ourselves. My story was awful, truly the worst I've ever told. And forgive me—but your poem was awful, too."

Stelinda smiled warmly. "Of course it was. Do you imagine that I didn't know? That I didn't *plan* for it to be awful?"

"But surely Yoss noticed."

"Do you truly believe," asked Stelinda, placing a hand on Jack's shoulder, "that my brother felt disappointed by our words?"

"I don't know."

"Then let me tell you. He couldn't have been happier. He was *delighted!*"

"How is that possible?"

"My brother believes only what he wants to believe."

Jack felt somewhat more confident as he listened to the princess. Then a new worry crept into his mind. "It's not just Yoss who matters," he said. "What of the people? What if we persuade the people precisely of what we want them *not* to believe? What if my stories and your poems persuade them that Yoss is the wise, brave, thoughtful king we claim he is?"

Stelinda didn't answer at first. Instead, she held out her right arm and touched the dark blue sleeve covering it. She asked, "What color is this cloth?"

"Blue," Jack answered promptly.

"No, it's red," Stelinda told him.

"It's blue."

"You're mistaken—it's red."

"Stelinda, be serious. It's obviously blue."

"Let me convince you otherwise." At once she sang a song that compared the color of her sleeve to apples, roses, blood, and rubies. Then she asked again, "What color is this cloth?"

"It's still blue."

"And what would you call me for claiming so earnestly that it's red?"

"If I didn't know you so well," said Jack, "I'd call you a fool."

"Indeed!" was Stelinda's only comment.

☙ 54 ❧

When the royal party returned to Callitti, King Yoss's response to the day's events confirmed Stelinda's prediction. "Well done!" he declared. "Now even more people have heard the news of who I am and what I can do. You will perform again and again until the entire Realm understands how glorious my reign will be!"

And so Jack and Stelinda went about proclaiming the glories of Yoss's reign—first in Callitti itself, then throughout the provinces. But they didn't venture forth on their own. Instead, they traveled with King Yoss, Zephyrio, a select group of councilors, and a large retinue of courtiers and servants too numerous to count: cooks, maids, tailors, cobblers, carriers, valets, and others. A squadron of soldiers also marched before, after, and alongside the procession—a full contingent of guards necessary to protect the king from any possible harm.

How disgusting, Jack told himself, that so many people would attend to just one boy. But the number of people didn't matter. The demands of travel didn't matter. The fatigue that he and Stelinda felt didn't matter. What mattered was simply the effort to undercut Yoss's authority.

Thus the king and his entourage proceeded deeper into the Realm—sometimes traveling for a week or two, sometimes for a month at a time—to present the new monarch to his subjects and to light the bonfire of their loyalty with the twin torches of Jack's stories and Stelinda's poems.

I should mention that no carriages existed in the Realm of Sundar at this time, but this lack didn't meant that the young monarch had to suffer the indignity of walking. Instead, footmen carried King Yoss—and, for that matter, all of the high-born travelers, as well as Zephyrio, Stelinda, and Jack—in sumptuous sedans. The ten or twelve footmen who carried each sedan were brawny youths trained in the task of providing a steady ride even though the men themselves struggled, muttering and gasping, along the road. Within each box-like sedan two plushly padded benches faced each other, which allowed the persons seated within the vehicle to ride in comfort and converse easily. A roof and sides made of heavy fabric shielded the voyagers from wind and rain. Curtains provided privacy. Despite the absence of wheels, these plush compartments offered a relatively smooth means of conveyance in a land where most roads were little more than rock-studded paths.

As you can well imagine, the royal entourage provided a stirring sight. Peasants in the fields dropped their hoes and planting sticks and came to stare. Villagers peered out from their windows. Dogs barked. People shouted. Bells rang in the towers. Never before had a king of Sundar made such a remarkable series of trips into the provinces. And once the royal trumpeters announced the king's arrival, Yoss made sure that his soldiers rounded *everyone* up for Jack and Stelinda's presentation. The people had no choice but to attend.

But one sunny morning an event took place that no one could have predicted. It was, in fact, an occurrence so completely unanticipated—indeed, so preposterous—that even Jack himself wouldn't have dared to introduce it as a plot twist in one of his stories.

The king and his retinue were passing through a forest called Sycamora. This region lay about three days' walk from Jack's own village, Yorrow, and the terrain had begun to look familiar to him. Jack knew that he had visited this place at some point in his life, but he couldn't quite remember how or when. In this way his memory served him well—but not well enough. He should have recalled more than the sweet leaf-scented air as the royal procession wound its way into the dim, cool woods. He should have felt some concern as he rode in the royal sedan with Stelinda, Zephyrio, and King Yoss. He should have let his mind stray to less cordial landscapes than the dappled forest scene surrounding him. As it happened, though, he was preoccupied with King Yoss, for the boy was scolding him with particular intensity.

"And I'll warn you only one more time: don't look so grim when you praise me among the people," the king told him in his shrill voice. "It's not enough that your stories honor me. You have to *smile*. My presence in these peasants' lives is a feast, not a funeral. So *smile*. Smile *intensely*. Smile *radiantly*. Smile so that my subjects—"

Without warning, something fell through the sedan's cloth roof and crashed like a sack of potatoes onto the floor. Something—or rather, *someone*.

It was Garth Golden-Eye.

The sedan swayed wildly, then steadied as the bearers regained control.

Wielding a small crossbow in each hand, Garth pulled himself up onto the bench next to Jack and Stelinda and across from Yoss and Zephyrio. This move allowed the highwayman to aim his arrows at both the king and the illusionist, who tried to lean away from the fearsome sight before them—this raggedly attired figure with his white-whiskered jowls, bulbous nose, and solitary hostile eye! Yet there was nowhere to retreat inside the box-like sedan.

"Guards!" Zephyrio shouted.

"I say! This is offensive!" Yoss protested.

Garth merely laughed. "Offensive it may be, but I wouldna make any soodden moves, noone o' ye, if ye wish to live a long an' 'appy life."

Stelinda, pale with fear, eased away from the ruffian beside her. At once Garth shifted his weapons so that one crossbow kept both Yoss and Zephyrio at bay while the other targeted the princess.

Jack felt an almost overwhelming urge to lash out at his old enemy, but he restrained himself, since even the slightest move against Garth might doom Stelinda.

"Surrender at once!" cried the king. "Or I'll order my guards to attack!"

A great commotion reached Jack's ears then—shouts and cries of outrage—and this racket made Yoss's threats seem plausible.

Garth only smiled, revealing his brown, broken teeth. "I'll let ye go in the foolness o' time, m'boy, rest assured o' that. Meantime, I suggest ye sit still rather than putting so mooch troost in yer minions."

"Better do what he says," Jack suggested.

The highwayman now turned to Jack. "Well, well—if it ain't our fine yoong storyteller. An' what a grand day it is, too, when our paths cross again."

"You know this man?" asked Stelinda in astonishment.

"I'm afraid I do," Jack stated gloomily. "He's Garth Golden-Eye."

Garth nodded toward the princess. "Good morrow, m'lady," he said, tipping the brim of his rough leather hat with one of the crossbows. "I 'ave indeed had the pleasure o' meetin' this admirable lad."

Shrugging, Jack told Stelinda, "He robbed me once—or at least, he tried to."

Garth turned back to the storyteller. "'Twas a grand waste o' me time," he complained, "as ye possessed noothin' to joostify me trooble. Nivver again will I exert meself to rob a commoner. But it seems ye're keepin' a better class o' coompany than in the past, eh, laddie? Ain't the commonfolk good enough for ye now?" Before Jack could object, the robber said, "Well, enough idle chat. I have a wee bit o' business requirin' me full attention."

"Business!" Yoss exclaimed.

"Business indeed," Garth responded. And with those words, the robber motioned for everyone to leave the sedan.

Jack, Stelinda, Zephyrio, and King Yoss climbed out.

Emerging with his hostages—both crossbows again pointed at Yoss and Zephyrio—Garth soon made his intentions clear. "Listen to me now, all ye high-born folk!" he shouted. "Climb out o' yer elegant means o' coonveyance. Stand facin' them trees what grow so plentifully all around. Then obey me fine friends' biddin'. Do ye grasp me words?"

The situation soon revealed itself to the players in this unexpected drama. Garth and his cronies—a much larger band of ruffians now than formerly—had ambushed the entire royal entourage. A multitude of robbers had emerged from the forest—not just men but women and children, too, as Jack soon noticed, all of them ragged, filthy, and armed with crude weapons. Although the king's retinue included a squadron of soldiers, the Royal Guard had lost the skirmish even before it started. Garth, lurking in a tree as the procession approached, had jumped from a limb and plummeted into the royal sedan. This gambit had allowed him to take King Yoss hostage and thus confound the guards' efforts to fight their assailants. Once the impasse became evident, even a huge army would have had no recourse but to surrender.

The king, the princess, the courtiers, the guards, the servants, and everyone else were now forced to spread out carefully among the trees. Soon each person stood isolated from the others.

"If iv'rybody would be so kind as to hand over yer necklaces, bracelets, tiaras, rings, earrings, an' amulets—and o' course any available gold doubloons, doocats, and sovereigns," said Garth, "I'd be most obliged."

The band of robbers first confiscated the soldiers' weapons; then they collected everyone's precious possessions.

As Garth himself started to pocket the king's jewels and gold, Zephyrio spoke with ominous hostility: "I hope you realize that your fate is the execution block."

Yoss himself cried out: "Indeed! This is outrageous! Don't you know who I am?"

Garth stroked the stubble on his rough chin. "Well, now, let me ponder the facts a moment. Robes o' royal blue . . . ermine collar . . . crown set upon yer noggin. Seems unlikely ye're an itinerant peddler, eh, or 'ave ye simply prospered in yer trade?"

Yoss lashed out against this impudence. "I'm the king, d'you hear me?" he shouted. "The Sovereign of Sundar, Monarch of the Land, and Lord over All Subjects of the Realm!"

"Well, well," said Garth Golden-Eye, "thank ye kindly fer presentin' yer credentials. All most 'elpful. Ootherwise I might 'ave mistook ye fer a servin' boy what slipped into one o' Majesty's fancy outfits."

At once Yoss flew into a rage. "You have no right to speak to me like this! To doubt my authority! To compare me to a servant!"

Garth bowed elaborately. "Beg pardon, m'boy. I troost ye willna take me comments too personal. It pays to be careful these days, eh, what wit' winds o' change blowin' through the Realm. Besides, I nivver did have mooch con-fie-dence in the gooverment."

"Silence!"

The robber smiled patiently. "Wit' all due respect, boy, I'd say ye're not in a good position to be silencin' old Garth Golden-Eye." He leaned closer, pushing the blind side of his face and the shiny doubloon embedded there toward the king.

King Yoss stared at the highwayman. "How hideous! You have a *coin* stuck in your eye!"

Garth Golden-Eye chuckled in dark amusement. "Well, 'tis true, true indeed. But I reckon 'tis far better to 'ave a coin stoock in me bloomin' eye than a ruby stoock up me bloomin' nose."

With those words, snickering and guffaws wafted through the woods like a sudden breeze. Many of those who laughed were Garth's henchmen—but some were members of the king's own retinue.

"*Silence!*" Yoss bellowed.

"As you wish, m'boy," said Garth. He turned to Jack and Stelinda and nodded once. "Fare thee well, me fine yoong storyteller. Farewell, m'lady. I've 'eard tell amoong the commonfolk that ye're quite a poet." Then Garth pulled back and signaled his accomplices. "Me deed now doone," he announced to everyone present, "I bid ye all a fond good-bye. Seems there's a party o' travelin' noblemen na far away what's requirin' me professional attention."

"Halt!" cried the king. "Halt, surrender, and submit to my authority!"

But the robber simply went about his business. By now his henchmen had filled eight or ten leather bags with jewelry and coins, and they had removed other valuables from the royal sedans. Herding everyone back onto the road, they prepared to depart.

How, Jack wondered, would Garth accomplish his departure without triggering a final fight? Surely the Royal Guard would pursue him through the forest. But Garth forestalled this gambit by taking Jack, Stelinda, Zephyrio, and Yoss with him, then abandoning his hostages one by one deep within the woods.

As he vanished into the maze of foliage, Garth shouted: "Tell this story, too, laddie! 'Tis a good un!"

⚜ 55 ⚜

Garth Golden-Eye! As if Jack didn't have enough problems already, that hairy, foul-smelling, one-eyed ruffian had arrived unbidden once more in the storyteller's life. Even returning to the safety of the royal retinue didn't ease Jack's dismay, for the procession continued on rather than returning at once to the Royal City. Seated now in one of the other sedans, he considered the implications of the encounter with Garth. Everything about the incident troubled him. Being ambushed in the woods was bad enough. Being held captive was worse. Worst of all was the realization that not only Jack himself but also his beloved Stelinda might have come to harm.

And yet another aspect of the robbery troubled Jack. Although he had taken great pleasure in seeing Yoss humbled by Garth Golden-Eye, the robber's parting words plagued Jack like stinging insects and caused his worries to swell. *Tell this story, too, laddie!* Garth had shouted as he and his cronies retreated. *'Tis a good un!* Yes, Garth's humiliation of Yoss would make a fine tale—but how could Jack ever tell it without incurring the boy-king's wrath?

Jack wasn't the only person who had heard and remembered the robber's final exclamation. King Yoss summoned him and Stelinda that same evening. He glanced at Zephyrio, who stood nearby, and said, "Storyteller—prepare a story about what happened in the woods today."

Jack was surprised. Wouldn't that incident be the last thing Yoss would want proclaimed to his subjects?

"And you, bard—write a poem celebrating what happened."

Stelinda, too, seemed taken aback.

"You will, of course, omit any pointless details."

"Details?" asked Jack.

Zephyrio stepped forward, his cape swaying behind him. "What I believe Majesty intends to say," he stated, "is that you must clarify what matters most. How the ruffians streamed out of the forest like ravenous wild dogs. How they brutally assaulted us. How their leader, Garth Golden-Eye, threatened to execute not just King Yoss but all members of the royal retinue. How the highwayman robbed everyone and subjected men, women, and children alike to brutal treatment."

Stelinda protested: "But that's not—"

The illusionist raised a hand to caution her. "There's more. You must describe how our valiant young monarch rebuffed these highwaymen. How King Yoss snatched Garth's own crossbow and turned it upon him. How the king fought off the minions who pounced on him like snarling jackals. How, upon rallying the Royal Guard, our beloved ruler sent the attackers fleeing for their lives."

Jack said, "I think it's important to tell—"

"What's important is revealing Majesty's strength, cleverness, and generosity. Emphasize that King Yoss not only routed the ruffians, he also distributed their ill-gotten jewels and coins to needy peasants in the area."

"Needy peasants?" Jack asked in amazement.

"Starving farmers, widows, orphans—people of that sort," said the illusionist.

"Widows and orphans," said the king. "I like that."

"Have you any questions?" asked Zephyrio.

Stelinda and Jack glanced at each other. "No, I don't believe so," said the princess.

"None at all," Jack stated.

Later, Jack visited the princess in her tent. King Yoss allowed them only a few moments of privacy each day, and the brevity of such visits made their time together all the more precious. They could talk. They could hold each other. They could pretend for a few moments that they controlled their fate. That evening, however, something other than their own concerns demanded their attention.

"They're mad!" Jack exclaimed. "Not just your brother—that oily illusionist, too! I don't know which of them is worse!"

Stelinda put an index finger to her lips. "Of course they're mad," she whispered.

Jack lowered his voice. "To claim that Yoss fended off Garth— what a joke! They have no shame. They'll claim that night is day and day is night, that candy is sour and lemons are sweet, that pigs can fly and pigeons make good bacon."

"Let Yoss claim all that. Let Zephyrio prod him on, too."

"What!"

"Let them say whatever they desire," said the princess.

"But they're lying!" Irate that Stelinda would so willingly agree to Yoss's and Zephyrio's distortion of the truth, Jack rebuffed her. "Well, then, let them say whatever they desire. But I can't imagine collaborating with them and becoming the mouth that tells such lies."

Stelinda reached out, took Jack by the shoulders, and embraced him. Then, whispering in his ear almost too silently to hear, she said, *"The stories they make you tell—and the poems they make me recite—will become stones in the prison that Yoss and Zephyrio build for themselves."*

❧ 56 ❧

hen good King Yoss smote the highwaymen!" Jack proclaimed to a crowd of haggard peasants in a rain-drenched town several days later. "Scattering like rats before a cat's attack, they fled for their lives. And the lord of these vermin, Garth Golden-Eye, saw his efforts come to grief! Soon victorious, good King Yoss showered kindness upon the Realm that fell like warm rain from the sky."

Stelinda was right, Jack told himself. If he told preposterous stories about the king, his audience would perceive them as the lies they were. Jack felt especially pleased with his comparing Yoss to the downpour that drenched these miserable folk even as he addressed them.

And indeed, the gathered peasants, huddling in miserable clusters and anticipating a reward for having listened so patiently, called out with only the vaguest signs of enthusiasm: "Yes indeed," "Yes, help us," and "We need your help, Majesty."

Zephyrio ascended the staircase to the platform where Jack had told his story. "Is this how you would honor the monarch who protects you?" he asked irritably. He gestured toward the king, who stood to one side beneath a canopy that six armed guards held aloft to protect him from the downpour. "Is this how you thank him for all he's done? You should be ashamed of greeting him in such a pitiable manner—and you should compensate Majesty for this insult. Pay him now with your praise." After a brief silence, Zephyrio suddenly called out, "Long live King Yoss!"

"Long live the king," said the peasants indifferently. "Long live King Yoss."

As if unaware of how feeble this response was, Yoss basked in the glow of his subjects' words like a man warming himself before a hearth.

Stelinda allowed her brother to savor the people's praise for a moment, then stepped forward. "I shall now recite a poem in honor of good King Yoss," she stated, and, in her clear, high voice, she began.

"A beehive hung from a sycamore tree,
And a very fine hive it was.
All the bees were happy with their lives because
The life they lived was free, free—
The life they lived was free.
        "Buzz, buzz, buzz!

"And the bees flew out from the hive each day
To go find nectar in the field.
Then they all flew back to make a great, rich yield
Of honey for one and all, all—
Of honey for one and all.
        "Buzz, buzz, buzz!"

Stelinda's poem went on to explain how, following the Bee King's death, his son proclaimed himself King Buzz and took over the entire hive. The other bees submitted to his rule even though King Buzz claimed all the honey for himself. Why shouldn't they? Surely the king would provide for everyone.

"The king would give to all, all—
The king would give to all.
        "Buzz, buzz, buzz!"

But the bees soon noticed that they worked harder than ever—spending long hours gathering nectar and toiling in the hive making honey—and they felt more and more exhausted even as they gained less and less to show for their efforts. Still, King Buzz assured them that a splendid future awaited them.

> "Trust your lives to me, to me—
> Trust your lives to me!
>   "Buzz, buzz, buzz!"

Abruptly she fell silent, curtsied, and walked away.

Stelinda's sudden departure caught Zephyrio and Yoss off guard. While Yoss glowered at his sister, Zephyrio turned to the crowd and called out, "Long live King Yoss!"

A few peasants weakly echoed him: "Long live King Yoss."

Jack hastened to catch up with the princess. "What are you doing?" he asked her.

"Doing?" she inquired. "Isn't it obvious? It's a sugary pill I've offered, but there's poison inside."

Jack understood Stelinda's words, but he worried about their effect. He went on: "This is too much too soon. Didn't you see how your brother glared at you? He and Zephyrio surely grasp your ploy."

"Let them grasp it, then."

"Stelinda—"

"They have no antidote to counteract my poison."

"Stelinda, please. If we don't step carefully, Yoss will dismiss us. He'll . . . *dispose* of us. What good can come of that?"

She turned to him, held him, stroked his hair. "Jack," she said, "I understand your concern. You're right—we *must* be careful. But not *too* careful. How long can the Realm tolerate the crushing burden of my brother's rule?"

He shook his head in sadness and bewilderment. "I wish I knew."

Whether these stories and poems affected their listeners, Jack and Stelinda couldn't be certain. But the listeners certainly affected the storyteller and the princess. For Jack, the sight of the miserable, fearful peasants inspired unease and dread. He feared failing the mission that King Yoss had forced upon him, for doing so would mean his death. He also feared succeeding, for doing so would mean helping a cruel monarch oppress his people. Perhaps he also feared having to return someday to a farm boy's hard life in Yorrow—a life of hunger, toil, fatigue, and uncertainty.

He sensed a different kind of unease in Stelinda. Having only recently emerged from the cocoon of palace life, the princess resembled a butterfly that, flitting about, marveled at the world's size and complexity. Jack watched his beloved and observed her fascination, surprise, and bafflement. The breadth of the land . . . the damp, complex odor of a farm . . . the honking of geese overhead . . . the scarlike road cut into a hillside. These and many other sights, sounds, and smells caught Stelinda's attention. She seemed especially troubled by what she saw among the people. A farmer struggling to carry a huge load of hay on his back . . . a one-legged boy walking with a crutch . . . a woman toting a baby in a threadbare shawl . . . two little girls begging near the marketplace . . . a farmer whipping a stubborn mule . . . four men shouldering a coffin as they walked down the road. The princess stared at everything around her and, unable to request explanations in the king's presence, fell silent.

But each evening, when Yoss and Zephyrio withdrew to plan the following day's activities, Stelinda took advantage of her brief time with Jack to ask him questions. "The peasants we saw today . . . why do they wear nothing but rags?"

"Most people in the Realm have only rags," Jack explained.

The princess laughed in astonishment. "How is that possible?"

"Because they're too poor to own anything else."

"And if they get wet in the rain?"

"Then they huddle by the hearth until their rags are dry," Jack told her. "Assuming, of course, that they have wood to burn."

"What? No wood to burn?"

He shrugged. "If they have no land, they have no trees to cut for firewood."

"But of course they could *buy* some wood," she suggested.

"Most of the king's subjects have only the crops they grow—and the king's tax collectors take much of that to sell for the king's benefit."

Bewilderment spread across her face. "So couldn't they exchange their crops for firewood?" she suggested thoughtfully. "Or else trade the crops for new clothes?"

"They could—but they need their crops as food to eat."

The princess fell silent for a long time. Then she said, "So what you're telling me is that most people in the Realm live wretched lives."

Jack didn't know how to respond. "Well—yes," he said at last. "I'd have to call their lives wretched. Which doesn't mean they don't feel certain satisfactions. Family members love one another. People help their neighbors. They have hopes for the future."

"Yes, surely their love and hope must compensate for their wretchedness."

"It helps," Jack noted. "But when you have no food, love won't feed you. When you're wet and cold, hope won't keep you warm and dry."

The princess gazed past Jack. Yoss, Zephyrio, and the councilors stood near a campfire twenty paces away. "And your own family," she asked suddenly. "Have they, too, suffered? Have they felt hardship, scarcity, and hunger?"

"Of course," Jack replied.

"Often?"

"Yes, they often have less food than they need, so hunger is part of their lives."

"Still?" she asked. "That is to say—*now*?"

"I suppose so."

Stelinda smiled an odd, half-mocking smile. "You *suppose* so? You're not sure?"

Jack felt more and more uncomfortable as Stelinda asked these questions. In truth, he hadn't thought about his family for a while. He hadn't considered what his mother, father, brothers, and sisters must have been through over the past several months. Stelinda's questions now reminded him. He felt a sudden, deep pang of longing for his family. Were they doing well? Were they getting enough to eat? Were they in good health? He couldn't help worrying.

Yet he also wondered how much time and attention he could devote to them. Yes, he was concerned. Yes, he wanted them to be happy. But the most crucial task, he told himself, was to undermine Yoss's reign. That would help his family more than anything else. Whatever distracted Jack from his bigger task would harm, not help, all the people of the Realm.

≈ 58 ≈

Just as he missed his family, Jack missed someone else: Loquasto. He hadn't seen the bird in many weeks. Where was he? What was he doing? Perhaps, tiring of Jack's delays and excuses, he had set out alone to find Artemisia. Perhaps he'd simply left in frustration or disgust. Jack missed the bird's chatter, his tart observations about the world, and even his occasional scoldings. He felt diminished by his friend's absence, and he worried about Loquasto's safety. Was he all right? Was he even still alive? It was so unlike him simply to disappear.

Loquasto's absence also prompted Jack to worry about his *own* safety. If the bird had remained with him, Jack could have asked his opinion about his new role, his efforts to undermine Yoss and Zephyrio. He realized now that no matter how irritating Loquasto had been at times—pressing his point of view, challenging Jack's plans, squawking at inconvenient moments—the bird had offered useful insights into the challenges Jack faced and the decisions he struggled to make. Loquasto had saved him from danger more than once. Now he was gone.

One day, as King Yoss's entourage passed a wheat field, a flock of black birds crossed the sky and alit on a hedgerow near the road. Jack was instantly alert. "Loquasto!" he called out, then silenced himself, embarrassed by everyone's stares, for he saw that the birds were just ordinary crows.

What have I done to drive away my friend? Jack asked himself.

❧ 59 ❧

Garth's brazen forest ambush didn't prompt King Yoss simply to rave against the robber. The king also issued a harsh new edict:

> Be It Known: *The vile, despicable, evil, wicked, nasty, low-born, stinky, contemptible, greedy, traitorous, uneducated, violent, and*

ugly robber known throughout the Realm as GARTH GOLDEN-EYE *is nothing but a* DEAD MAN. *Having forsaken all rights within the Realm of Sundar, including the right to live, the afore-mentioned Garth Golden-Eye is* FAIR PREY *to any loyal subject of King Yoss. Any such subject of the king may* PUT GARTH GOLDEN-EYE TO DEATH. *And, upon presenting the* LIFELESS HEAD OF GARTH *to the Lord High Chamberlain, he or she will be rewarded with a* BOUNTY OF TEN GOLD DUCATS.

"Dead man indeed," said Jack with a shudder as he read this edict. Posted everywhere—on houses, shops, barns, and trees—it was the biggest news in the Realm. "I can't believe Garth will survive more than another week."

"We shall see," said Stelinda.

"If one of the commonfolk doesn't kill him to claim the king's reward, his own henchmen surely will do so."

"We shall see."

In fact, nothing happened in response to King Yoss's edict. A week passed, two weeks, three. Word still came of Garth's robberies—not robberies of commoners but of nobles traveling on royal business. The news arrived, too, that Garth had begun to distribute the booty from these robberies among villagers and peasants.

Yoss's reaction didn't surprise either Jack or Stelinda. "That man must die!" he shouted. "If ten ducats isn't enough to seal his fate, I'll raise the bounty to a hundred." He motioned to one of his servants. "Scribe! Rewrite the edict! Raise the reward! *Now!*"

This command, too, did little to doom the robber. No reports suggested any attempts against his life. On the contrary, royal spies among the villagers told of growing sympathy toward Garth and his band of ruffians. Their number had grown, the frequency of robberies had increased, and the amount of loot distributed among the poor had risen. As a result, no commoner spoke ill of Garth Golden-Eye, much less planned to kill him.

"What are you telling me?" King Yoss screamed at a messenger one day.

"Garth Golden-Eye is still alive," said the boy, trembling.

"Alive? *Alive*, you say?"

"Indeed. Majesty—the people are protecting him."

"Nonsense! Who would hesitate to kill Garth Golden-Eye for the reward I've posted?"

"Majesty, forgive me for saying so, but people *admire* Garth Golden-Eye."

"Admire?" Yoss pouted in silence. Then he said: "Very well, I'll raise the bounty to a thousand gold ducats. You hear me? A *thousand*! Scribe—rewrite the edict!"

Which, as it so happened, still did nothing to cut short Garth's life.

☙ 60 ❧

As Garth's fame spread throughout the Realm, King Yoss tried to counter it, but he was helpless to harm the robber's reputation or destroy his influence among the people of Sundar. Perhaps this explains why the king tried to control the situation by issuing a different kind of edict:

> *Whosoever shall be caught in possession of the royal jewelry, coins, gold ingots, or any such items of the* KING'S OWNERSHIP *will be summarily* PUT TO DEATH.

But when even this latest proclamation brought no response, King Yoss lashed out at the entire kingdom. No longer would he endure these insults. No longer would he tolerate the losses he suffered through Garth's robberies. No longer would he risk losing the nobles' support as the Realm's wiliest outlaw relieved them of their most precious goods. He issued yet another edict:

> HENCEFORTH *all of the king's subjects shall give four-fifths of their worldly goods each year to the* CROWN, *whether such goods be crops, crafts, or creatures; and any person failing to* SURRENDER SUCH GOODS *shall be* PUT TO DEATH.

"How can he proclaim such things?" Jack asked when he found them posted on a wall. "I can't believe that even a selfish, foolish boy would send people to their death."

"Neither can I," said Stelinda, "but Yoss has long delighted in cruel deeds. As a child he often tormented dogs and cats in the most awful manner."

Jack said, "But now it's people he'll condemn to Young Moribundo's ax."

"True."

"Does he understand the consequences?"

"I doubt it. If it affects other people, it's not real to Yoss. It's just a game. Only *things* move him."

Jack had noticed this aspect of Yoss's behavior. The king often stared at his crown with an expression of delight. He caressed the royal scepter like a pet. He stroked the gold embroidery and fur trim of his robe. He marveled at what he held and warmed himself with whatever strange heat he felt emanating from his riches.

"Your brother certainly likes his possessions," Jack remarked to Stelinda.

"I don't know if he likes them or not," said the princess. "What I know is that he *craves* them. Craves them as an injured man craves a bandage for his wound."

"Which wound would that be?"

"I have no idea. I've never understood him. Perhaps Yoss feels that people blame him for our mother's death in childbirth. Perhaps he blames himself."

"But why, then, should he punish everyone else?"

"I wish I knew," said Stelinda.

❧ 61 ❧

The royal journeys continued. Jack and Stelinda told stories and recited poems to persuade everyone that a glorious day had dawned in Sundar. Jack dreaded these presentations but participated anyway, hoping that they would soon have the opposite effect from what Yoss intended.

Would they? He couldn't be sure, but certain rumors made him optimistic. Yoss's harsh taxes sparked outrage against the new king. His royal edicts ignited hostility throughout the Realm. Perhaps Jack's stories and Stelinda's poems helped fan the flames. But Jack soon realized that it was Garth Golden-Eye who had lit the biggest fire. By robbing the rich and giving to the poor, he challenged the king as no one else had done. Some villagers had started to complain more loudly and even to resist more actively—driving off the tax collectors and chasing away the king's emissaries.

Was it possible that Yoss's days as king might be numbered?

Jack could only hope.

Then one day, the royal entourage arrived in a village called Satch-itorra. The Royal Guard rounded up the peasantry, and Jack and Stelinda prepared to face the reluctant crowd. But almost at once the presentation took a new shape.

First, Jack noticed eight or ten unfamiliar people lingering close to the wooden platform that members of the Royal Guard had built for the storytelling. Some were peasants wearing ragged, dirty clothes. Others, dressed in fine attire, were clearly members of the nobility. Seeing peasants and nobles wasn't what surprised Jack—it was seeing them *together*, standing side by side and chatting amiably like longtime friends.

Then he realized that these people *were* longtime friends. They were members of the King's Artists: Ned Painter, Eliza Singer, Edwin Flutist, Hildegard Harpist, and others. Delighted, Jack approached them. "Eliza! Ned! How wonderful to see you. But, tell me—what are you doing here?"

The Artists turned to face him. "Jack!" Hildegard exclaimed.

"I'm so glad you're here," Jack said. "I thought you were all sent away to the mines and forced to work in the foundries."

"We were," said Mog Dancer.

"But we're back," Eliza told him.

"We're all performers now," said Hildegard. "We're presenting a play on the king's behalf."

"A play?" Jack inquired. "What is a play?"

Ned shrugged. "It's a new kind of entertainment—something to amuse the people. I don't know more than that. You don't ask questions when you're given a chance to escape from the mines."

"Anything is better than the mines!" Edwin exclaimed.

Before Jack's friends could say more, Zephyrio began to address the crowd. "Good people!" the illusionist called out to the weary villagers massed in the town square. "I bring you wonderful news."

The audience grew irritable. A man shouted, "Nothing wonderful has ever come from the Royal City."

A woman added: "The news is always bad!"

Jack flinched, expecting Zephyrio and Yoss to lash out against such impudence. But Zephyrio only smiled, while Yoss watched in silence from beside the platform.

"The wonderful news will be obvious soon enough. Behold the glories of your future!" Zephyrio proclaimed, and with those words he snapped his fingers.

Almost everyone in the crowd edged forward to get a better look.

Jack looked inquiringly at Stelinda.

She shook her head in bafflement.

Fog materialized in the air above the village square, shifted, and congealed—soft and swirly—until it settled and obscured the platform. As this cloud intensified, swirling faster and faster, Jack felt more and more uneasy. He reached for Stelinda's hand just as she reached for his. Several courtiers standing nearby backed away several steps. Many of the peasants did, too, and Jack could hear the muffled sounds of people praying and weeping.

"I hear sounds of dread and worry," the illusionist called out to the crowd. "I hear sounds of deep foreboding. Rest easy, all of you, for no one should feel alarmed. King Yoss loves you all like brothers and sisters. He wants no harm or hardship to befall you. I stand before you now to reveal what lies ahead during the reign of our beloved young king."

Stelinda turned to Jack and whispered: "Like brothers and sisters? Will he subject *everyone* to that wretched fate?"

Jack didn't reply; like everyone present, he felt his attention drawn by what was transpiring on the platform before him.

The spinning cloud parted suddenly to reveal an unexpected scene. A peasant shoveled dirt from one pile to another. His wife dug potatoes from the ground. Their children worked at tedious chores: chopping wood, carrying water, sifting grain. A mood of deep fatigue weighed down the scene, and even the platform—which now resembled a garden plot—looked bleak and barren.

At first Jack wondered who these people might be—and how they had materialized so abruptly. Then he recognized individual Artists: Mog, Edwin, Ned, and others, all wearing ragged clothes.

"So *this* is our glorious destiny?" a member of the audience called out with a harsh laugh.

Zephyrio smiled. "Ah, good people, don't despair!" he said. "How well Majesty knows of your toil! How deeply King Yoss understands your exhaustion! Believe me, the scene you see now isn't the future—it's the present. But look again. See what is yet to come."

With those words, the fog descended once more, obscuring the people on the platform, swirled with great intensity, and lifted suddenly. The platform now revealed a completely different scene. The family wore newer, cleaner clothes. A lush garden surrounded them. The children held up carrots, squash, and corn. The wife raised a sheaf of golden wheat. The husband lifted onto his shoulder a basket of perfect, bright red apples.

"*This* is your fate!" the illusionist proclaimed. "*This* is the legacy you'll inherit during King Yoss's reign!"

The new, vibrant scene prompted murmurs of delight and astonishment from the crowd. Such an abundance of food! Even Jack was impressed by what he saw. But how had this spectacle come about? The fog . . . the stark first landscape . . . the splendid garden it became! Was this all Zephyrio's doing? Jack had no idea. In any case, what appeared on the platform clearly captivated the audience and put everyone present in a state of childlike eagerness for more.

"This is merely a taste of what Majesty will bestow upon you!" shouted the illusionist. "King Yoss understands the hardships you face!" Now the air grew cloudy once more, swirled wildly, and clarified again to reveal a large family—parents, children, and a scattering of other relatives—huddled in a dark, dirty house. The children clung to their parents or crouched on the filthy floor. A few sticks smoldered on the hearth. These people stared outward from their squalor. The fog returned once more, swirled, dispersed, and revealed a far different scene. The sticks on the hearth now sprouted hearty flames. The table in the room had grown wider; some pathetic little biscuits there had swelled into heaps of meat, bread, potatoes, and other vegetables; and the peasants' clothes had been transformed into elegant woolen garments trimmed with fur and studded with copper buttons. The sight of all these changes inspired cries of delight and admiration from the crowd.

Zephyrio called out again: "*This* is your fate, good people! *These* are the benefits you gain simply because your king loves you so deeply!"

Jack turned to Stelinda. "How does he conjure such visions?" he asked.

"I wish I knew," said the princess. Then she added: "Or perhaps it's better that I don't."

Visions indeed! Within a short while Zephyrio provided many more splendid sights for his audience. Visions of comfort. Visions of abundant food. Visions of wealth and well-being. Visions of village harmony, peace, and bliss.

The more the people saw, the more they marveled at what appeared before them. And the more they marveled, the more they warmed to the illusionist's claim that good King Yoss was the source of all benevolence, safety, and delight in the Realm of Sundar.

"This is what the future holds!" Zephyrio proclaimed to the villagers. "This is the glory that awaits you all!"

A murmur of astonishment and delight rippled through the crowd.

"Are you pleased?" asked the illusionist.

"Yes!" shouted some of the people.

"Greatly pleased!" cried others.

"I should hope so," Zephyrio stated, "for King Yoss will bestow these gifts upon you."

A man somewhere in the crowd called out: "Long live the king!"

Others took up the cry: "Long live King Yoss!"

Jack and Stelinda looked at each other in dismay.

"Long live King Yoss!"

Soon the whole village shook with the people's united voice.

And as everyone cheered, King Yoss turned to face his people, he smiled in delight at the acclaim they bestowed upon him, and he opened his arms wide as if to embrace every man, woman, and child at once.

Zephyrio, clearly pleased, called out: "Go now, all of you. Spread the news of the splendid days ahead."

⚜ 62 ⚜

The plays quickly improved Yoss's status throughout the Realm. Watching the Artists act out these dramas, the king's subjects began to feel new emotions toward their monarch, and they started to admire the handsome boy who ruled over them. Even where the crowds had recently failed to respond, they now eagerly chanted, "Long live the king!"

Jack and Stelinda observed these changes with bewilderment, frustration, and alarm. True, the plays pleased the eye and ear alike.

No doubt they appealed to bored, weary, hopeless people and fed their eagerness to believe that better days awaited them. But weren't these dramas too good to be true? Few people among the gathered crowds seemed to think so. "Long live the king!" they cried. "Long live King Yoss!"

What appalled Jack and Stelinda most was that the people's enthusiasm increased even as their well-being declined. King Yoss's new taxes drained each family's funds. The poor peasants grew still poorer. Yet somehow his popularity swelled like a hideous mushroom. Watching the spectacle of the plays, people seemed ready to believe almost anything.

"How does Zephyrio do it?" Jack exclaimed in bewilderment one evening. "He conjures such wondrous illusions—but illusions all the same."

"Here's what inspires *my* wonder," said Stelinda. "Not the illusions, but the people's eagerness to accept them. They see images of food and decide they're no longer hungry. They see images of fire and decide they're no longer cold. They see images of a smiling, friendly king and decide that Yoss loves them. People don't care about their true situation. All that impresses them is the spectacle on stage."

"It's true," Jack replied gloomily. "As Zephyrio told me once, illusion is what matters."

"We have become a kingdom of fools," said the princess.

"What then shall we do?" asked Jack.

Stelinda ran both hands through her wheat-colored hair. Her downcast eyes revealed her despair. Then she looked up. "You and I, too, have become fools. Not by falling prey to Yoss and Zephyrio, but by failing to fight them powerfully. Our weapons have been dull, our tactics feeble. Small wonder that my brother and his adviser have gained the upper hand."

"But you yourself suggested that we battle them by stealth and undermine their cause by seeming to advance it."

"True. But I was wrong."

"So what should we do instead?"

"Something different!" exclaimed Stelinda. "Something better! Something that's more powerful than nipping at their heels like a pesky puppy! Something that chases them, corners them, and holds them at bay like a fierce, snarling dog!"

Jack had never seen Stelinda so upset—her face tight with anguish, her hands shaking—and the sight alarmed him. "But surely—"

The princess reached out and rested her hands on his shoulders. "Surely *you*, dear Jack, should understand. It's *you*, not I, who have lived a life of hunger and toil. It's *you* whose family still labors so hard. It's *you*—"

"Stelinda, please. Don't get carried away."

Her expression revealed her puzzlement. "Don't get carried away?"

"I understand why you're angry," Jack said, "but surely our efforts will undermine Yoss and Zephyrio in the fullness of time."

"Time is no longer full. Time is leaking away, like water from a cracked pot."

"Then let me ask you once again: what should we do?"

"I don't know," she answered wearily. "Something that inspires the people to rise up against these tyrants. Something . . . something like what Garth Golden-Eye is doing."

⫷ 63 ⫸

"Perhaps it's just my imagination," said Zephyrio when he summoned Jack to his tent the following day, "but at times I question your loyalty."

"My loyalty?" Jack asked irritably. "I'm here, am I not?"

"You're here, yes, and I'm glad of that. Make yourself comfortable." Zephyrio gestured to the chair opposite his own. A plate of pastries and two cups of tea rested on a small table nearby. "Help yourself." When Jack ignored his hospitality, the illusionist only smiled. "You're here in body, of course, but where is your heart, Jack? Is your heart loyal to King Yoss? Or do its loyalties lie elsewhere?" Zephyrio took his cup and sipped the tea. "Not hot enough," he stated. He pointed at the cup with his right index finger until the beverage began to steam; then he sipped from it again and smiled.

Jack shivered at this sight. "I'm in Majesty's service," he said, ignoring the impulse to ask how the illusionist had warmed his tea. "You know that. I'm doing whatever I can to assist him."

"I hope so," Zephyrio said, sounding impatient. "It's certainly your duty as a loyal subject. You might show a little gratitude, too— for the fine food and elegant clothes you've received and for the chance you've been given to see the Realm. What more could you possibly want?"

Unable to restrain himself, Jack blurted, "I want to free what's in my heart! I want to tell my own stories!"

Zephyrio merely smiled his calm, reassuring smile. "Of course you do," he said. "That's what any artist wants: to practice his art. And that's exactly what King Yoss will grant you—once you finish your new task."

"New task? What new task?"

Zephyrio raised his right forefinger to counsel patience. "The task of easing worries, soothing fears, and diminishing the confusion that's rampant throughout the Realm."

"Isn't that what we've been doing?" Jack asked irritably. "Isn't that why we've been telling stories and reciting poems?"

"Of course," said Zephyrio. "You're altogether right. But somehow the commoners aren't sufficiently soothed by mere stories and poems. The plays we're presenting now are far more effective in easing people's concerns. They reassure everyone of a serene future. They inspire the people to love their king. The plays are, in fact, the key to winning trust throughout the Realm."

Jack could only shrug. "Fine," he said. "Maybe you're right. But if so, you don't need a storyteller, do you? Release me from my duties. Let me attend to other matters."

"Such as?"

"My own stories. You said the ones I'm telling serve no purpose. So you don't need me."

Zephyrio smiled. "You've grasped half the truth, Jack. We don't need your stories."

"Good." Jack started toward the door.

"Instead, we need your presence in the plays."

"My *presence?*"

"We want you to act in them."

"But that's not my role!" Jack exclaimed.

"No matter," said Zephyrio. "I'll explain everything you need to know."

"I can't do it," Jack said. "I *won't* do it."

"No?" asked Zephyrio, arching an eyebrow. "That's unfortunate."

Jack felt queasy. "What do you mean, *unfortunate?*"

Zephyrio gestured quizzically. "We live in dangerous times, Jack, and the danger requires everyone to make sacrifices. Your sacrifice is to place the common good above your artistry. To serve the king. To help overcome the threats facing Sundar. But later—once the tide of danger ebbs—King Yoss will grant your wish."

"Explain yourself."

"If you don't behave foolishly and incur the king's wrath, you'll soon be freer than you ever thought possible," said Zephyrio. "You'll have your current title—royal storyteller—but you'll be free to go about your business."

Jack blurted, "To tell my own stories—"

"To tell each and every story in that crowded brain of yours."

☙ 64 ☙

Leaving Zephyrio's tent, Jack could scarcely restrain his excitement. Soon he'd be finished with King Yoss. Finished with spewing nonsense. Finished with pretending to do one thing while actually doing something else. Instead, he'd practice his art, perfect his techniques, and release the stories trapped in his mind like restless animals caged in the royal zoo.

But he would have to earn this freedom. *Your sacrifice is to place the common good above your artistry.* Of course. Yoss would have his way no matter what. If Jack resisted, he'd lose the struggle; worse yet, he'd die under Young Moribundo's ax. What would *that* accomplish?

No, it would be far better to pretend to give in, play the game, and win.

Then he would be free, Jack told himself—free to tell each and every story that needed to be told.

❦ 65 ❦

That afternoon, during his brief time alone with Stelinda, Jack explained what he planned to do, and why. The plan made even more sense to him as he spoke with her. "Keep in mind that just because I'm acting in the king's dramas doesn't mean that I've submitted to his will," Jack told her. "On the contrary, I'll struggle against him. I'll influence him. I'll sway him from the madness of his whims."

"Sway him?" asked Stelinda. "How would you sway my stubborn, selfish brother?"

"By gaining his confidence, then persuading him to change his ways."

Stelinda didn't reply at first. Then, speaking quietly, she said, "You'll peddle his chains."

Startled, Jack said, "Chains?"

"You'll act in these little skits and convince everyone how much they crave imprisonment."

"You're not being fair, Stelinda!" Jack exclaimed. "It's just a ruse. Although I may *seem* to praise King Yoss, I'm really persuading the people to rise up—"

"You'll struggle against the king," said the princess, "but you'll do so by persuading the people to admire him. To love him, even."

"No—by outraging them with Yoss's foolishness. Just as you yourself have suggested in the past. Just as we've been doing together."

"True, that *is* what I suggested," said the princess sadly, "and that's what we did. But as I told you, our strategy was too feeble to defeat the enemy we face. The people who heard us praise Yoss didn't understand our real message."

Jack grew impatient. "But only this plan can work!" he exclaimed. "We can't fight the king directly—he's too powerful! Our one chance is to undermine him from within."

The princess was silent.

Jack went on, speaking louder: "I'll sow brambles when he thinks I'm sowing wheat. By the time he understands what's happening, his field will be choked with thorns."

She just gazed at him.

"His tyranny will end. He'll fall from power."

Still no response.

"*Talk* to me!" Jack told her.

"You clearly have no use for my opinion—so surely will you be my brother's minion."

"But not in rhymed couplets!" he shouted. He couldn't believe that she'd stab *him*, of all people, with those double-edged poetic daggers!

"No? Then there's nothing more that I can say. I love you—but my love is choking on dismay."

"*Stop.* My plan will succeed. I'll break Yoss's hold over the Realm."

"Jack—of this sorry plan I want no part. What you intend will truly break my heart."

Angry and hurt, Jack said, "Oh, leave me alone."

"If that is what you genuinely prefer, then it's time for me to take my leave, good sir."

With those words Stelinda turned and left the tent.

⚘ 66 ⚘

Jack didn't see the princess that evening, nor did he receive word from her. Neither did he hear from Stelinda the following day. Still hurt and angry, he made no effort to visit her. Let her stew in her own stubbornness!

But the next morning, while he stood talking with Zephyrio and the king, Jack saw a young messenger approach.

The messenger bowed deeply. "A thousand pardons, Majesty—"

"Even a million wouldn't excuse this interruption."

"Forgive me."

"Oh, stop it!" snapped the king. "Why are you bothering me?"

"To bring bad news, Majesty. Regarding the princess Stelinda—"

"Where is she, anyway? I haven't seen her since yesterday."

"Majesty, the royal spies have discovered that your sister—"

"Yes? Out with it!"

Trembling, the messenger said, "Princess Stelinda has left to join Garth Golden-Eye's band of ruffians in the forest of Sycamora."

FİVE

She left?

She left.

Why did she do that?

Why indeed! Jack himself wondered why Stelinda would abandon him. Worse yet, why would she abandon him to join forces with Garth Golden-Eye, of all people?

A highway robber.

Exactly. Garth had been doing more than anyone else in the kingdom to cause Yoss trouble, but he was still a filthy, sneaky old outlaw. Jack could not imagine why Stelinda would willingly choose Garth's company. What could she possibly have had in mind, running off to the forest of Sycamora? Stelinda's actions left him confused, angry, and hurt. In recent weeks she had clearly changed, but he didn't know why. Now, following their most recent argument, she was gone. And of course this wasn't the first time that Jack had felt abandoned.

Loquasto . . .

Right. First Loquasto had left him; now Stelinda had.

☙ 67 ❧

I wouldn't worry too much about your fine, fair princess," Zephyrio said a few days later, when he, King Yoss, and Jack had returned to the Royal City. "In fact, I wouldn't give her a moment's thought. You have something far more important to occupy your mind—the final task on the king's behalf. After that, you're free."

"Entirely free?" Jack asked.

"Free indeed. Free as that crow you released from captivity a while ago."

Hearing the illusionist mention Loquasto made Jack flinch. "What must I do?"

"Simply what you've already agreed to do: travel one last time and speak to the peasantry."

"And peddle the king's dramas."

"That's a crass way of putting it," said Zephyrio. "There's no need to peddle something that the people so eagerly desire. But we must proceed with urgency, given what's at stake. Is that not true?"

"I don't know," Jack said without much interest. "Maybe so."

"Splendid. That's your mission."

Jack didn't have the energy to argue. "When do we leave?"

Zephyrio smiled calmly. "Soon."

✄ 68 ✄

And so a week later, Jack joined the king's entourage again and set off on his last journey, a journey intended to reach twenty or thirty villages, each destined to witness a play now called *The Glory of the King*.

"Listen, all of you!" Jack shouted in the village square of Lorritia. "See for yourselves what our fine young monarch has in store for you."

Fog engulfed the platform; the play commenced.

Here we go again, Jack thought. He was no longer able to see the peasants crowding around the elevated stage as Zephyrio somehow generated all this vapor. But he could hear their exclamations: "*Ooh!*" "*Aah!*" "*What's happening?*" And he could hear the Artists' footsteps as they scrambled into place to play their parts.

The fog dispersed.

More oohs and aahs. The peasants had never witnessed such a spectacle as now appeared before them. But for Jack, *The Glory of the King* was a tedious sequence of events: the poor family's hardships, King Yoss's arrival in their midst, and the marvel of lights, sparks, and mysterious changes that accompanied the transformation from squalor to prosperity. Lightning! Thunder! Wildly growing vegetables! Stark trees sprouting blossoms and bearing fruit! While some members of the Artists acted out these scenes, others took up harps, flutes, and fiddles to play melodies that intensified the sadness, grief, shock, amazement, delight, and eventual joy that the audience felt while witnessing *The Glory of the King*.

Jack now played one of the poor peasants whose life changed so wonderfully, and he cringed with each word he spoke to Ned Painter, who played the king. "Oh, Majesty!" Jack exclaimed, kneeling before Ned. "What can so lowly a creature as I—a worm, a maggot—do to repay you for your generosity and kindness?"

Dressed in blue fur-trimmed robes and wearing a lush golden wig, Ned looked remarkably like the king. He smiled warmly. "Good people! Despite all I've done for you, you needn't thank me," he proclaimed. "I am here only for your benefit. I may be your lord and master, but I am your servant, too." He bowed gracefully, then went on: "Everything I do, I do for you. I'll help you. I'll improve your lives. I'll banish suffering. And in return I ask only for your devotion—the devotion that people owe their king."

The Artists onstage with Jack—Brynne, Mog, Ned, and the others—couldn't seem to believe their good fortune in having the king present in their humble home.

"Long live King Yoss," Jack said flatly.

At once Brynne echoed him: "Long live King Yoss!"

The actors playing their children joyfully yelled the same words.

Then Yoss—the king himself, not the actor playing him—

climbed the stairs onto the stage to receive his subjects' acclaim and praise. And as the king reached out to hug the actors—the parents one by one, then all the children in a big embrace—the villagers, too, cried out: "Long live King Yoss!"

From out of nowhere, white rose petals fell onto the Artists and their audience like the gentlest of snowfalls.

Jack knew that Zephyrio was responsible for making these dramas so effective. But how? How did he make blossoms spring forth from a dead branch? How did he make fruit swell from those same flowers? How did he make real flames spring up in a fake hearth? How did he make petals flutter down from an empty sky? Jack didn't understand these marvels any better than he understood Zephyrio's other deeds. He never had. Perhaps it didn't matter. Perhaps, as Stelinda had suggested long ago, it was better not to know. What mattered was simply that Zephyrio managed to play a vast trick on the entire Realm. But the situation was even worse than that. The people of Sundar were playing a trick on themselves. No one was obliged to gaze at these foolish dramas, yet people did. They stared and stared, helpless as mice transfixed by a snake preparing to devour them. They could have fled for their lives, but they didn't.

Was that surprising? Maybe not. The people of Sundar lived harsh lives. They worked too much and rested too little. They suffered many hardships. All they wanted, really, was relief from the burdens they carried. Jack could understand why they'd cling to fantasies about King Yoss.

So be it, Jack told himself. Let King Yoss, Zephyrio, Jack, and the Artists put on *The Glory of the King*. Let the villagers find relief from their toil. Let them feel momentary hope for the future. At least he could stop wasting his time and talent on Yoss once he fulfilled his participation in these garish performances. He could return to his art. He could tell his own stories. He could track down Loquasto and resume the quest to unite him with Artemisia. Most important of all, he could locate Stelinda, beg her forgiveness, and win her back.

☙ 69 ❧

The royal entourage traveled across the Realm presenting *The Glory of the King*. Sometimes they visited one village a day, sometimes two or three. In all of these visits, Jack would give a little speech, then step into the drama itself, and it was always he who offered the first shout: "Long live King Yoss!" at the play's end.

Stelinda was right, Jack told himself grimly after yet another presentation in yet another village. *I'm just selling Yoss's wares. I'm no better than a peddler who claims to offer gold jewelry but knows that his goods are only gold-painted tin.*

Onward to Silver Ridge. To Speth. To Orilia. To Ford-at-the-Narrows.

"How many towns do you think we've visited on this journey?" Jack finally asked Zephyrio late one evening as they stood by the illusionist's campfire.

"How many?" repeated Zephyrio as he warmed his hands. "I couldn't say."

"Thirty-five," Jack stated.

"I haven't been counting."

"*I* have. You said this last journey would include twenty or thirty towns. We've visited thirty-five, which means I've fulfilled my part of the agreement."

"Who cares?" Yoss said, approaching the fire. "The number of villages makes no difference. You'll be done when I say you're done."

"Majesty." Jack bowed reluctantly. "Zephyrio said that my duties would last only—"

"Your duties and Majesty's whims," the illusionist interrupted, "are one and the same."

Like a pot left too long on the hearth, Jack boiled over. "You *promised!*"

"I promised nothing. I told you you'd be free on finishing your final task. That task is not yet completed."

"But *when!*" Jack shouted. "Will we wander through the Realm forever?"

"If that's what I want, then, yes, we'll wander forever," Yoss stated.

"Listen, Jack," Zephyrio said. "Majesty is eager to grant your freedom, but the situation is . . . complicated. There's so much unrest in the Realm." He shook his head. "As if the peasants weren't enough trouble already, Garth Golden-Eye is sowing resentment. So are his misguided followers. Not just commoners, but even one of the nobles."

Jack couldn't hold back. "*Stelinda*—what have you heard of her?"

"Nothing!" Yoss snapped. "She's a fool!"

"No news at all?" Jack asked in dismay.

"None whatsoever," said Zephyrio. "But it makes no difference. Forget the princess—she's irrelevant. What matters is that the sooner we persuade people to trust King Yoss, the sooner you'll be free. And the way to persuade them is for you—"

"To do your duty!" Yoss shouted, trembling.

Jack felt hope die within him.

❦ 70 ❦

Saviolu . . . Deer Paddock . . . Niff . . . Kendar's Pass . . . Figget-on-the-Gifford . . . Zooth . . . Every town led to another, then another, then another. In each town, Jack and the Artists presented *The Glory of the King*. In each town, they heard great acclaim for King Yoss. In each town, the entourage arrived amidst signs of rebellion and departed with order and calm restored.

Jack did nothing to resist because nothing mattered to him anymore. He played his part. He helped beguile the people with lies. He did whatever Yoss and Zephyrio asked of him.

❦ 71 ❦

The weather grew cold. Autumn in Sundar was always rainy, so the royal entourage now proceeded more slowly and in far less comfort than before. One morning, the king and his retinue reached a village in weather so wet and foggy that no one among them could see the features of the place.

"What *is* this wretched little town?" asked the king as he stood watching his servants set up camp in the square.

"Who knows," said Zephyrio. "These settlements all look the same. The name doesn't really matter." Then, spotting Jack nearby, he inquired, "Lad—is this a town you recognize?"

"No," Jack replied. Through the billowing fog he could barely see the shops and cottages around the square, but they could have been anywhere in Sundar. What difference did it make?

Once the preparations were complete, the heralds blew their trumpets; the villagers came forth; and, despite the foul weather, the Artists got ready to stage *The Glory of the King*.

At the last moment, Zephyrio approached Jack. "There's a little problem," he said. "Ned Painter has taken ill. The man can scarcely walk, he's so sick."

"Cancel the performance," Jack said at once. Though concerned about Ned's health, he saw this illness as an opportunity to scuttle the play for at least one performance.

Zephyrio glanced about. The town square was packed with at least a hundred wet, shivering peasants. "Nonsense," said the illusionist. "We must proceed."

"But who will play the king?" Jack asked—and immediately realized his mistake.

"Oh, that's easy," Zephyrio said with a smile. He held out the robe and wig that Ned would have worn to impersonate King Yoss.

Jack raised his hands as if to fend off a blow. "No, *please!* I don't know the lines!"

"Of course you do. You've performed this drama so often that you could take any role." Zephyrio reached out and jammed the blond wig onto Jack's head.

"No!" Jack shouted in desperation. It was bad enough to play a peasant swayed by the king's cheap promises. How much worse to play Yoss himself.

"Get ready," Zephyrio commanded. *"Now."*

Dizzy and sick to his stomach, Jack put on the robe, stood with Zephyrio by the staircase, and awaited his cue to ascend to the stage.

The Glory of the King began. At the proper moment, Jack—now playing King Yoss—entered the scene, gazed out at the miserable peasants in the square, and began to recite his lines. Doing so took no effort, for the words were etched in his memory. . . . *"And this great* bounty shall be yours for nothing but the willingness to embrace your king—"

Suddenly, Jack froze. Gazing deep into the crowd, he spotted his father, his brother Fergus, and his sisters Sally and Eleanor. *This town was Yorrow!* He had returned to his own village.

Jack was so shocked that the once-familiar words vanished from his memory.

"Go on!" whispered Zephyrio.

Jack stared at the crowd in bewilderment.

"Don't waste their time," King Yoss commanded, "or *mine*."

A wave of nausea struck Jack. He turned, stumbled down the staircase, and scarcely managed to get away from the audience and out of sight before he crouched and vomited.

Luckily, it wasn't difficult for him to convince King Yoss and Zephyrio to relieve him of his duties. They assumed he'd caught the same illness that had afflicted Ned Painter, and they certainly didn't want him throwing up onstage! Zephyrio grabbed the robe and wig, and Jack headed toward his tent, supposedly to rest. But the moment Yoss and Zephyrio couldn't see him, he suddenly changed course, sought his family members, and pulled them away from the crowd.

"Jack!" Father exclaimed as he hugged his son. "You're back!"

"Jack! Jack! Jack!" cried Fergus, clinging to his brother's arm.

Sally and Eleanor, too, embraced him.

Standing there in the rain, Jack suddenly didn't know what to say or do. He looked around. The king and Zephyrio were right across the village square. "Where's Mother?" he asked abruptly.

"At home," said Father. "She's feeling poorly."

"And the others?"

"Caring for her."

Jack wondered: could he leave to visit his family? Impossible!

Zephyrio and Yoss would never allow it. Yet he said at once, "I want to see her. Let's go home right now."

They rushed off through the rain and fog.

When they arrived at the cottage, Jack found his mother propped up in bed and looking pale. "I can't believe you're back!" she exclaimed, holding Jack. "It's been so long . . . I was afraid I'd never see you again."

"I'm sorry," Jack responded. "I've been—busy."

"We heard you're the royal storyteller," Mother said. She smiled, but Jack saw Father turn away, averting his gaze as if from an unpleasant sight.

Suddenly, Fergus asked, "Why are you helping him?"

"The bratty king!" Gwynne added.

Jack flinched at these words. "Well—I'm not really *helping* him."

"No?" said Father. "What would you call it, then? Traveling about and telling grand stories about King Yoss. Acting his part in a play."

"Well, I'm trying to undermine him . . . to work against him from—from within," Jack stammered. "I've tried. Believe me, I've tried."

"He's making us *miserable!*" Sally cried.

"Life is even harder now than when Alphonse was king," Mother added.

"Maybe it isn't hard for *everyone*," Alfred said, reaching out and stroking Jack's sleeve.

"What are you saying?" asked Jack, astonished and hurt by these words.

"Such pretty clothes!" exclaimed Eleanor. "You must be rich now."

"You don't understand," Jack protested. He glanced around uncomfortably. How long had he been away from the royal entourage? Such smoky air . . . The smell of his family's unwashed clothes made him feel sick. "I shouldn't be here," he blurted. "I need to go."

"What?" exclaimed Mother. "You've just arrived."

"I have to go."

Jack's family gazed at him in bewilderment and pain.

"I'm sorry," he said sadly, but he wanted only to leave.

"Well, then, go," his mother replied. "We know you're a busy man."

"That's not it," Jack said quickly. "If I don't leave now, the king will send his guards to find me. Then all of you will be in grave danger. In fact, I hope I'm not too late already." He headed for the door.

Before he stepped outside, though, Mother said, "Someone came looking for you not long ago. A young lady, and high-born, too. She spoke with great cultivation and refinement."

"I've never seen such a fair maiden," Father stated, an odd smile on his face.

"Such a good poet and singer," Mother said. "She sang a song for us."

"*Stelinda!*" Jack whispered. Stelinda—visiting Yorrow! He asked, "What did she want?"

"We wondered the same thing at first," Mother told him. "Such an elegant guest in our humble home. Why *would* she visit us?"

"She said she wanted to make sure we were all right," Father said, "and to warn us about what's coming. Hard times first, she said, then better times, free of Yoss's tyranny."

"She told us to be wary of the king's spies," said Eleanor.

"And she asked us not to say anything—to anyone—about you," Mother added.

Jack nodded uneasily. "That's all?"

"The money!" Alfred whispered.

"What money?" Jack asked.

"The coins her companion gave us," Father said. He stepped over to the hearth and pulled out a brick. Then he reached into the hole, removed a small leather bag, and gave it a shake. The contents made the unmistakable clink of coins.

Jack ignored the sound and focused on his father's words. "Her *companion?*"

Jack's parents looked at each other, then at Jack. "He stayed outside, so we didn't see much of him," Mother said. "But the lady called out just before she left, and he came to the door and gave her this little bag. That's how we caught a glimpse of him."

"Yes?"

"He had only one good eye. The other eye was covered by a gold coin, which means he must've been—well, *you* know. But instead of taking our money, he gave us some."

"Lots," Fergus said blissfully. "Lots and lots!"

"He and the lady gave us more money than we'd ever dreamed of," Mother said. "But even better, they gave us hope."

❧ 72 ❧

Jack left the cottage in a state of roaring confusion. Stelinda had visited his family—and Garth had, too. They'd warned Mother and Father. They'd helped them. They'd predicted hard times . . . then good times.

And what was Jack doing, meanwhile? Hawking Yoss's wares. Helping Zephyrio and Yoss tyrannize the Realm. Strengthening the power of the two people he despised most in the entire world.

He stood in the road and listened to the rain mutter and stutter.

At that moment Jack reached a terrifying insight about himself. He realized that he didn't exist. Once he had been a storyteller; now he was one no longer. Once he had been Jack—a living, breathing, thinking, feeling person—but now he was a mere puppet. Not someone but something. Something that was nothing.

Worst of all, he had ceased to exist as a result of his own choices. Bit by bit he had thrown out parts of himself: his concern for others, his curiosity, his delight in the world, his loyalty to family and friends, his love for Stelinda, his outrage at the king's misuse of power. And now he was no longer Jack Storyteller—he was only a character in someone else's story. Yoss's story.

Very well, then, he decided suddenly, *I'll undo what I've done.*

❦ 73 ❦

Rain drenched Jack as he walked back toward Yorrow's village square. Where could he go? He didn't know. What would he do? He wasn't sure yet. All he could think about was running away. Later, he'd figure out a plan.

"There 'e is!" shouted someone close by.

Jack spotted a squadron of guardsmen on his left: five or six soldiers, maybe more.

"Jack Storyteller!" cried another voice. "Halt!"

He faltered for a moment, then turned and ran.

"Halt!"

He skittered up the street and ducked down a slick alleyway. A volley of crossbow darts shot past him—*fssst! fssst! fssst! fssst!*—but all of them missed. Jack sprinted off, slipped, and fell in a puddle. He

lay still for a moment, then forced himself up, rounded a corner—
and slammed at once into two more guardsmen, toppling both.
Wearing chain mail and wielding battle-axes, they couldn't move
fast. Jack was up and off again, and they could only shout after him:
"Jack Storyteller—halt!"

Jack knew the town's maze of streets, and the fog hid him in its
folds. Soon he was alone. But where could he go? If he returned
home, he'd risk his family's safety. If he stayed out in the open, the
guards would find him. All he could do was leave Yorrow. Without a
coat and supplies, he was ill prepared for travel of any sort, least of all
travel in rough weather. Yet he had no choice. He stumbled through
the town until the cottages thinned out, the street ended, and he
found himself in the countryside.

He left the road and put Yorrow behind him.

⚘74⚘

Jack didn't know how long he staggered about. He simply
shoved his way through the storm, crossed the fields, and
avoided the few cottages he saw until he reached the woods.
Which woods, he didn't know. It hardly mattered. This forest
would conceal him from the Royal Guard. He'd gain some time to
figure out a plan.

Thus Jack found himself cold, hungry, tired, scared, and lost.
Tucking his hands under his arms, he lurched through the whirling
rain. Branches thrashed his face. Sometimes he gained a dozen yards,
sometimes less, before falling. He started shaking hard and couldn't
stop. Night fell.

Jack realized that he'd soon exhaust himself, collapse, and die from the flesh-numbing cold. So much for his splendid life! His story hadn't turned out as he'd expected.

He didn't care. At least he wasn't telling *Yoss's* story.

The only thing that saddened him was realizing that he'd never see Stelinda again, he'd never have a chance to apologize, and he'd never get to explain his change of heart.

Where was she? Was she safe? Or was the Guard tracking her down, too?

Jack tripped, lost his balance, and fell yet again. Shaking hard, he lay still for a moment—and caught sight of a dull glow off to the side. He forced himself up and peered hard at the sight. There, just a dozen yards away: yellow firelight glowing in a window.

He stumbled over to the cottage and, desperate now, pounded on the door.

No answer.

Jack couldn't stop shivering. He pounded and pounded.

At last the door creaked open.

Standing there was Queen Celestina—the Woman of the Woods. Jack stared at her but couldn't speak. He had told so many people about her—how she lived in the forest in a house shaped like a huge bird's nest, how she ruled a kingdom of woodland creatures—that he'd forgotten she was a real person, not a character in a story.

"Majesty," he said at last.

"Jack."

"You're here."

"Of course," she replied. "This is the only kingdom I've been allowed to rule. But look at you—you're a fright! Come in from this awful storm. Honor us with your presence."

With these words, Queen Celestina ushered Jack into her cottage and shut the door behind him. He was so relieved to be in a warm, dry place that tears came to his eyes.

A great commotion greeted him: the squeak, chitter, and shriek of many animals as they scurried, hopped, and slunk about inside Celestina's home.

"Be still, dear ones!" their queen commanded. "All is well." At once they fell silent. Then, turning to Jack, she said, "Half of a queen's work is easing her subjects' fears."

"As it ought to be," Jack replied, "for this is a time when there's much to fear."

"Is that so?"

"It is indeed. Sundar is in upheaval."

"I wouldn't know, would I, living as I do in my own little realm."

Jack took off his wet outer garments, and the old woman draped a rough blanket over his trembling body. He seated himself at Celestina's table. Then she ladled out a bowl of soup from a pot simmering on the hearth, placed it before him, and handed him a spoon.

"Thank you. I can't tell you how glad I am to be here," Jack said. Then, between spoonfuls of the hearty soup, he told his tale. "The Realm is plagued with troubles," he began.

"What troubles, Jack?"

"Hunger. Poverty. Weariness. Sickness of the body and the spirit, too—despair, confusion, rage. Deep suffering."

"But you, Jack—you're damp and cold, it's true, but you seem well fed. And look at your fine attire! Velvet, satin, and the finest leather! *You* aren't suffering."

"I wish that were so," he replied.

Puzzled, Celestina asked, "Haven't you thrived by telling your tales?"

Jack shook his head. "Thrived, yes, but at a cost."

"What cost could there be for telling your own goodhearted stories?"

"I have no idea, for those aren't the ones I've told."

"No?" The old woman looked uncertain. "Which stories, then?"

For a moment Jack couldn't reply. At last he said, "There's a new king who rules Sundar—a young but evil king. I serve that king. I tell *his* stories, not my own."

Celestina averted her gaze. "Hmm—that's not good at all."

Jack nodded. "I've become nothing more than a character in someone else's story. In fact, we're all characters in this ghastly tale."

"I am as well?"

"You are indeed."

"That's deplorable."

"For me, what's most appalling is how much I've assisted my two worst enemies: Yoss and his henchman, Zephyrio. In doing so, I've angered my best friend, Loquasto. Worse yet, I've enraged my true love, Stelinda."

"Stelinda," said the old woman. "What a fine name—a name fit for a princess."

"She *is* a princess."

"Then you've done well indeed, Jack, falling in love with royalty."

"But how well am I doing if she flees from me in anger? I drove her straight to my third-worst enemy, a ruthless highway robber named Garth."

With these words Celestina grew alert. "Surely you don't mean Garth Golden-Eye?"

"You know him?" Jack inquired in astonishment.

"Of course. Garth and I have long been friends."

"Friends!"

"He's a charming fellow," said the queen, "though he sorely needs to be domesticated."

"Are we speaking of the same person? Garth, the notorious

231

robber? The heartless ruffian who deprives so many people of their belongings?"

Celestina sighed. "Garth is like a young child—he has trouble distinguishing what belongs to him from what belongs to others. This leads to many misunderstandings."

"He robs people every day!"

"If someone taught him right from wrong, no doubt he would behave himself."

Jack slumped in despair, demoralized once again that Stelinda had chosen Garth's company over his own. "What you've said may well be true," he told Celestina. "Who am I to judge? I serve a king I loathe. I've submitted my powers of storytelling to his will. I've relinquished any claim to my art. And now, partly through my own fault, the people of the Realm are all prisoners."

"So it would appear," said the old woman. She watched him a moment without speaking. Then she continued. "Well, you must reject this awful young monarch and reclaim your art. You must help your friend Loquasto. You must win back Princess Stelinda. Doing so will solve your problems—and, indeed, the problems afflicting all of us."

"*How, Celestina? How?*"

"We'll figure that out," she stated firmly. "But I'll be blunt: you'd best get started. You've let your story take the wrong direction. You've let the plot run out of control. Worst of all, you've allowed your own character to develop in unseemly ways."

"Not on purpose," Jack protested.

"No excuses! You're a storyteller, Jack. Practice your art. Use it well. Remember your obligations. The characters must be fulfilled, the plot fully realized, the story well told."

Chastened, Jack knew Celestina was right. What she'd said confirmed his worst fears, yet he felt relieved, too, for her words set him on a new path. In that he found a degree of consolation and—to his surprise—a kind of freedom.

✎ 75 ✎

J ack talked late into the evening. He told Celestina all about his recent past—every sorry tale. How he'd betrayed Loquasto's trust and turned his back on his friend's quest to be united with Artemisia. How he'd selfishly followed his own interests and assisted Yoss and Zephyrio. How he'd let down Stelinda in so many ways. Celestina listened without interruption. When, at last, he finished speaking, he bowed his head. "What, then, shall I do?" he asked humbly.

"I'm not sure yet," replied Celestina. "Perhaps I'll have a plan by morning. Now, though, we must sleep."

Jack was too exhausted to protest. He simply curled up on the floor beside the hearth, slept all night, woke late, and ate the breakfast that Celestina gave him.

Only then did she reveal what she was thinking. "I had a dream last night," she told Jack, "and dreams, of course, tell the best stories of all. This is what mine told me: you must start by correcting the first big mistake you made. How? By helping your friend Loquasto undertake his quest."

"What!" Jack blurted.

"Mark my words."

He was appalled. "The Realm is in flames! Yoss, Zephyrio, and their minions will make prisoners of us all. Surely resisting them is more important than aiding Loquasto."

"What you say is true," said Celestina. "Equally true, however, is your obligation to undo the grave error you committed a long time ago."

Jack started to interrupt, but the old woman cut him short with a stern gaze. Then she continued: "Doing so will free your heart to honor the love you feel—the love, at least, that you *want* to feel for Stelinda."

"I *do* love her," Jack stated firmly.

"Then you must regain her trust."

"But how?"

"That is for you to discover."

"And meanwhile I should let the Realm burn to the ground?" he asked in outrage.

Once again Queen Celestina silenced him with her sky-blue eyes. "I can't be sure," she told him, "but I feel deep in my heart that you'll gain your opportunity to save Sundar by following the course I've set. First, make amends to your friend Loquasto. Second, right the wrong you've committed against Stelinda. Only then should you attempt your third task: to save the Realm from disaster."

"I don't understand!" exclaimed Jack, gesturing helplessly.

"Jack, dear Jack—sometimes you can't understand what's necessary except by striving hard to do it."

For a long moment Jack simply sat at the table. He wanted to give up. He wanted to lie down on the floor, go back to sleep, and never wake up.

Then, forcing himself to face his fate, he said, "All right, then. I'll strive hard to do it."

Celestina helped Jack get ready. Although his clothes had dried overnight, she gave him a rough, heavy cloak to wear over them. This garment would both keep his body warm and help disguise him during his perilous journey. The storm had erased his footprints of the night before, but Jack would need to wear something far less conspicuous than court attire if he was to evade capture. Celestina's cloak wrapped him in forest hues and textures. She also gave him a leather pack so finely stitched and oiled as to be waterproof, plus several loaves of bread she'd baked overnight.

Jack took them eagerly. "Thank you for everything," he told her.

"You're most welcome," she replied. "But remember: tell your own stories."

"I shall."

"Help others tell their own stories, too."

"I'll do that as well," Jack said. He embraced her and set off.

At once he faltered and turned back.

"Celestina, with all your knowledge of forest creatures, tell me— where on earth would I find a talking fish?"

"There's a lake in Sycamora that's full of them," she replied without hesitation. "I've visited it myself, though not recently. You should go there. They'll talk you silly. One fish in particular will tell the story you want to hear."

"A fish princess?"

"Indeed. Her name is Artemisia."

☙ 76 ❧

Sycamora lay only a few days' walk from the Twilight Woods, but Jack needed almost a week to reach his destination, for he took roundabout paths to avoid detection. His caution was well founded. Time after time he spotted squadrons of the Royal Guard marching through the farmlands. Twice, he caught sight of King Yoss, Zephyrio, and their retinue.

When he arrived at long last in Sycamora, he was exhausted, muddy, bruised, sore, and hungry. How odd, he thought, to have reached the site of such alarming experiences—not just one encounter with Garth Golden-Eye but two—only to feel a deep sense of relief. Yet that was what he felt. And he felt it despite the depth of the forest's gloom, the vagueness of its paths, and the strangeness of the cries drifting among the trees. For Jack now believed that this place, alarming as it was, would somehow reveal the way out of his predicament.

For a whole day, Jack wandered through the forest in hopes of finding the fish kingdom. But his search led nowhere. He saw no other person and no animals except for a few birds. Then, near dusk, he heard voices. He eased through the foliage and warily sought their source.

It wasn't fish he heard but people—forty or fifty of them sitting around three campfires in a clearing. Wearing ragged clothes made of rough leather and homespun wool, they looked as tired and cold as Jack himself felt.

Yet despite their haggard appearance, he had never seen such a happy group. Sitting together, huddling close, they sang a song whose words kindled a fire in Jack's heart:

"Arise, friends and loved ones, why crouch ye like cravens?
Why cling to a life full of hunger and pain?
Why let the king's soldiers attack like harsh ravens—
Why suffer the harm of the tyrant's disdain?

"Think of the wrongs ye bear!
Think of the rags ye wear!
Think how your children cry
As hardships multiply!

"Your minds are as keen as the minds of your masters,
In swiftness and strength ye surpass them by far!
Your brave hearts have taught ye to weather disasters,
Ye vastly outnumber your foes in this war!

"Why, then, accept these lords?
Why not resist their swords?
What right have they to take
The things ye toil to make?"

Jack realized then who was leading the singing. It was Stelinda. Sitting right beside her was Garth Golden-Eye. And clustered around them were humble village men, women, and children of all ages—as well as Garth's band of ragtag rebels—now joined together to rebel against the monarchy.

"So rise, O my brethren, and bear it no longer—
Rise up and confront the king's hideous powers!
Show Yoss and his minions which side is the stronger
When we, the Realm's people, take back what is ours."

Watching and listening, Jack felt a mix of envy and admiration. He started forward, ready to join the princess. But before he'd taken more than two steps, a noise across the clearing caught his attention.

Like fierce wolves, dozens of Royal Guardsmen leaped from their hiding places and surrounded the group. Some of these soldiers carried crossbows; others wielded swords or battle-axes. In the blink of an eye, they took everyone captive.

Then a voice called out: "There! The storyteller!"

Jack hesitated for a moment. He couldn't imagine abandoning

Stelinda at her time of greatest need. Yet if he stayed, what help could he possibly offer?

He bolted, shoving his way through the foliage and darting between trees. Crossbow darts hissed all around: *fssst! fssst! fssst!* He could hear men crashing after him. Yet precisely because he was smaller than they and not burdened by weapons and armor, he moved faster and with far greater agility. He soon left them far behind.

❧ 77 ❧

Night fell. Jack knew that the guardsmen wouldn't pursue him in the dark; they had trouble maneuvering even by daylight. As he crouched in the forest waiting for sunrise, he struggled to keep warm and to make sense of his predicament. These few hours of contemplation led him to an unexpected decision: he would resume his search for Artemisia. This went against all his instincts, for it meant abandoning Stelinda. But he realized that any attempt to rescue his beloved would result only in his own captivity, whereas finding the fish princess—as Queen Celestina had insisted—might provide him with a later, better opportunity. And it might well start the process of freeing everyone from King Yoss's tyranny.

But deciding to find a talking fish is one thing. Actually finding one is quite another. Jack looked everywhere. He followed streams and rivulets. He sniffed the air in hopes of smelling water. He climbed hills in an effort to spot reflections.

At last he found three lakes linked by a channel. In the first— more of a bog than a lake—he saw few signs of life. In the second, the scattering of fish he spied were only minnows that came and went like sparks. In the third lake, a big gray fish swam lazily under-water, rose to the surface, and released a bubble that burst with a single syllable: "Buh!"

So much for talking fish.

Jack searched all day. He crisscrossed a sparsely wooded area, shoved his way between bushes and brambles, and waded through swamps. At nightfall, soaked and shivering, he found himself trapped in deep darkness. Once again he had no choice but to crouch, hug his knees to conserve warmth, and hope that no further misfortune would befall him before dawn.

Then, without warning, he heard an unexpected sound.

A splash.

Jack stood and listened closely.

Another splash.

He moved carefully toward the sound, guiding himself through the foliage by touch alone. What had been thick darkness began to thin. Splinters of moonlight soon stabbed through the canopy of trees: first a few, then more and more.

Jack found himself by a lake—a lake large enough to reveal a patch of sky and a crescent moon. By this pale light Jack saw a splendid fish cruising back and forth at some distance from the shore. It submerged briefly and then leaped into the air, flashing for an instant like hammered gold before disappearing once again into the water.

"Hello!" Jack called out. "Hello?"

A sudden splash; a glint of gold.

He felt like a fool, speaking to a fish! But what did he have to lose? "Hey! My name is Jack! I come on behalf of a bird, Loquasto! A bird who loves a fish named—"

"Artemisia," said a silken voice.

Gliding toward him was the most beautiful fish he had ever seen.

"If I hadn't been so caught up in my own concerns," Jack explained to the fish princess as he finished telling his story, "I'd have devoted more time and attention to helping Loquasto. That's all he ever asked of me—help in figuring out how to be with you."

Jack was sitting at the edge of the lake now. Artemisia drifted in the shallow water nearby. Her fins and tail billowed and furled. She remained silent for a time; then she said, "Your words are honorable, Jack, but the sad truth remains: no matter what you might have done on our behalf, it wouldn't have helped. There's no way that a fish and a bird can live together."

"But there *must* be."

"Jack Storyteller, no person or creature alive could make our wish come true by force of will alone. Certainly not you, not I, not Loquasto."

"There may be someone," Jack said hopefully. "Someone, in fact, whom both you and I already know."

"Who could that be?"

"Queen Celestina."

"The Woman of the Woods?" asked Artemisia in her lilting voice.

"By either name, yes—that's who I mean."

"How could *she* help?"

"I can't say. All I know is that Celestina is wise in the ways of all creatures."

"I didn't even know she was still alive. She must be old and frail by now."

"Old, yes," Jack said, "but not so frail."

"Then Celestina is our one hope," said Artemisia.

ᵺ 78 ᵺ

This was their plan. The well-crafted leather pack that Celestina had given Jack would serve as the perfect container for transporting Artemisia. He would lower it into the lake and fill it with cold, clear water. She would then swim into the pack and allow Jack to seal it. Enclosed in this supple tank, the fish would be safe for the journey back to the Twilight Woods. Jack would leave Artemisia in Celestina's care. After that, he would set off again, this time to locate Loquasto. If all went well, he would explain what had happened, regain the bird's trust, enlist his help, proceed to find Stelinda, and liberate her from Yoss's captivity. And then—

"It's hopeless," said Artemisia. "I can't imagine how we'll accomplish even one of these tasks, much less all of them."

"You told me that your greatest desire is to be with Loquasto," said Jack.

"It is indeed."

"If that is your goal, then you must take the actions necessary to reach it."

Artemisia hesitated a moment, then said, "Lower the pack."

Jack held it down in the water and let it fill.

With an elegant leap, the fish flipped into the leather bag.

Jack sealed it, slung it onto his shoulder, and set off.

In the morning, the sun shone brightly and the ground dried underfoot. For these reasons Jack could advance faster now and in much less discomfort. He worked his way quickly through the forest in hopes of reaching Celestina's cottage in a few days. He checked Artemisia now and then—opened the pack, spoke with her, then sealed the pack again—and proceeded.

But that afternoon something caught Jack's attention: a shred of dark green velvet fluttering from a branch.

Jack pulled it off the twig. This cloth resembled the fabric of Stelinda's gown. At once he glanced about, convinced that she must have been nearby.

You can imagine his delight and dismay when, pushing his way through the forest, he found her. Delight, because he'd never expected to locate her so quickly. Dismay, because he soon discovered that she was held captive in a most appalling manner: tied to a tree next to Garth Golden-Eye.

The two prisoners faced away from Jack and stood side by side with their arms bound overhead to a horizontal branch. They looked like garments hung up to dry. Jack couldn't even imagine how painful this position must be. The sight filled him with such rage that he rushed forward at once, desperate to free his beloved.

Stelinda's hair caught his attention as he approached—hair as radiantly golden as ever, but shorter now. As short as—

Jack stopped and understood his mistake.

At that moment, both Stelinda and Garth turned to face him.

But they weren't Stelinda and Garth.

They were King Yoss, clad in a cloak the same color as his sister's, and Zephyrio, wearing a rough deerskin tunic similar to Garth's. Both of them smiled at Jack's bewilderment.

"You're late," said the illusionist, letting go of the branch above him and lowering his hands.

"Very late," said the king, lowering his hands as well.

Soldiers swarmed out of the forest and grabbed Jack.

~ 79 ~

Bound to a pole by his wrists and ankles and carried like a dead deer between two guardsmen, Jack suffered through the long trek out of Sycamora. What pained him far more than this mode of transport, however, was having no knowledge of Stelinda's or Garth's fate. Or Artemisia's. His captors had confiscated the pack containing the fish princess, and they made no mention of the others.

When the group finally emerged from the woods, the guards removed Jack from the pole and cut his bonds. He could scarcely walk, his legs hurt so much. The guards fed him bread and water. Then one said, "Go with him"—and motioned toward Zephyrio.

The illusionist stood a few yards away. Resplendent in his usual fine attire, he watched Jack stagger toward him. "Let me guide you," he said, offering his hand.

Jack pulled away. "I can guide myself!" he snapped. "Besides, you already have a puppet."

Zephyrio's gaze hardened. "I'm just trying to be helpful."

"I've had plenty of your help, thank you."

"Maybe you have," said the illusionist. "Maybe you have."

"Where is Stelinda?" Jack demanded.

"I'm keeping her safe until she reaches certain . . . insights."

Jack could scarcely contain his anger. "Insights? She'll never cooperate with you and Yoss. She'll fight you to the end. And even if you kill her—or me—Yoss's reign is almost over, and so is yours. The people will rise up against you."

Zephyrio smiled, gesturing to his left. At that moment, a squadron of the Royal Guard marched by with a group of prisoners in tow. Men, women, even children: twenty-five or thirty haggard peasants, their hands tied behind their backs and their right ankles connected to a long chain. They stumbled and staggered as the guards prodded them with sticks. "We know who's plotting against us," the illusionist stated calmly. "We know everything about Garth and Stelinda. We know everything about their followers."

"That's not possible," Jack protested.

"It's not only possible," said Zephyrio. "It's certain. We know *everything*."

The look on the illusionist's face showed such confidence that Jack felt his own certainty crumble. "How?" he asked. "*How* do you know?"

Another smile. "Oh, a little bird told me." With those words Zephyrio snapped his fingers. At once, a midnight mynah flew over and alit on Zephyrio's outstretched hand.

"Loquasto!" Jack exclaimed.

The bird glanced at the storyteller and immediately averted his gaze. "Not what it seems!" he squawked. "Not what it seems!"

Jack couldn't speak. He couldn't accept the sight before him and couldn't believe what it seemed to mean: that during the months of the bird's absence, he had been working for Yoss and Zephyrio. No, that wasn't possible. Loquasto had to be tricking them. Yet without a doubt, there he was, perched on Zephyrio's hand as if it were the safest, most comfortable resting place in the world.

"We should go," said the illusionist. "We have a long trip ahead of us." Then he launched Loquasto back into the air.

With sinking spirits Jack realized how vast were the forces arrayed against him.

✺ 80 ✺

Zephyrio ushered Jack into a sedan—one of those man-carried compartments that he'd shared with the illusionist in the past. He almost refused. Jack hated remaining in Zephyrio's company, but he felt so battered and weary that his desire to sit overwhelmed his will to resist.

"Since you seem so fond of stories," Zephyrio said as the carriers lifted the sedan and set off down the road, "let me tell you one."

"Don't," Jack snapped. "I don't want to hear it."

"Oh, but you do. You've wanted to hear it for a long, long time," Zephyrio said. "You've wondered: Who *is* this mysterious, elegant gentleman? How *does* he perform the remarkable feats that have so dramatically changed everyone's fate throughout the Realm? Is he a wizard? A demon? Or just an astoundingly clever man?"

Seated on the opposite bench, Jack shoved himself as far away as possible, folded his arms tightly across his chest, and wished he could be anywhere else on earth. But Zephyrio was right: He *had* asked himself these questions, and he wanted to know the answers.

Zephyrio sensed Jack's curiosity. As alert and amused as a cat toying with a cornered mouse, he said, "I could, of course, reveal the truth by more powerful means than mere storytelling. I could dazzle you with visions, frighten you with conjury, leave you dumbstruck with revelations! I *could* do that," he noted, snapping his fingers and releasing a burst of blue-white sparks. "But for once I'll restrain myself. I'll resort to the words you find so delightful. I'll cure the malady of your ignorance with a dose of your own medicine."

"Just tell the story," Jack muttered.

Zephyrio nodded. "All right, then—the story."

Once upon a time (the illusionist began) a farm boy lived in one of the Realm's squalid, distant provinces. This boy toiled hard to help his family survive, but his efforts made little difference, and he, like everyone else in the village, staggered beneath a burden of poverty, hunger, and fatigue. He hated working from dawn till dusk. He wearied of watching the crops grow. He despised herding his family's feeble sheep. He detested eating the boiled turnips, rough barley bread, and half-spoiled mutton that made up his daily meals. And this boy, outraged by his fate, swore that he would somehow throw off the burdens of country life. He would flee the provinces. He would seek his fortune in the Royal City! He would find a clever way to accomplish his goals, attain success, and avoid the hardships that afflicted almost everyone else in Sundar.

But you'll interrupt me, won't you, Jack? You'll shout, *Stop! I know my own story!* Well, lad, this isn't just *your* story. It's mine as well. Yes, Jack—for I, too, have humble origins. I, too, hail from the provinces. Are you surprised? Of course. For when you hear my refined accent, when you note the elegance of my manners, you can't help concluding that I'm of noble birth. Isn't that so? Admit it! Well, Jack, my elegance and refinement are illusions. Everything about me, in fact, is an illusion. For I decided years ago that I wouldn't sink into the helplessness that half drowns the Realm. I'd master a discipline that would grant me the power to wade out of the stinking swamp of village life. I'd take control and rise above the pathetic common people.

Ah, Jack, the expression on your face suggests that you find my story unnerving. Is that not so? Are you disturbed by the possibility that my background so resembles your own? That I, like you, am just an ordinary farm boy from the provinces? Or do you struggle to believe what I've just told you? Well, Jack, rest easy. Nothing I've just told you is true. Nothing! Not a single word! It's all a pack of lies.

Allow me to start over. I'll tell a story more to your liking.

Once upon a time a young nobleman grew up in Callitti. Handsome, rich, and well-educated, he saw the good life spread out before him like a banquet. Grand houses, armies of servants, vast treasuries of gold and jewels, and a lifetime of comfort were his for the asking. This young aristocrat wouldn't have to exert himself to achieve any goal that suited him. But can you grasp, Jack, how these circumstances affected the young man? Do you imagine that he felt pleased to have all advantages, all accomplishments, all successes presented to him on a platter? No, the situation appalled him. Worse: it disgusted him. What challenge was it to live like that, with a splendid outcome guaranteed in advance? The young man decided early on that he would reject the nobility and the easy life. He would forgo all the privileges set before him. Instead, he would pursue a different course. He would play a different game.

So how's that, lad? A more convincing tale? You look a little more comfortable with this story. Well, once again my words are just smoke and mirrors. Lies. All lies!

Let me try again.

Once upon a time a young man—a spy from the kingdom of Vmatta—entered the Realm of Sundar intending to depose King Alphonse and take over the government. He did so in the guise of a well-bred illusionist. His plan: to insinuate himself into the court, gain allies among the courtiers, gradually find favor with the prince—

No, that's not really true. Here's another approach.

Once upon a time, Lord Derek, son of Lady Mercuria—the noblewoman from Navatte betrothed long ago to King Alphonse—plotted to gain control of Sundar, the kingdom that Derek believed to be his own birthright.

No, that's even more far-fetched. Let me try again.

Once upon a time. Once upon a time. Once upon a time. . . .

Enough. Listen to me, Jack: these stories don't matter. Not a single one. Whether I'm lying or telling you the truth doesn't matter. My background doesn't matter. What matters, Jack, is *power*. What counts is *power*. There's no magic but *power*—and I have it. Do you think I cast spells to entrance people? Do you? No—I simply overpower them by any means that serve my purpose. It's easier than you think. People are willing victims, believe me. Victims not of magic, but of the *illusion* of magic! Transparent birds! Pink lightning! Winged loaves of bread! Visions of King Yoss protecting and nurturing his people! Does it matter if these visions are real or false? Not at all. What matters is simply that I have the power to make people feel wonder in their souls, terror in their bones, dread in their bellies, and hope in their hearts. That they marvel at the sights I reveal. That they'll do anything I say. *That's* what matters.

Zephyrio leaned back on his bench and stared at Jack, his eyes revealing more pity than anger. "Believe me, Jack," he said. "You count for nothing. You are weak. The same holds true for your sorry friends—Garth, Celestina, and the princess Stelinda. Even Yoss counts for nothing, for he has no power. None, at least, beyond what I've granted him. Do you understand me now?"

Jack didn't reply. How could he respond to what Zephyrio had said? Never in his life had he felt so sure that someone was wrong—that every syllable the man had spoken was in error. Yet he felt powerless to oppose the illusionist.

Jack shifted his weight and let his head droop, feigning sleep. Exhausted, he soon had no need to pretend.

✒ 81 ✑

Jack wasn't surprised when, on arrival in the Royal City, he was taken at once to the palace dungeon. Guards opened a massive iron door and shoved him into a cell. He landed hard on the stone floor. For a long time he just lay there.

It was night. The only light entering the cell was a single moonbeam, narrow as a tree branch and flatly angled, that filtered through a hole in the high ceiling. Otherwise, the room was a tank filled with darkness. Jack could scarcely see the walls around him.

After a short while, however, as he came more fully into awareness, he realized that he wasn't alone. A man-shaped shadow emerged from the far corner's deeper darkness and crossed the cell.

"Who's there?" Jack asked, suddenly fearful.

"Who would ye think?" replied a gruff voice.

Jack hesitated a moment. "Garth? Is that Garth Golden-Eye?"

It was indeed the robber. "Ye're that *storyteller*," he said. "That storyteller what serves the king—"

"Listen," Jack said urgently.

Garth took a few more steps toward Jack. "I don't listen to nobody what serves King Yoss—what doose the most to 'elp 'im tighten 'is grip around the bloomin' kingdom's froat."

At first Jack stepped back, alarmed by Garth's approach. Then he held his ground. "Attack me if you believe it suits your purpose," he said. "But before you do, hear my story."

"Ye've wasted quite enough o' me time wit' your stories, thank ye kindly. Ye've wasted everyone's time."

Garth was now so close that Jack could smell the robber's foul breath. Yet Jack forced himself to show courage that he didn't feel. "Do you believe that my stories have caused your problems?"

he asked. "That if I hadn't told my stories, life would be wonderful?"

"O' course not, lad, but it's *you* what's made me problems so mooch worse."

"And you believe that I'm the one who put you in this dungeon?"

"Don't be daft. It was King Yoss."

"I see. But if you do me harm, that will solve everything, won't it? Hurting me will somehow spring you out of prison and absolve you of trying to overthrow King Yoss."

"What are ye tellin' me?" Garth asked.

"A story," Jack replied. "That's what I'm telling you."

"What bloomin' *story!*"

"Once upon a time there was a storyteller, and this storyteller hated King Yoss," Jack said. "The storyteller worked to overthrow the king. But his efforts didn't succeed. In fact, the storyteller made the situation worse. When he realized that, he felt great despair, but he didn't know what to do."

"Ye're tryin' to fool me," Garth growled, grabbing Jack by the front of his shirt. "Ye're tryin' to pooll the wool over me eyes."

"Let me finish my story."

"Enough o' yer stories!"

"Stop!" a woman shouted. "Garth Golden-Eye, unhand that boy!"

Garth let go as another shadow emerged from the cell's dark corner. For a moment, the moonlight shone on long, white hair.

"Celestina. Is that—is that you?" Jack stammered.

"Indeed." The old woman touched Jack's face, and he reached out to embrace her.

"Yoss has imprisoned you as well?" he said. "For what crime?"

"For the crime of threatening his power," she told him. "Do you recall the story I told you long ago? How I once was queen of Sundar, though just briefly? It seems that Yoss has heard of this and considers me a danger."

"I'm sorry you're caught up in this web," said Jack, and he embraced Celestina once again.

"I nivver troosted this lad in the past," Garth grumbled, "nor do I troost him now."

"*I* trust him. I always have," Celestina stated firmly. "I believe every word he speaks. Although he may seem to have served King Yoss, it was only to work against him."

"But why?" Garth asked Jack. "Why na joost turn against 'im outright, like us rebels?"

"Because I'm a fool," Jack replied. "I thought I was being so clever. Thought that by chewing away at Yoss's power like a termite inside his house, I'd bring it down. I wanted to end Yoss's reign. Not for my sake—for Stelinda's. I've never wanted anything but her well-being."

"I don't believe you." A new voice joined the conversation.

Jack turned at once toward the dark corner. "Stelinda?"

"I wish I could believe you," said the princess as she stepped forward, "but I don't."

He wanted to rush over, to embrace her, to kiss her—but he didn't. He couldn't bear the thought that she might resist him.

For a long moment Jack was silent. "I spoke half the truth," he said at last. "I *was* a fool to think I could overthrow King Yoss from within. But I was an even greater fool to strike a bargain with him."

"Go on," said the princess.

"Zephyrio offered me elegant attire, fancy food, beautiful apartments—and I refused him. He offered me gold and jewels—and I refused him. Then he offered me total freedom to tell my own stories. All I had to do was serve King Yoss until he gained full dominion over the Realm. Afterward, I could tell my stories. And that offer, I'm afraid, was the bait that lured me into his trap."

"So it seems," said Stelinda. "So it seems."

❧ 82 ❧

They huddled together inside their cell. Cold, hungry, tired, and afraid, the four prisoners waited for night to end. The moon passed somewhere above the dungeon, its shaft of pale light slanting down the wall until it touched the floor. Jack felt as if he were sitting at the bottom of a well.

Celestina tried to keep their spirits up. "There's always hope," she stated. "After all, *I* escaped when facing execution long ago. Moribundo rescued me."

"I met his son, Young Moribundo, when Yoss sent me off to the chopping block," Jack said gloomily. "But the son lacks his father's compassion—he made no effort whatsoever to release me."

"Yoss and Zephyrio see us as the greatest threat to their power," Stelinda added. "Why should they let us live? They're far safer if we're dead."

"I wish ye wouldna poot the matter quite so bloontly," said Garth Golden-Eye.

In this dark state of mind, the four prisoners had no choice but to wait, wait, wait—and then keep waiting.

❧ 83 ❧

Now, a storyteller locked in a dungeon is someone with time on his hands, and time is the warp on the storyteller's loom. The weft, of course, is words—the yarn that shuttles back and forth across the warp and weaves the fabric of a story. A storyteller locked in a dungeon can always amuse or distract himself by telling stories. He can amuse and distract other people, too. And this is exactly what Jack did now.

He told a story about the floor he sat on, which, viewed in the dim light, became a mysterious landscape. The uneven stones were a range of hills sloping into farmland. The crack in the middle was a river that had carved a canyon in the land. The spider who lived in the crack was a monster—Yossillo by name—who preyed on any wayfarers foolish enough to enter his realm. Jack told a story about crossing this harsh landscape, tricking Yossillo, and setting off down the river on a raft to safety.

Celestina told a story to lift everyone's spirits.

Once upon a time, a greedy little mouse named Yoff gazed out of his comfortable nest and watched the other animals go about their business. The squirrels gathered nuts. The birds picked berries. The wild pigs dug up mushrooms. The deer nibbled tender leaves. The forest was full of delicious things to eat, and there was plenty of food for everyone. But Yoff wanted it all for himself.

"If I were king of the forest," he said, "then all the food would be mine. But I'm just a mouse, so that's impossible."

"It's not impossible," said Zerio, a clever rat, who had been lurking nearby. "All we have to do is turn you into a bear—for bears are huge and powerful, and all the creatures of the forest obey them."

"But how?" Yoff asked.

"Bears rub their backs against trees—leaving tufts of fur on the bark," the rat explained. "We'll gather up all that loose fur, bundle it together with twigs to form a fake bear, and put you inside it. Then you can rule over the forest kingdom."

Overnight, they did just that, and as day arrived, the mouse surprised all the other animals. "I am the king!" Yoff exclaimed from his hiding place behind the bear's fierce face. "Bring me food! Otherwise, I'll gobble you up!"

Terrified, the forest creatures did as King Yoff commanded, then fled in terror. Each night, Yoff and Zerio feasted on this bounty. Each day, the creatures toiled to serve their king.

"See how easy it is to fool others?" Zerio said.

But a bird named Jackle the Grackle soon grew suspicious. "That bear doesn't ever move," he said. "He just stands there and orders us around."

"Don't anger him!" exclaimed the other animals. "Just bring him food—or he'll gobble us up!"

But as they grew weary—indeed, as they began to starve—Jackle knew he had to act. So one morning, as King Yoff made his usual demand for food, Jackle flew up, landed on the bear's head, and inspected his snout. The bear's nose was the place where Yoff hid to peer out at the animals below. Jackle plucked a feather from his wing and tickled the bear's nose.

"Ahh— Ahhh—"

A great sneeze burst forth from the bear, blowing all the fur off the skeleton of twigs beneath.

And at that instant the forest creatures saw that the king they feared and obeyed was just a pathetic little mouse.

Garth told a story, too—the story of his hard life.

"Me own moother didna loove me," he told the others. "As a lad I 'ad no toys and no food neither. So 'oongry was me family that we soometimes didna 'ave a thing to eat but stones. Aye, noothin' but stones. Is it such a big surprise, then, that I'd seek me fortune deprivin' ladies and gentlemen o' their pocket money? Them folk 'ad more than they needed, and I 'ad noothin' a-tall. 'Twasn't fair. O' course, it was nivver me plan to keep all the booty—no, me friends, I'm a ginerous soul at 'eart. That's why, when King Yoss came round to make our lives miserable, I decided to start all over. I told meself:

Garth, old boy, 'tis a new day now, so roll the dice again, turn over a new leaf, poot yer best foot forward, take the 'elm o' the ship o' fate, and do things different from what you doone in the past—"

"Garth," Jack interrupted. "There's something I've been wanting to ask you."

"Wha's that, laddie?"

"If it's not rude of me to ask—how did you lose your eye?"

"Me eye?" Garth said, puzzled.

"The eye you've replaced with a golden coin."

"Och, *that* eye," said the robber with an awkward laugh. "I nivver did lose it. No, laddie, 'tis right where it's been all along." With those words he reached up, plucked out the doubloon, and revealed a perfectly good eye staring out of its socket.

Jack, Celestina, and Stelinda stared back in amazement.

"'Tis rather sensitive to light, that eye," Garth went on, "so one day long ago I coovered it with a coin to protect it. To me great surprise, I discoovered that what I'd doone stroock fear into the 'earts of all what be'eld me. So I joost left it there, reckonin' it provided some 'elp in me difficult profession."

When it was Stelinda's turn, she offered a story of a different sort— one that she sang to her companions until it lulled them to sleep:

> "'Go to bed,' my mother said—
> 'The wind's in the leaves
> And the rain's on the pane.
> We'll harvest the sheaves,
> We'll winnow the grain,
> We'll bake the bread
> In the morning.'"

≈ 84 ≈

The prisoners had barely slept an hour before footsteps sounded in the corridor. The locks clanked, the great oak-and-iron door swung open, and four men walked into the cell. One of them was enormous; the others were merely huge. But aside from their size, they looked almost identical. They were all shirtless, revealing great round shoulders, massive bellies, and vast expanses of pink flesh. They all wore black boots, black trousers, and black leather hoods.

Jack recognized the largest man at once: "Moribundo!"

"Indeed," the man said. "Good morrow, ladies and gents."

"You *can't* be Moribundo!" Celestina exclaimed. "I met him fifty years ago, and you don't look a day over forty."

"Tha' 'twould be me dear departed dad you're speaking of—Old Moribundo," the man replied. "I'm Young Moribundo."

"I see."

"And me sons, here, are the Little Moribundos—"

"Enough o' this nonsense!" Garth shouted suddenly. "Who gives a whit about yer family 'istory?"

The three Little Moribundos—youths of fifteen or sixteen—shuffled about with a shyness that Jack found surprising, but Young Moribundo took offense at Garth's interruption. "Now, listen 'ere. We don't mean no 'arm, honest. We just come by to introduce ourselves an' beg yer pardon."

"Our *pardon?*" asked Stelinda, turning pale.

"Yes, m'lady. For what will 'appen on the morrow."

Jack felt a chill seep into his flesh. "We're to be executed, aren't we," he said flatly.

"I do apologize," Young Moribundo told him. "'Tain't my decision."

"Listen," Celestina said abruptly. "Many years ago your father did me a great favor—"

"Sorry," the executioner responded before she could finish. "No favors. I'd like to 'elp ye out, o' course, but i' 'tain't possible. I can't do no favors—I got a family to support."

"Please?" asked Stelinda.

"M'lady, 'tis 'ard enough already, keepin' three big young'uns fed. Sorry."

"Sorry," said the first Little Moribundo.

"Sorry," said the second.

"Sorry," said the third.

After bowing deeply—the father and his sons simultaneously— all four Moribundos left the cell.

❦ 85 ❦

Jack drew Stelinda aside and related all his recent misadventures in hopes of winning her forgiveness. "I've told you everything, and everything I've told you is true," he said when he finished. "Will you trust me now?"

"I want to," she replied sadly. "I truly want to. But something inside me . . ."

"What is it?"

"When I needed you most, Jack—when we had the best chance of defeating my brother—you refused to help."

"Stelinda—"

"You chose to help Yoss instead."

"Surely you understand why, though. You've heard my story."

"Of course. I've heard your story. I've thought about your story. But now, after hearing *all* your stories, this seems like just another—story."

"It's not."

"How do I know that?" she said sadly.

"Perhaps you *don't* know," Jack told her. "Perhaps you simply have to trust me."

⚘ 86 ⚘

Weary down to the marrow of their bones, they slept. At once Jack began to dream, and in his dreams King Yoss appeared, laughing and taunting him, and Zephyrio showed up, too, floating in a bubble, and Young Moribundo strode toward Jack with the three Little Moribundos behind him, each of them wielding a massive ax. Then, as Yoss screamed *Off with their heads!* Jack found himself lying face-up and watching an ax drop toward him. But when the blade struck his neck, he felt only a peck against his skin. Then another peck . . . then another . . .

He awoke suddenly, clutching his throat, and sat upright.

Something fluttered away in the darkness, then fluttered back.

"Loquasto!" Jack whispered.

"Shhh!" The bird landed beside him.

"I'm so glad to see you!" Jack exclaimed. "But what are you doing here?"

"I want to have a few last words with you."

"And I with you. I want to apologize. I've been a bad friend—I know that. I used you. I didn't mean to, but that's what I did. I got so involved in my own concerns that I forgot about yours."

"Indeed," said Loquasto. "Mine and everyone else's, too."

Jack was long past trying to defend himself. All he wanted now was to follow Queen Celestina's advice and make amends for the errors he had committed. "I won't make excuses," he said.

"Good."

"I've caused enough damage as it is."

"True."

"But hear me out, Loquasto, please. I found your beloved. I found Artemisia—"

"I don't believe you."

"—and I brought her to you."

"Oh?" said the bird, glancing about. "That's wonderful! Where is she, then? Over there in the corner? In your pocket? How odd—I could have sworn I saw her in the palace not long ago, when Zephyrio and King Yoss showed her to me."

Jack felt despair welling up inside. Once again his enemies had triumphed. "I found Artemisia in the forest of Sycamora, and I brought her out," he said. "When they captured me, Loquasto, they captured her as well."

Loquasto huffed in contempt. "Interesting! How convenient that on finally keeping your promise, you just happened to lose precisely what would prove your good intentions."

"I'm telling you the truth," Jack stated.

"I don't think you know what the truth is anymore," the bird told him. "You've told so many stories you can't keep them straight."

"This isn't a story!" Jack exclaimed. "I'm just asking your forgiveness."

"It's too late for that," Loquasto said. He arched his wings and flapped them a few times as if ready to take flight.

Jack grew angry now. "Do you know what? You should beg *my* forgiveness, too," he told the bird. "For you betrayed me in turn. And not me alone, but Stelinda as well—and the entire Realm—by joining forces with Yoss and Zephyrio."

Loquasto fidgeted. "They lured me with a promise I couldn't resist."

"Apparently so," Jack noted bitterly.

"They promised that if I helped them, they'd find Artemisia and bring us together. And they kept their promise. Just yesterday they brought her to the palace."

"Have you spoken with her?"

"Not yet. But they showed her to me. She's in a glass tank. There's water inside, of course, and a hole at the top so they can drop in food."

Jack felt great pity as he heard Loquasto's words. "They put your beloved in a *tank?*" he asked. "She who has spent her whole life swimming freely in a beautiful, clear lake? Isn't that just typical of Yoss and Zephyrio?"

"They promised me they'd release her at the right time."

"And you trust them?"

"I have to."

"Well, good luck!" Jack said with a laugh. "First *I* find Artemisia, and now the two most dishonest people in the Realm say *they* did, and you believe them."

"Jack, they've kept their promise—"

"And you're together at last!" Jack exclaimed, scarcely restraining his mockery.

"I should peck your eyes out for saying such a thing."

"Go ahead. It won't make my situation any worse than it is already."

Loquasto didn't move. "If Yoss and Zephyrio had said, *Do as we ask and you'll be with Stelinda forever,* wouldn't you have complied?"

Jack didn't reply. Though still furious, he suddenly grasped why Loquasto had made his choice.

"You won't answer," said Loquasto, "because you know the answer is *yes*."

Jack sighed. "Nothing I say matters," he told the bird. "Believe anything you want. Do whatever you want. But go talk with Artemisia! Hear the truth from *her*. Ask who found her in the forest of Sycamora and who brought her out. Was it Yoss and Zephyrio— or me? *Ask* her!"

Loquasto's only response was to flap his wings, spring into the air, and fly out through the hole in the ceiling.

❧ 87 ❧

When morning came and a little more light dripped into the cell from above, the four prisoners felt the full burden of their captivity. They glanced at each other but didn't speak. What was there to say? They had no plans to make, no plots to hatch, no insights to share. With damp stone walls surrounding them and a massive door blocking their escape, they knew they were trapped. They'd all be dead within a few hours.

Jack considered telling the others about Loquasto's visit. But even if they believed his story, the tale would be pointless. It made no difference whether Loquasto sought Artemisia or not. A bird, even a talking bird, could do nothing to change their fate.

Once so full of stories and so eager to tell them, once so confident of their power to change the world, Jack now fell silent.

❦ 88 ❦

The clanking of the locks tolled the prisoners' doom. The door swung open. In marched a squadron of guards and, right behind them, the four Moribundos. In a matter of moments, Jack, Stelinda, Celestina, and Garth had been bound, gagged, and led from the prison to the palace square. There Jack found himself facing what he had dreaded most: a huge wooden platform with four chopping blocks resting atop it.

The executioners led the four prisoners up the platform staircase. Jack somehow succeeded in catching Stelinda's gaze as they climbed. And in that brief, speechless moment, using his eyes alone, he managed to tell Stelinda this story: *I love you.*

The executioners forced each prisoner to lie face-up on a chopping block. Then they checked their axes. "Sorry," said Young Moribundo, stroking the blade with his thumb. "Don't take it too personal."

Suddenly, trumpets sounded: heralds drawing everyone's attention. Glancing sideways, Jack saw King Yoss and Zephyrio climb the stairs, cross the platform, and stand before the crowd that filled the courtyard.

"Listen to me, all of you!" shouted Yoss. "These four traitors are a menace to me, to you, and to our kingdom! They've spread trouble everywhere with their lies and nonsense. Now it's time to put an end to their stories and poems! To storytellers and poets! *All* of them— forever!"

Some members of the crowd clapped and cheered, but by no means all. Jack wondered what their silence revealed. Were they afraid? Were they appalled by what they were seeing and hearing? Would they resist the king and rise up to stop the execution?

Nothing happened.

Then Zephyrio, clearly angered by the people's feeble response, shouted, "Is *this* how you thank your brave monarch for all he's done on your behalf? This meager applause? These paltry cheers? Well, let today be a lesson to any other traitors among you. Enough of stories! Enough of poems! Long live King Yoss!"

A scattering of voices reached Jack and the others on the platform: "Long live King Yoss."

"That's pathetic," said the illusionist in a scolding tone. "Try again."

Once more a few voices called out.

"Well, then," Yoss said, "*be* that way. *Don't* praise me. *Don't* thank me. But believe me, you'll see who's in charge!" Turning to the four executioners, he shouted: "*Off with their heads!*"

Jack turned to gaze at Stelinda one more time. He felt oddly calm about dying, but the thought of Stelinda's death filled him with unbearable sorrow.

"'ey, you!" said Young Moribundo. "Look up 'ere, now!"

A drum rolled.

Trumpets blared.

Jack gazed upward and saw the huge ax high above him, almost floating, ready to descend. *This is it,* Jack thought. *The end.*

⌇ 89 ⌇

Without warning, a small black object appeared, darting this way and that, swooping at Young Moribundo and diving at his sons. With each swoop this object moved faster and more abruptly, catching all four executioners off guard.

It was Loquasto.

Jack doubted his eyes at first, then believed them. Sharp-clawed and dagger-beaked, black as a wedge of midnight, the bird was back. But what could a small bird do against four huge men? To Jack's astonishment and delight, Young Moribundo lowered his ax and let it fall to one side, the better to fend off his feathery assailant with both hands. His sons did likewise as Loquasto pestered them, too, shooting from one to another to another, stabbing at their faces time after time until they cowered.

"What's the meaning of this?" shouted Zephyrio.

"Get the crow!" yelled Yoss.

Loquasto landed on one of the flagpoles angling out from the platform, and from this perch he called down to the crowd in his piercing voice: "Listen to me, all of you! Listen to a talking bird—one who has seen a lot and knows a lot about Yoss and his henchman."

"Silence him!" King Yoss shouted to his guards. "Chop down the flagpole! Kill him!"

At this point Zephyrio interrupted. "Good people, don't be fooled!" he yelled. "This is part of Jack Storyteller's trickery. He controls that bird! He's throwing his voice like a common puppeteer! He's trying to make fools of you!"

Surprising Jack, Young Moribundo turned to the illusionist and said, "No—let 'im speak."

Then Jack heard voices from the crowd: "Let the bird speak!" "Let us hear the bird!" "We want to hear him!"

Young Moribundo further startled Jack by raising him to a seated position. He didn't untie Jack's restraining ropes or remove his gag. He did, however, signal to his sons, who helped Garth, Celestina, and Stelinda in the same manner.

All this time, Loquasto cawed loudly from his perch. "Listen to what I tell you! It's a wretched story, but one you need to hear." Then he related what he knew about Yoss and Zephyrio. How they had plotted to steal the throne from King Alphonse. How they had taken advantage of the king's illness and, in fact, had deprived him of medicine in a way that had hastened his death. How they had bribed and threatened councilors and courtiers to place Yoss, not Stelinda, on the throne. And how, once Yoss was in power, they had squashed resistance throughout the Realm and subjected everyone to their complete control.

"And that," Loquasto concluded, "is why you should rise up against this foolish boy and his terrible puppetmaster. You must prevent them from executing the four people who would release you from tyranny."

Once or twice during Loquasto's speech, Yoss had attempted to interrupt, but Zephyrio had restrained him. The king quivered with rage, yet neither he nor his henchman tried to leave. Now, as Loquasto finished, the illusionist raised his hands again and called out: "Good people! What a remarkable story this crow *seemed* to tell you! I commend Jack Storyteller for his skill in creating such an impressive illusion! A talking bird! A clever trick indeed! But should you believe your eyes and ears? I recommend otherwise."

Yoss interrupted: "I protest—"

"Silence!" the illusionist told him sharply. Then, turning once again to the crowd, he went on: "I offer you a simple choice: believe Jack—or me. Believe the far-fetched tale that Jack no doubt will tell you, or believe me when I assure you that King Yoss offers you generosity and love."

Jack wasn't sure what Zephyrio meant, and Stelinda, Garth, Celestina, and Loquasto seemed equally perplexed by this abrupt turn of events.

"Release the prisoners," the illusionist commanded.

"No!" Yoss exclaimed, stamping his foot. "I won't have it!"

"Silence!" shouted Zephyrio. "You aren't in charge here." He waited while the four Moribundos untied Jack and the others. Then he addressed Jack: "Come forth."

Reluctantly, Jack obeyed. He walked over to where Yoss and the illusionist stood.

Hundreds of people stood below in the palace square. Courtiers, valets, guards, cooks, gardeners, maids, kitchen boys, bricklayers, farmers, craftspeople, and children of all ages pooled before him in a great lake of humanity. Staring. Waiting.

"What would you have me do?" Jack asked.

Zephyrio laughed gently. "Do?" he inquired. "Well, that should be obvious enough." Then, raising his voice, he shouted: "Listen, all of you! If what the bird says is true—if Yoss and I are so terrible, and if you're truly better off with the king stepping down and someone else taking over the government—if all that is true, then let the reign of King Yoss come to a speedy end!"

"You can't do that!" Yoss shouted. "I'm the king!"

"You're the king if *I* say you are," the illusionist snapped. "Now be silent and listen."

King Yoss backed away, glowering, but he restrained himself.

"Here's how we'll decide," Zephyrio continued. "Let Jack tell you a story—a story so rich and wonderful that he'll convince you that his view of the world is right. Afterward, let me show you a better view of the world. A view that shows how wonderful your lives will be. Then *you* decide."

Jack was thrilled by these words. He'd have a chance to save Stelinda, Garth, Celestina, and all the people of Sundar! What could be better? Yet he also was terrified. How could he accomplish such a daunting deed? How could he beat Zephyrio in this strange contest? What tale could he tell to achieve his goal?

He stood without speaking. So many stories cluttered his mind.

Stories about faraway lands . . . stories about animals . . . stories about magic charms and mysterious spells . . . stories about warriors, shepherds, ghosts, and witches . . . stories about wondrous musicians and enchanting songs . . . stories—

"Well," said the illusionist. "Is silence the best story you have to offer?"

"Jack," said Stelinda. "Speak the words in your heart."

He gazed at her a moment, surveyed the others on the platform, and then turned to the crowd. "I have no stories," he said.

☙ 90 ❧

The illusionist smiled with delight when he heard Jack's admission. "What?" he said. "Our story peddler has run out of trinkets to offer his customers?"

"I thought so!" Yoss shouted.

But at once Jack called to the crowd: "I am a storyteller, it's true. It's also true that I have no more stories to offer you now. At least none worthy of you. For it's not *my* stories that matter—it's *your* stories. They have at least as much power as mine! Tell stories about the work you do. About the people you love. About the deeds you've done or want to do. About the changes you long for. *These* are the stories you should be telling, all of you. *Your* stories! Not *mine*, and certainly not *theirs!* Yoss and Zephyrio want you to believe that only the king's story matters—but that's not true. Tell your own stories! Speak the words in your hearts."

After a pause, Zephyrio asked, "That's all you have to say for yourself?"

Jack nodded once.

"Just as I expected," the illusionist called out to everyone below. "Jack Storyteller has nothing to offer. But I offer you *this*." He held out his palm, allowed a shiny bubble to sprout from it, and extended his arm as the sphere grew large. "Behold!" he exclaimed. "*This* is your story! *This* is your future—a future worthy of your greatness!"

Within the shimmering sphere, images began to appear. Images of perfect fields. Perfect villages. Perfect houses. Perfect hearths cooking perfect meals. Perfect health for everyone. Perfect work for everyone. Perfect families for everyone. Perfect everything for everyone. And all these images swirled together, all somehow identical with the promise of King Yoss's reign— until Loquasto, launching himself into the air, jabbed his beak into the bubble, which burst and disappeared without a trace.

"Which will it be?" the bird asked loudly. "Will you tell your own stories? Or have Zephyrio and Yoss tell them for you?"

For a moment, no one responded.

Then from below a voice called out: "Down with King Yoss!"

Like fire spreading in a dry forest, more cries quickly raged through the crowd. "Down with Yoss!" "Down with the king!"

Yoss glowered at the illusionist, stamped his foot, and shouted, "No! I won't *have* it! You said this wouldn't happen to us!"

Zephyrio smiled. "It won't happen to us," he said without a hint of alarm in his voice. "It will happen to *you*." With those words he walked over to the staircase, descended, and quickly entered the crowd, which parted for him in alarm.

Jack watched him cross the palace square. He expected the illusionist to send off protective flames, a shower of thorns, or a pall of smoke to surround himself in a shield so frightening that nobody would make a move to touch him. But Zephyrio did nothing of the kind; he simply walked away. Everyone was so afraid of him that they backed off to let him pass. Soon he disappeared from the palace grounds.

Silence reigned for one brief moment. Then, as people truly understood what had happened, a new cry—timid at first, then confident, soon raucous—arose from the people: "Long live Queen Stelinda!"

A splendid commotion erupted on the platform. Jack and the princess rushed over to each other and embraced. Celestina and Garth drew close and hugged the young couple. Loquasto swooped about overhead. And Young Moribundo and his sons surrounded Yoss and took him captive.

Over and over the people shouted, "Long live Queen Stelinda!"

SIX

So that's the end of the story, right?

Almost—but not quite.

What happened to Jack and Stelinda?

I'll tell you in a moment.

They lived happily ever after, didn't they?

Well, that's certainly how most stories of this sort would end. But our story is more complex, so I need to guide you through a few more tangles in the plot. One of the tasks that every storyteller faces is tying up all the loose ends left dangling in the weaving of a tale. I admit I've left more than a few such loose ends: threads of plot, strands of characterization, a wide fringe of incidents. So listen now, and I'll knot them all together for you.

With Yoss in captivity and Zephyrio in flight, Sundar could now be entrusted to safer hands. The royal councilors proclaimed Stelinda queen. By this means, Princess Stelinda, true heir to the crown, re-gained her claim to rule over the Realm.

I'll tell you in a moment how she made use of that claim. First, however, I should describe something else—the resolution of a far different conflict.

"Do you believe me now?" Jack inquired once the morning's crisis had ended and he and Stelinda found a few moments together. "Do you believe me now that despite all my mistakes, my intentions have been good?"

"Jack, only a fool—" she began.

"Only a fool?" cried a shrill voice, interrupting her.

It wasn't Jack who expressed such outrage; it was Loquasto. As I mentioned earlier, sometimes you need a talking bird to set things right. This had certainly been true on the execution platform. Now it seemed to be true again, for the midnight mynah landed on Jack's shoulder and at once started regaling Stelinda.

"Listen hard to what I have to say," the bird cawed. "Everything Jack has told you is true. True, true, true! Even if he's sometimes not too clever, his heart is good. He's been positively obsessed with you from the start! Why do you think it's taken so long for me to be reunited with Artemisia? It's because this fellow has been so smitten with you that he—"

Stelinda reached out and grabbed Loquasto by the beak. "Enough," she said. "I need no convincing. What I was trying to say is this: Jack, only a fool would have doubted you. I was a fool. I know your heart is good. Please forgive me."

"You have no need to ask my forgiveness," Jack replied.

Stelinda embraced him. "Then the terrible tale of King Yoss's reign is now fully told," she said. "We can leave behind that time of fear, doubt, and suspicion. And we can start a new story—a story in which my plot and yours are one and the same."

And so Stelinda became the queen?

Well, the situation wasn't quite so simple. The councilors' proclamation didn't make her happy. Why? Because she didn't want to be queen. She never had. This young woman, like her father before her, had no desire to wield power or run the government. On the contrary, she felt a deep aversion to these roles. She regarded the crown as a source of sorrow, not of joy. She wanted only the freedom to practice her art. To write poems and recite them. To compose songs and sing them. To enjoy the world with the clarity and delight that an artist can attain.

For this reason, Stelinda renounced her claim to the throne. Not immediately; that would have thrown the Realm into further upheaval. But following an interval of some weeks and with Jack at her side, she stated her intentions to the royal councilors.

"Who, then, shall rule in your stead?" they inquired in alarm.

"Surely not your sisters Giselle and Mythunia—they're almost as unsuited as Yoss."

"No, their rule would be disastrous, too, although for different reasons."

"So who should carry the scepter and wear the crown?"

"The rightful heir," Stelinda said without hesitation. "The true heir. Someone who has already served as queen of Sundar but was unjustly unseated from the throne: my great-aunt Celestina."

To clarify the situation, Jack recounted the story that Celestina had told him when he'd first met her in the Twilight Woods. Following her parents' untimely deaths long ago, Celestina had inherited the Realm. But a conspiracy much like Zephyrio and Yoss's had put her brother Mackaroe in power and condemned Celestina to death; only Old Moribundo's mercy had allowed her to escape into exile. Many years later, in the aftermath of Mackaroe's death, Alphonse had become king and the realm had gone into decline. But now, following her long exile as ruler of her own forest kingdom, Celestina could resume her rightful role as queen of Sundar.

"She is a kind and wise woman," Stelinda told the councilors. "With your assistance, she will spread happiness and prosperity throughout the Realm."

What came of this decision was a glorious coronation. Thousands of commoners flocked to Callitti from all corners of the Realm. The nobility attended, too. Stelinda, Jack, and Loquasto joined as the guests of honor; and even Garth and his fellow rebels joined the festivities. With all these people massed together, Celestina took her vows of office, accepted the crown and scepter, blessed everyone, and ascended to the throne.

"Long live Queen Celestina!" proclaimed the prime councilor, Lord Jeremy, in his squeaky voice.

The crowd shouted in response: "Long live Queen Celestina!"

Bells pealed in the towers. Fireworks rose into the sky. Everyone cheered. Happiness and peace reigned. That is how the kingdom began a new chapter in its history, and how Jack and Stelinda found themselves free to proceed with their own lives.

Did they get married?

I'll answer your question in a moment. First, though, I need to describe what became of some other characters in our story. Garth, for instance.

Garth! I've wondered a lot about Garth Golden-Eye.

I'm pleased to say that the robber's tale has a happy ending. By all accounts Garth had lived a contemptible life—a life of greed, crime, and deception—so it's difficult to imagine that such a person could ever change his ways. That, however, is precisely what happened. During Yoss's harsh rule, the highwayman so clearly saw and understood the people's suffering that he underwent a profound change of heart. He renounced his past and reformed. Henceforth, his mission wasn't to deprive people of what they owned but to provide them with what they lacked.

The truth is that even before Yoss fell from power, Garth had devoted himself to unearthing his hidden booty: boxes, barrels, and chests full of stolen jewels and coins. He dug these up, located as many of his former victims as he could, and returned to them whatever precious belongings he had taken from them. These acts of compensation eventually struck Garth as insufficient, as he wasn't helping the poorest citizens of the Realm.

"Promise me," he had begged Stelinda at one point during their weeks of backwoods conspiracy, "that if we ever throw yer bloomin' broother off the throne, ye'll give ol' Garth Golden-Eye some work 'elpin' the people o' this long-soofferin' kingdom."

As it turned out, it was Celestina who granted Garth's wish. She appointed him royal alms-giver, with responsibility for distributing money to the poor, and he did everything in his power to honor her trust.

What did Celestina do about Yoss?

Well, his fate was different from what you might imagine. In most places, a dangerous and unpredictable deposed king would have been sent into exile—or locked in a dungeon. But Queen Celestina was a far different monarch than the one who had preceded her. She took pity on that sad, angry boy while at the same time gently punishing him for his cruelty and greed.

How?

By giving him what he wanted—or what he thought he wanted. Celestina appointed him accountant for the Royal Treasury. Confined to the palace vaults, Yoss undertook a task he had relished in the past but soon found unspeakably tedious: counting out all the doubloons, ducats, sovereigns, and other coins; weighing and measuring gold and silver ingots; and assessing the jewels, ornaments, and medallions stored there. Thus he served a useful purpose while closely guarded and unable to cause any harm. As he tired of those opulent baubles, perhaps he grew up and attended to other people's needs rather than to his own desires. But that would be another story.

What about Zephyrio the illusionist?

Well, you might imagine that the terrible deeds he committed against the people of Sundar would lead to an equally terrible fate. Surely such a devious, selfish, harmful person deserved punishment. He should have languished in prison or performed hard labor until he somehow paid back his debt—if, indeed, such a debt could ever be repaid at all. There would be justice in such a fate.

I regret to say, however, that Zephyrio suffered nothing of the kind. On the contrary, yet another act of trickery allowed him to escape punishment altogether. He employed his powers of illusion to disguise himself as a fishmonger, and he escaped Callitti driving a wagon piled high with fish heads and entrails. This cart gave off such an appalling stench that even if someone had recognized him, no one would have tried to stop him from leaving.

After that? If I were to tell the tale, I might say that Zephyrio took up residence in Vmatta, a kingdom to the west, or that he fled to Ettai, located to the south. But the exact location makes no difference. Wherever he went, he would find a realm full of people willing— no, eager—to be duped by the illusions he offered.

And Loquasto . . . did he find happiness with Artemisia?

Ah yes, Loquasto. The unanswered question regarding the talkative bird was whether or not he could live at last with his one true love. The fish princess now resided in Callitti, for Jack had located a large decorative pond for her in one of the palace gardens. The bird lived in the nearby trees, so surely some sort of accommodation should be possible. But what? Fish can't fly. Birds can't live underwater. The situation certainly presented some difficulties.

Jack offered the best solution to this quandary. Building a spacious birdhouse for Loquasto right at the water's edge, he provided the perfect dwelling for his friend. "Ducks live on the water, though not in it," he explained. "The same holds true for geese, loons, gulls, and swans. Fish come up to the air, though they can't dwell there. If you truly love each other, spend time where the fish world and the bird world meet."

I can't claim that this arrangement solved all their problems. But I'll tell you this much: the bird and the fish chose it, and chose each other, with open hearts.

Tell me about Jack's family. What did they think of what he'd done?

Well, for a while they actually didn't know. Rumors about the end of Yoss's reign spread through the Realm, but few people fully understood the events that had taken place. Jack's family didn't altogether grasp what had happened until he showed up a few weeks later.

I mentioned earlier that one of the oldest stories in the world tells of a young man leaving home to seek his fortune. That's certainly true. But another old story tells of his return following his adventures.

And so, not long after Yoss ceased to be king, Jack found himself standing before the door to his family's cottage in Yorrow. *Should I knock?* he asked himself. *Or should I just walk right in?*

As Jack tried to answer these questions, the door suddenly swung open. There stood his brother Fergus. The boy stared in silent confusion for a moment, then abruptly yelled, "He's back! It's Jack! Jack, Jack, Jack!"

The rest of the family rushed out at once, everyone shouting, crying, and hugging Jack in a raucous embrace. He hugged them, too, delighted and relieved to be home. Then, as everyone settled down, his brothers, sisters, and parents started pelting him with questions.

"Is it true that Yoss is no longer king?" Father asked.

"And that the Woman of the Woods is now our queen?" Mother asked.

"Someone told us that you knocked the boy-king off the throne," said Alfred. "Is that true?"

"Are we safe now?" asked Gwynne.

"What's going to happen next?" asked Sally.

Dizzied by all these questions swirling around him, Jack stood a moment without answering. Then he reached out to his family. "It's so good to be back," he told them. "Let's go inside and sit. There's a long story I want to tell you—and I want to hear *your* stories, too."

What about Jack and Stelinda? You said you'd tell me more about them as well.

And so I will. You're right to ask. For they are, after all, at the very center of our story.

I told you that Princess Stelinda renounced her claim to the throne. All she wanted now was to be with Jack, to practice the arts she loved, and to live in peace. Thus, once Celestina was safely established on the throne, Stelinda left the Royal City, traveled through the provinces to Yorrow, and joined Jack in their new life together.

They got married?

That's what they chose. There was a great wedding in Yorrow, a wedding that everyone in town attended, both to celebrate Jack and Stelinda's love for each other and to rejoice in their victory over Yoss and Zephyrio. Garth, Celestina, and even some of Celestina's animal courtiers also took part in the celebration. This jubilant wedding party gathered in the town square as Lord Jeremy, the prime councilor, presided over the couple's ceremony.

"Jack, tell Stelinda why you've chosen her to be your wife," said the tiny old man.

"You are what matters most in the story of my life," Jack told the princess. "You are the best character, the perfect plot, the most delightful source of surprises, the most satisfying resolution."

Now Jeremy turned to Stelinda. "Stelinda, tell this young man why you've chosen him to be your husband."

"You are the song my life is singing," she told Jack. "You are the most moving melody, the most amusing lyrics, the most enjoyable refrain, the most delightful final cadence."

"Then I proclaim you husband and wife," said the prime councilor, "and I wish you happiness until the end of your days."

Jack and Stelinda kissed.

The crowd cheered.

One last thing.

What matters most is that you live your own story to the fullest and that you tell it well. Make sure you fully develop your main character. Fill the tale with lots of other characters—men, women, children, even animals—who tell their own stories. Make your listeners laugh or cry . . . or even sneeze. Have lots of twists and turns in the plot, but not too many, before you reach your final resolution. Then, when the day is done, you can feel confident that your characters have been fulfilled, your craft mastered, your story well told.

Be off now. The world awaits you.